DARKSTORK MAEDAY

Ashley Barnhill

One year earlier, maybe…

MAE STEPS OUT of the pizza shop still in her gym wear. She didn't actually go to the gym. Hasn't set foot in a gym in months. Once a second skin, her tight cycle shorts and push-up gym bra are now just a force of habit, relics from when she was a different person. Younger and fitter. Kinder – possibly. But shit like that isn't sustainable. The pizza box she's cradling is warm and damp against her forearms. The smell of undercooked dough, BBQ sauce and greasy cheese assaults her senses. A final dinner bought as a peace offering of sorts while Rob packs up his things.

Mae sighs, joining the last of the sweaty stragglers stumbling home from their post-work drinks as the sun sinks into the mighty Colorado River. The late June Texan summer is already oppressive – the air, arid and unforgiving, has stolen all the moisture from the city leaving the pavements cracked and the people charred. The drone of cicadas, nature's sirens, harmonize with the murmurs drifting from nearby bars. Mae can almost feel the electricity in the air. It keeps her on her toes. Reminding her of the wider purpose.

The traffic lights on the corner turn green just as Mae reaches the crossing. Goddamnit. She crouches to hit the button with her elbow, then straightens up and balances the pizza box on one arm. Releasing her right hand, she extracts a slice. What does Rob care anyway? Not like a pizza will really make anything better. She's not even sure why she bothered. Mae licks her fingers as the intersection stoplights change to yellow, and then to red, and as they do her eyes fall on a dark figure in the middle of the road. A stork. Ink black and stoic. It turns its head and tilts its long blood-red beak. It blinks, slowly. Taunting her with its unwavering stare.

Mae steps off the curb, and out of nowhere a car speeds round the corner; headlights glaring, accelerator down. The smell of burnt rubber rises from the tarmac. What the–? The stork takes flight and swoops toward Mae, she ducks and something wet splatters in the corner of her mouth. Holy hell in the name of God and Texas. The bird has marked her.

Wiping the rancid taste from her lips, Mae looks up to

find the car still speeding toward the red light. She hesitates for longer than she should. The sun gleams off the hood of the car. Closer. Closer.

At the last second Mae comes to her senses. She attempts to sidestep, juggling the pizza box but just as she's about to step into the clear, the car swerves missing Mae by inches. She staggers, startled as she looks up through the windscreen, coming face-to-face with familiar, hardened eyes.

The world switches to half-speed as Mae steps back into the road and hurls the pizza box at the fleeing car. That's when she notices the ambulance coming from the other direction. She watches in slow motion as it swerves to avoid the car. BBQ chicken pizza soars through the air, greasy slices landing with a wet splat, smearing across the ambulance driver's windshield.

There is no time to scream. Mae's body falls back, and as her head hits the burning pavement the car has already disappeared straight through a red light, leaving her in a smoke cloud of smoldering tires.

The stork meanwhile lands gracefully on the curb. It perches there, calmly taking in the scene.

I

Mae

"Is it still the same dream you're having?"

"I reckon it is." Mae pulls her gaze from the window, her eyes once wild as the Texas plains are now glazed and despondent. She lifts a hand and traces the web of scars across her scalp. "I mean, maybe. Or no. I think I dreamt it was a BBQ chicken pizza this time."

"Mhmm," her psychologist, Dr. Abernathy, uncrosses her legs, then recrosses them the other way. "And the flavor before was…"

"Pizza marinara," says Mae with defiance. She hates it when people do this. And they do it all the time. Like this whole thing is just some big game instead of her life. Her actual real godforsaken life. "It was balls-basic marinara. The kind without the cheese. It was Rob's favorite, basically cuz it's the only pizza made for people who can't have meat or cheese for pleasure. Gross tasteless crap-sauce bread. I don't remember my favorite, maybe smoked brisket. I probably used to do nasty shit to meat lovers pizza. You know like those violently graphic scenes in pizza delivery pornos, but to the pizza not the spotty delivery boy. Even when I watch pornos like that all I can think is what a shame the pizza's getting cold. But now I can't stand the sight of pizza, whatever kind." Her hands are shaking. She clenches and unclenches her fist, an anxious tick she's developed since the accident. She tucks them between her thighs.

Dr. Abernathy looks up from her clipboard and smiles. "Yes, Mae. It was a vegan pizza." She removes the lid from the end of her Mont Blanc pen (psychologists always have Mont Blanc pens) and seals the tip. "You know," she says, slowly and calmly. Condescending, if Mae were to define it bluntly. Dr. Abernathy seems to sense this feeling. She rolls her shoulders and sits foreword, resting her elbows on her knees to close the space between them. "Alright, Mae. I'm going to be very real with you here because I don't think there's any point in chasing what we can't get back. We're now a year after the injury. Six months after regaining consciousness. I think we need to start accepting that these memories are lost. Unless a twist of fate intervenes."

Mae waits, poised for the punchline. "What– that's it?

But that's years of my life! They can't just be gone. They must be inside me somewhere. That's what you said! You said you were going to help me unlock them. That it was just time." Mae stands up and casts around, then sits again, unsure what she'd stood for in the first place. Lifting a hand to her hairline, she traces her fingertips along her scalp again, over the ridged stitches and buckled skin. A mountain range of trauma. "Chronic Amnesia is like free-falling off a cliff. All your memories are around you but you're moving past them too fast to grab a single one. Like Alice down the rabbit hole."

"I know, Mae. But you know picking at scar tissue won't help you get any closer, it will just prevent the wound from healing. It's like sailing with a hole in your boat – you'll sink before you make progress." Dr. Abernathy moves to take Mae's hand, but then pulls back at the last minute, as though thinking better of it. "I understand that it's hard to hear, really I do. But this is the brutal truth, and you need to accept it. Otherwise you'll end up living in a world of open wounds that thinks itself whole."

*

Mae gets home around noon. Their loft is sleek and luxurious, decorated in a minimalist décor that she can't quite believe she'd have chosen herself. Rob likes to keep things pristine clean – even if a burglar broke in, he'd make them take their shoes off. Mae, on the other hand, would happily drink juice from a vase and eat straight out the air fryer basket before bothering to clean a single dish.

The condo extends over two floors, connected by a staircase that winds its way upward like a snake. They have floor-to-ceiling windows with views of the city. Mae moves toward the window and looks out over Austin. It's a hazy afternoon, a smorgasbord of pathogens and possibilities. The downtown skyline is bathed in a warm otherworldly glow, light shining from the ever-changing landscape of towering skyscrapers. Mae hasn't always lived in the city. She grew up in Hereford, in the rustic Texas Panhandle Plains – a wide-open gone-yonder countryside where the buses don't run, and you have to drive a good five hours to find a decent coffee shop. It was growing even quieter now, since the cattle started shriveling in the rising heat. Despite having two brothers, she always felt alone out there. Even as a young child, she was always dreaming of something brighter and busier. This feeling, by some cruel swipe of hand, was part of herself that the accident let her keep. She'd had to relearn her family name, learn to recognize her brothers from photographs and even how to walk. But the loneliness – that stayed with her. Mae casts her eyes out to the tallest shape on the horizon – the gleaming, crescent-shaped Frost Tower, and home to D8N App headquarters, which takes up the entire top floor of the glassy pyramidal skyscraper. The building is iconic in Austin. The locals call it Owl's Perch, hinting at the distinctive circles near the tower's summit – a watchful, wide-eyed presence over the neon haze of the city.

Mae pulls herself away and rubs at her eyes. She should be proud of herself, she knows. That was it, after all. The last of her insurance-paid rehabilitation sessions. She's free now. Ha! No more guided walks. No more babysitters and pureed meals. No more wearing a helmet. Now she just needs to relearn basic life skills and spend the rest of her life living with massive memory gaps where the force of the oncoming car knocked them from her skull.

From somewhere above, Rob's voice comes snaking down the stairs. Mae has always loved Rob's voice – his deep, British accent with its velvety undertones evokes an authority that can both fill and silence a room. But Rob isn't home, Mae knows this. Rob is never home these days. She must have left the TV on in the bedroom.

Turning from the view, Mae makes her way upstairs, lingering only momentarily over the pictures hung in a collage up the staircase. Pictures of her and Rob. Young and not so young. Pictures of them at parties, dressed up in matching Halloween costumes on Austin's dirty 6th Street, tailgating at Longhorn football games, Mae teaching Rob to make smores over a campfire, and on holiday visiting Rob's parents back in the UK, posing in front of the London Eye and Rob's proposal on top of The Shard with views of the sunset. Rob used to bring these into the hospital to try and jog her memory. She used to lie and act up excitement to make him feel good, but she can't honestly remember most of the occasions in the photos. The guilt she feels for this is something she still can't figure out how to live with – half the reason, most likely, that Rob doesn't like being around so much these days.

At the top of the stairs, Mae takes the second door on the right and pushes into their velvet-plush bedroom. Sure enough, the TV is on. It's showing a replay from the morning news, and on screen her tousled brunette fiancé, Rob Malthus, with his chiseled cheekbones, is talking with the anchor.

"If you're single, you're on it. A global phenomenon – no one's swiping anywhere else. It's completely obliterated the market," she says, eyeballing Rob like he's such an exquisitely groomed god that she wants to stab herself in her face with his dick. When did women start looking at him that way? "Hailed as a masterpiece, it's the biggest geosocial app in the world. That's right, today we're talking about D8N App, with the British creator tech titan guru Thomas Robert Malthus."

"Cheers, Katrina. I'm absolutely chuffed. Just don't Google my name – that whole bodies in the cellar thing was just a smear campaign from a disgruntled wanker neighbor." Rob winks, topaz blue eyes glistening like a melting ice sculpture. "I'm just being daft, darling."

"And he's funny," the Anchor swoons. "So, tell me Rob, what inspired you to create D8N App?"

Rob straightens his back. At 6 feet 3 inches, he's the tallest man in most rooms, and a good three heads taller than the presenter. His staple black tee is clinging to his sculpted frame, accentuating his shoulders. He hasn't always been muscular, Mae realizes, and she can't fathom how he became to be so in such a short space of time. When they met at University, Rob had been mal-nourished and sinewy, living off vegan instant noodles and Mountain Dew. This new Rob, however, oozes with cerebral elegance and power – the sort of man who could tell you to go to hell and make you look forward to the trip.

"Well Katrina, as a kid I volunteered at a shelter and saw a puppy get euthanized because it had Von Willebrand's disease, and they didn't have the space to keep a sick animal. Bloody hell, that hit me pretty hard. I was 8 years old, and I was gobsmacked – absolutely gutted. I wanted to help make sure other animals didn't suffer like that puppy. I started a community outreach scheme that paired aspiring owners with their perfect rescue pet. It was based on things like your personality, hobbies, how active you are, your location, and any other pets you have. We'd also spay and neuter the animals for free to help safeguard your pet's health, possibly improve certain behaviors – and provide pet food, of course. So, I guess I peaked at age eight." Rob shrugs, trying to look modest.

The reporter lets out a fuck me laugh, visibly spellbound by Rob's Oscar-winning performance.

"Yes, well anyway. I was in university when I started programming D8N App. My purpose wasn't just to match people, but to build a new world of soulmates. Rebuild humanity for future generations. I'd like to say it all starts with love, but I guess it really starts with the science of love."

"Okay, Mr. Do-gooder. How many successful matches to date?" she asks, twirling her hair.

Rob smiles with such boyish charm you can practically hear the 'ting' of light bouncing off his smile. "We're about to clock up ninety million users and nine hundred thousand successful matches. Its algorithm will decide the fate of billions."

"So, it's for everyone? The entire world. Love at first swipe."

"That's right, Katrina. Love at first swipe. And it's about to get even better with our latest update. A proper smash hit for prosperity."

Mae hears them talking on screen but isn't really listening. She can't comprehend reality right now. God how she wishes she could escape her own head. She grabs the remote and turns the TV off. She needs voices. People. A human touch. Rob. She needs Rob's dick in her heart.

Mae runs back downstairs and digs her cell out of her bag. She dials Rob's number and waits, chewing on the soft skin around her thumbnail. He doesn't answer. She rings again. They have a piano in the far corner of the living room. Mae crosses and sits at it as the dial-tone reverberates in her ear. She opens the lid and tries a chord, then another. It's Für Elise. Playing the piano is a place where her memory gaps fade away. Her fingers glide over the ivory keys with ease, the melodies presenting themselves instinctually, like they're a physical part of her. The part of her that wasn't shattered.

"Hello?"

Mae strums an off-key as Rob answers.

"Howdy," she says, scrambling to organize her thoughts. "Are you home soon? I could order in for us. Have a date night?"

"Oh, hi Mae. It'll be a late one, I'm afraid. I'm slammed with work. Sorry babe, I told you I've got a thousand and one things to do. If I cock up this launch, shit will hit the fan and we'll all be covered in it."

"Yeah, I remember," says Mae, stroking the piano keys. "Okay, well, how about you work another hour or two and then I'll come meet you? We can go out tonight. It feels like it's been years. It's starting to feel like the last time I opened for a guy was a cranioplasty."

Rob sighs audibly over the line, and Mae can almost see him pulling his hand down his face in that exhausted way he does. "I don't think so, Mae. You're not ready. Not yet. Baby steps. Look, tomorrow night it's the DarkStork launch party. Wait till then, alright? You can get all dolled up. Sorry, love, I've got to dash. Pop the kettle on and sooth yourself with a cuppa. I'll likely crash at the office again tonight. There're ready meals in the fridge."

The line goes silent. Mae sits listening to the dead air until frustration washes over her. "Fuck you," she yells into her cell, bashing the piano keys so hard she hopes they smash. "You're busier than a funeral-home fan in July."

Mae slams the piano shut. She's not had a drink in – how long has it been now? Six months in a coma, six months out. A year. Crossing to their marble-topped kitchen, Mae throws open the drinks cabinet and pulls out the first bottle she sees – Buffalo Trace bourbon. She yanks a tumbler out of the cabinet, pours a hearty slug of liquid courage, tops it off to the brim with Topo Chico, then downs it. "Thank the Texas Ranch Water gods. Hell, all water's dirty brown murk now." The liquor burns her gums and the back of her throat, tracing flames down her esophagus. But it's not unpleasant. If anything, it feels like a relief. It puts some slap back in her jaw. She takes the bourbon and drinks straight from the bottle. She's not eaten since breakfast – well, lunch was 8 gummy worms – and can already feel the alcohol numbing the front of her skull, making it heavy, filling out all the empty space she's been left with. Fuck Rob. Take those ready meals and wedge 'em up your wankwaffle arse. Mae reaches for her cell and orders an Uber.

2

Mae

She chooses somewhere expensive. A cocktail bar on West 5th Street with leather stools, a large decorative gong hanging behind the bar and shelves of backlit bottles – vodka, whiskey, bourbon, gin – lining the walls. The door swings closed behind her and the sultry notes of *It's Hot!* by T Bird and The Breaks welcome her in, raspy vocals resonating in the pulsating heat.

The vibrant city of Austin is everything her young self hoped for. The streets bustling with activity even on a weeknight, the bars and restaurants around the city already filling with post-work gatherings. Austin also has a thriving arts scene Mae always intended to dabble in. She was a good pianist, a mediocre songwriter and had even tried her hand at a bit of stand-up comedy during her college years – a hobby she'd forgotten since graduating. Or so it seemed.

Mae zigzags her way through the frat bros, sorority sisters, yoga moms and tech dudes, interspersed with couples or soon-to-be couples eyeing each other over cocktails. She wonders how many of them were matched through D8N App? Despite her hand in co-founding one, Mae isn't sure she could ever do dating apps herself. She pulls up a stool at the bar and attempts to catch the bartender's eye. He's old-ish, late thirties maybe (is thirties old to her now?), with rugged hair and a beard that's both patchy and in need of a trim. He's clearly in a mood – concentrating on polishing one of the beer taps and actively ignoring any movement from the other side of the bar. Mae drums her fingers and sighs pointedly. This has no effect on the bartender.

"OH HEY!"

Mae turns to find a man pulling up the stool beside hers. He smiles widely and places a presumptuous hand on her arm. "How are you doing?"

Mae tugs her arm away. "Sorry, do I know you?"

"Hello? Do you want a drink or not?" The bartender is giving her a death-stare, having apparently decided he can be fussed to do his job.

"Yes, actually," Mae smiles without blinking. "Double tequila on ice." The bartender nods, already starting to turn away, but Mae interrupts. "Oh, and I mean a real double. Not a lazy, can't-be-half-assed-to-open-a-new-bottle-double." The bartender nods again, the muscles in his jaw visibly tightening. Mae finds she's enjoying winding him up. It makes her feel both uncomfortable and more like her caustic self than she's felt for a while.

The bartender grits his teeth. "What tequila?" he asks.

"Oh," Mae squints up at the shelves, but her visual impairment makes it hard to scan the labels in the way she once could. With peripheral vision all but gone, her range of sight is narrowed to barely half of what it was, allowing her to see only what's directly ahead. This, just another thing she now has to live with. The seconds pass as she tries to focus on each label in turn. She blinks furiously as her eyes start to water – another new motor spasm she can't figure out how to control.

"She'll have the Hornitos Anejo," says the guy now sitting next to her. "And the same for me please, though neat. Thanks, G."

Mae rounds on her new companion as the bartender turns away. "So, you're buying me drinks now?"

"You're welcome, Mae," says the man, tilting his white baseball cap with a seamless blend of streetwise-swag and the Mad Hatter's iconic madcap tip. Is he about to drop some sick beats or whisk her to his eternal tea party where the only rule is to expect unexpected madness? "What's say we ease off the smoke now, hey?" He's looking right at her. And not just at her in a general sense, but right into her eyes

– his, hazelly brown flecked with amber, seem to glow in the light. They hold a strange allure – intense but also distanced. Almost as though they're holding back on some great secret.

They sit there staring at each other while Mae assesses. This man feels familiar somehow, but she doesn't know him. Or doesn't remember him, at least, which must make him a fairly recent pre-crash connection.

The bartender appears from Mae's compromised left side vision – startling her so much that her whole body jolts. This is something she's getting used to – a lingering symptom of her half-blindness crossed with post-traumatic stress. The bartender places their drinks before them, and her mystery date breaks the eye contact to pay. Mae looks down into her drink, watching the golden liquid settle. How many friends has she lost to the black void of her brain? What sort of friend even was she? The sort who's salty to bartenders, apparently.

"I'm sorry for being foul," Mae says to her drink. "I'm not myself tonight." She hears the irony in this and almost laughs at herself. But the bartender doesn't hear or doesn't care for her apology. He's already gone back to his corner.

The brown-eyed man raises his glass and raises an eyebrow at Mae's. She lifts it to meet his. The glasses clink.

"To you," he says, "for cheating death. That was a hell of a wallop."

Mae takes a sip of her tequila. It's sweeter than she expected. Almost syrupy. And for a moment she feels like it's stirring a memory – of hot summer nights and boom boxes, keg stands, pick-up trucks and tractors in ranch pastures.

"So, how would you like to do this?"

Mae tugs her mind back to the present. The man she doesn't know has that same half-amused look on his face. "Do what?"

"Mhmm." The man makes a show of rearranging himself on his stool, then smiles widely and holds out a hand. "DB."

"D– what? That's not your name?"

"It is actually, and you said that last time."

"Right, okay. Well, I'm Mae but you seem to know that already."

"I do, but let's pretend I don't. It's more fun this way."

"Because you have all the cards? DB. Dickbutt."

"Exactly. Yo goofy-ass always called me that."

"It's a meet to pleasure you. Fuck. It's a pleasure to meet you. Goddamnit, I have the mental dexterity of a Jenga block."

DB's grin spreads to his eyes, which glimmer in the dim light of the bar. He's very obviously young – younger than Mae, but still, he has the early traces of crows' feet on his temples and laughter lines around his mouth. An old soul in a young man's body. It makes him feel trustworthy, for better or worse.

"Alright then, DB," says Mae, settling into the game. "Tell me, what do you do?"

"I work in IT," he says, taking a sip of his drink. "But

not the boring kind."

Mae laughs. "Okay, so what do you class as the fun kind?"

"I'm a cyber engineer." DB raises his eyebrows at her, the sort of look James Bond might give when luring in a target – or a lover. "You know, writing codes to track UFOs, building cyber bots to take over the White House, inventing the world's first digital chromosome to cure all genetic diseases, no flex."

Now it's Mae's turn to raise an eyebrow. "Oh, really?"

"No." DB shrugs. "Not, really. I could though. I am *that* good."

"I believe you." Mae smiles, amused. "Shame about that last one though. That sounded pretty ground-breaking."

"It will be," DB winks at her, and they lock eyes again. Being in his company feels natural, and Mae is reluctant to give the drink credit for that.

Mae breaks away and looks out at the room. It seems to be growing busier the later it gets. Someone has turned the music up and the hipster groups are dancing between the tables. She'd always been first on the dance floor in her college days. She wonders if she's grown out of that now. "Can I ask how you know me?"

"Seeing as this is a new beginning for you, we could just both agree to start over?" says DB.

"You make it sound like we fell out."

"I wouldn't say that."

"So, I fell out with you then?"

DB throws his head back in mock exasperation almost knocking that white hat off his head. "You're lost in the sauce, getting hung up on the facts here."

"What can I say? It's harder to trust people who seem to know more about you than you know about yourself." Mae downs the last of her drink and pushes the glass away. Is she a sad drunk? She hopes not. That's not what she came out for. She can feel DB's eyes on her. He shifts his body forward to speak in a lower voice.

"No, Mae. We didn't fall out. We met about one year before your accident, in the elevator actually, before you interviewed me for my job at D8N App. And now we're friends. We hit the nitty gritty streets, go for drinks on Fridays, and Tuesdays and most other days too. Your favorite drink is Hornitos Anejo on the rocks cuz it reminds you of your first summer after running away from home. You're a tough boss, but passionate, and you have this way when you talk that lets everyone know you're keeping the best of yourself close to your chest. It's what draws people in and keeps them there. Real talk, it's what keeps me coming out after work."

Mae shifts in her seat, then loses her balance and almost topples over. DB catches her arm to steady her. Mae shakes herself. He's right – she doesn't need these details. It only makes her miss what she doesn't have. Starting over sounds better. Healthier. She sits up straight. "Well, then. I guess it's a shame I'm not that person anymore cuz she sure sounds swell." Mae waves at the bartender. "Let's get some shots."

DB sits back and salutes. "You're the boss. Let me guess, more tequila?" He laughs. "You and your plant agave saving water nerd mission. You sometimes do come off as a girl who'd wash paper plates."

"Okay nerd. I bet when a girl asks you to fill up her box you complete a sudoku." Mae smirks. "Fuck it, more tequila."

The bar grows steadily heavier, then emptier around them as they order round after round of tequila. And the next time Mae looks up, she finds they're the last ones there beside a group of college kids taking drugs between arm wrestles. All boys, one girl – her main squeeze, the head honcho of the crew is the type that looks like he'd argue about religion in the comments of a snowboarding video. Mae watches as the main boy, playing cowboy wannabe in a too-clean Stetson hat, oversized brass belt buckle and a poser-prop piece of straw tucked in the corner of his mouth, looks around then pulls a plastic bag of pills out his pocket. God Mae wishes she could be young again.

Mae turns back to DB. "How about an arm wrestle?" She eyes his arms – scrawny but muscular. She has no muscle mass left after a year on bedrest. "Actually, scratch that. A thumb war. Loser buys kebabs."

DB rolls up his sleeves. "You're on."

They set their positions and grip right hands, staring each other down.

"One. Two. Three. Four. I declare a thumb war." Locked in, Mae grits her back molars. "Take your position.

Go!" They go at it. Mae yells, "Tag team!" Her left thumb tags her right thumb and then tackles DB's down.

"Yo! You're a cheat!"

"You didn't say no tag team." Mae raises a shot, downs it and throws the glass at the gong behind the bar. *Kerblanggggggg,* the clang echoes around the room and several people cheer. "Not bad for a half blind gal with a titanium super skull. I'm like Stevie Wonder Woman." Mae nudges DB and grins. "Come on then kebab boy, let's get out of here. Wait, no! I actually want pizza."

"Yeah, kebab confused me," says DB, sliding off his stool. "Last I knew you were a mental vegan."

"Vegan? Pfft, I was raised on meat, gnawing on bones and marrow."

"I know. Your fam are pasture-to-butcher's-block ranchers. They raise cattle and then partner with the nearby processing facility for the slaughter. You had me hack into their local slaughterhouse mainframe and change the breed of your family stock from cattle to dragon."

"Ha – no I didn't!" Mae doubles over laughing. "Man, I was quite the joker, hey?"

"One of the best."

Together they stumble from the bar and take to the street. The sky is dark, and the air is arid. It makes Mae feel thirsty. They grip each other's arms, trying to guide themselves in a straight line. Mae moves to DB's left side so she can see him. They're laughing and singing, and Mae's shoes are swinging from her fingers.

Outside Roppolo's, Mae lights a ciggie while DB squints at the menu on the door. "While I microdose death, get me the BBQ brisket," says Mae. "Large."

"Sure as hell not vegan anymore then. And since when do you smoke? Damn, you have changed."

"Vegan?" Mae frowns.

"Yeah, I just told you. You used to be a mental vegan."

"Ah sorry, these memory lapses are the real deal. My fiancé has moments he wants to tear his hair out cuz apparently I'm asking him the same thing for the millionth time. Whatever. Even if I was vegan, the new Mae reacts to the smell of a distant BBQ cookout the same way a shark reacts when a lone girl goes swimming on the rag. I would buy brisket out of a stranger's van." Mae dances her fingertips to her lips, as though savoring a kiss.

Fifteen minutes later, DB comes out with a pizza box and a disappointed face. "Okie dokie smokey. They didn't have any brisket. And they mad-judged me when I asked for it. All they had left was the pizza no one wants – Hawaiian."

"Um. Excuse me, I love pineapple on pizza."

DB raises his eyebrows.

"Shut up. I'm serious." She nudges him and reaches for the box. "Pineapple on pizza is God."

"You're a crazy freak." DB laughs. "This is unreal. I think we're like the only two people in this world that love pineapple on pizza."

"I know, this is like a never-happens meet-cute moment. Like um… *you* fuck kids? No way, *I* fuck kids!"

"Shh." DB hushes her, looking around to make sure no one heard. "I don't fuck kids."

"Phew. I was starting to feel like you hanging out with me there'd be one less amber alert tonight." Mae winks.

They eat, sat on the curb, dangling long strands of melted cheese into their mouths. And for the first time since the accident, Mae finds she enjoys every slice.

DB finishes up, a satisfied smile on his face. He turns and looks at Mae's eyes. "Yo, got any gum?"

Mae, her eyes sparkling with a mischievous glint, replies, "Gum? No, but I got something better." She reaches into her pocket and pulls out a small, blue-green canister. "It's a spray. Try it."

Without a second thought, DB gives the spray a quick spritz, sending a mist straight into his mouth. The spray hits his taste buds, and he immediately starts coughing, eyes watering. "The fuck is this spicy ass liquid fire?"

Mae, grinning ear to ear, leans in close, her voice a conspiratorial whisper. "That, my amigo, is Mace. Old habits die hard. Pre-accident me was a real prankster extraordinaire. I mean, what girl hasn't Mace-d a guy while playing hard to get?"

DB, still hacking, manages a weak smile. "Ayo, that's like puttin' my mouth on a 120-volt battery – straight-up whomp." He breaks into another coughing fit, doubling over. "Damn, there she goes. I remember you with your pranks. You were Trouble with a capital T." He shakes his head, then leans in, undeterred by the Mace, and kisses her.

It's a kiss that says yes to chaos, yes to the unknown, and yes to the trouble that comes with this fascinating, unpredictable woman. Then DB splutters and laughs.

"Let's get you some gum before we head back, hey Dickbutt?"

He plants a second kiss on the end of her nose. Mae closes her eyes to greet it, and when she opens them she's in a living room she doesn't recognize, a new drink in her hand. They're dancing around DB's place, cigarettes in an ashtray, lines of cocaine on the coffee table. The paintings on the walls blur into one as Mae spins and throws her head back. She sings at the ceiling, at the cute constellations of stars tacked up there. If she squints, she can almost pretend she's outside. Alive. God, how alive she feels. How herself. This is herself. She knows that now. This. Is. Herself. She feels reckless with energy, like one of those rebirth moments when you almost die, except Mae has been re-born, squeezed out of a bartender's rag. Her legs tangle with someone else's and she falls back onto a sofa, the rich, woody smell of DB's cologne surrounding her, engulfing them both as it has before, and then his lips are there again and Jesus Christ, she wants those lips. His lips ain't no prayer book. She presses her body into his and his mouth is on hers. DB tries to pull his buttoned shirt over his head, but it rips, and the buttons burst all over the room. His hands are under her top, unzipping her denim shorts, his fingers tracing over the tattoo she got that night when she first started dating Rob. The night at the strip club when the bouncer got shot with a bow and arrow. And they all got chucked out, only for Mae and Rob to stumble on a tattoo parlor, the "OH HEY" now inked along her hipbone a reminder of wilder times. DB lingers over it now, tracing the meaningless phrase before whispering words that Mae can only be half sure of in her drunken state: "He's lying to you, you know." Then DB slides down her body, ready to play a little lower.

3

Mae

Mae's head feels both heavy and empty, stuffed with cotton wool and pounding with the vibrations of the last song they'd been blaring. It's light. She blinks rapidly, trying to clear the blurry film from her eyes. She doesn't think she's ever felt this sick. What felt like a rebirth moment the night before, now feels like she's been brown-baggin' it since her cradle days. Mae groans and rolls over. She feels hot and her skin is weeping with sweat. Mae blinks and tries to focus. There's a man asleep next to her, but it isn't the man it should be.

"Shit." Appalled, Mae bites her fist. She sits up, her

heart rate accelerating. She's in what appears to be a kid's tent with pink and yellow nylon walls. She gropes for her clothes but comes back with nothing but stuffed animals, staring at her with wide traumatized eyes. Where are her clothes? She fumbles with the sheets to free herself and crawls out of the flap. They're in a child's bedroom. The walls are painted an iridescent shade of blue – it hurts to look at. There are shelves of Legos, and a box of soft toys in the corner. A train set lies partially broken on the floor. "What the fuck in tarnation? He has a kid?"

She wracks her brain, trying to remember any mention of a child, but comes up with nothing. He had no ring on his finger – did he? Mae crouches down again and peaks back into the tent, trying to see DB's hand, but he's too tangled up in princess-printed sheets.

Her denim shorts are on the floor, her boots and panties strewn over a row of now not-so-innocent teddy bears. She dresses frantically but still can't find her top. The tent rustles as DB stirs. Heart pounding, she spots it caught on the door handle. She grabs the tops and dashes from the room, treading on a Lego piece as she goes. Mae grabs her mouth to muffle a scream. No wonder Godzilla was so angry all the time. She presses the door gently closed behind her.

The living room is a mess: cushions on the floor, Corona bottles and crumpled dollar bills on the coffee table. Mae's bag is on the sprawling breakfast bar next to a fruit-bowl filled with candy bars and crumpled dollar bills. *Fuck it.* She grabs three Mars bars and makes a beeline for the door, only then spotting the photos of a curly-haired toddler. She stops, turns and reaches for a dollar bill before sprinting out.

The morning is too bright for Mae's eyes. She squints, her pupils constricting painfully against the searing glare as she searches for a bus stop. Finding one a safe two blocks from DB's house, she stumbles over to it and checks the times. Central, anything going central. She needs to get herself as far away from this as possible.

Mae digs through her bag for a candy bar and tears it open. She sinks her teeth through the chocolate-coated nougat, chews and takes another bite, as though eating it fast will somehow sweeten her shame.

The first bus that arrives is going as far as Lake Austin. Mae climbs right to the back and collapses in a corner. There's a foundation stain down the tee she's wearing, and the fabric smells strongly of tequila. She reaches into her bag and pulls out another candy bar. What the hell is she going to tell Rob?

Mae fits in very well on this bus. The woman in front of her is eating beets from a Ziploc bag – Mae watches her finish the last slice, then turn the bag inside out and licks it clean. On the other side a security guard is nodding off. The college frat boy spread out on the front seats still has powder around his nose and vomit on his boat shoes. Mae hooks her legs up onto the seat and feels the scars down the side of her left calf. She's no better than any of these people. She rests her head against the window. There's a D8N App banner on the back of the driver's box. Like she needs another goddamn guilt trip. She crams the rest of the candy bar into her mouth as penance and searches for her phone.

Shit. Where is her phone?

She rummages deeper, filtering through the broken lipsticks, receipts, and tampons and an old pregnancy test. A Ziplock bag of pills she'd forgotten she had – aspirin maybe, or meds she was supposed to have taken for her memory. Maybe all the blank years really were her fault after all.

"Fuck, fucking, fuckity, fuckshit." All eyes on the bus turn to look at her. "What?" she asks, unable to keep the frustration from her voice.

Mae throws her bag on the floor and buries her face in her hands. She must have left her phone somewhere. At the bar, or at DB's. She lifts her head only to be greeted by another hot pink D8N App ad on a billboard. Goddamn karma. There's no way Rob will buy she flushed her phone down the *"loo"* again, as he calls it. He's gonna have questions. And that's assuming he did end up staying at the office and isn't already changing the locks on her. How could she be so ding-dong dicks-for-brains stupid?

She looks down at the Rob <3 tattoo on her left index finger. With savage ferocity, she rubs at the ink, as though erasing the tattoo will erase the memory of her betrayal. But it's no use. She knows what she has to do – she can't start her new life with lies. Taking a deep breath, she scans the other passengers, searching for a savior. She zeroes in on a lone college kid two rows in front of her and slips out of her seat to tap him on the shoulder.

"Howdy-do," she says, leaning in just enough to invade his personal space. "I know this is forward as heck, but my phone died, and I need to make a quickie call. Any chance I could borrow yours?" She lays on the eye-batting and lip-biting, pulling out all the stops. "Please?"

The dude, clearly taken aback by her charm offensive, hesitates. Mae can practically see the thoughts swirling in his head: *why is psycho chick talking to me?* But she doubles down on the sincerity. "Please," she says. "It's an emergency."

The dude sighs, clearly unable to resist her hurricane of hot messness. He hands over his phone. "If you're quick. I'm off in a couple of stops."

"Thanks, you're a lifesaver," Mae says, her smile genuine. She stumbles back to her seat, already dialing Rob's number. She's sweating like a pig at a luau, her legs jigging as she waits for the line to connect.

"Hello?" Rob's voice crackles through the line, distant and distorted, thanks to the clusterfuck of tall buildings surrounding her.

Mae's heart pounds. "Hey, it's me," she says, her voice shaking despite her efforts to sound casual. "I lost my phone, and before I explain, I need to tell you something. I slept with someone else." There, she's said it. Now she just has to wait for the verbal bullets to start flying.

Rob's voice, fragmented and faint, cuts through the static. "–breaking up."

Mae cups her hand over the phone, trying to block out the noise of the city that's conspiring against her. "We're breaking up?" she asks, confusion mixing with her guilt and shame like a toxic cocktail.

"The call is breaking up," Rob clarifies, a little clearer this time.

"Oh, right" Mae takes a breath. "I cheated on you," she blurts out again, her voice loud and clear, carrying more emotion than she'd like. The dude who lent her the phone shoots a curious glance over his shoulder, no doubt wondering what the hell kind of soap opera he's stumbled into.

"When? How?" Rob asks, his voice faint but now audible.

"Last night," Mae whispers, her cheeks burning. "I got drunk, and it just happened. I'm so sorry, babe."

"Speak up! I can't hear you!"

Mae leans in closer to the phone, practically mouth-humping it. "It was a mistake."

Silence.

"How could you do this?" Rob's anguish is raw and exposed, like an open wound.

Mae's chest tightens like a vise grip of guilt. Why did she have to be honest? Why didn't she just stay home like Rob told her to? "I know, I dang bungled up big time. But we can fix this. It meant nothing, I promise. I don't even remember it. It might not have even been good—"

"I can't hear you," Rob says, frustration creeping into his voice. "I can't—I just can't process this," Rob stammers. "I can't forgive you. You've ruined everything. You were my reason for living, and now— I don't even think I want to go on."

The way he says this, so flat and definite, chills Mae to the core. "Wait, Rob? You don't mean that. Are you talking about—like, you're talking about offing yourself?" Mae can't breathe. Her vision starts to cloud, erasing the bus around her.

"You've ruined everything," he says again. Then, suddenly, there's the sound of barking in the background. "Down, Bella."

Mae's brow furrows. "Who's Bella?" she asks, confusion clouding her brain as she realizes the voice on the other side of the line isn't as deep as Rob's. That this might not even be Rob at all.

"You know why I got Bella? For you. Now I'm taking it out on her – just a little puppy. I knew you always hated Bella. And you know what, Bella hates you too."

Mae's eyes widen. Shit. Shit. Shit. "Lord a'mercy. I got the wrong number. Sorry! Don't kill yourself. Bye." She hangs up, her hands shaking.

Stunned, she looks down at the phone, but she can't bring herself to call Rob after this shitshow. Maybe it's a sign. A sign that she should just keep her cowpatty cunt mouth shut.

Resigning herself, Mae stumbles back down the row to return the phone. "Thanks, sorry 'bout that. Whoopsie-poopsie."

The dude, looking bewildered, takes back his phone and Mae escapes before he has chance to comment.

Throwing herself back into her seat, Mae stares out the window. She chews at the skin around her thumb nail, the way she used to do as a kid hiding in the garage to escape confrontation with her father and brothers. She should go home and take a long bath, but some deep, irrational part of her brain just wants to see Rob now. Needs to see the love in his eyes. To prove to herself that it isn't broken. That he hasn't by some terrible force of osmosis already sensed her betrayal. She jabs the button in front of her seat, and the bus stopping light pings red.

The D8N App offices are on Congress Avenue. Mae stumbles through the glass revolving doors and tries to give off an air of composure as she approaches the front desk.

"Hi – morning," she says to the guy behind the security desk. Her voice is raspy from sleeplessness and alcohol. She clears her throat. "I've left my pass at home. But you know me, right? Mae from D8N App."

The guy looks at her blankly. "Full name?" he asks.

"Mae Day."

He nods and turns to his computer screen, searching for her ID.

Mae shifts her weight from foot to foot, clenching her

fist. She's trying to resist the urge to look around in case she sees someone she knows – or someone who knows her. She doesn't want to see anyone but Rob.

The man coughs. "Alright miss, through you go."

Relieved, Mae passes through the glass gates which swing open as she steps toward them. She dives into an elevator and rams the button for the 45th floor. As the doors slide closed, Mae turns to the mirrored wall behind her and looks at herself properly for the first time that morning. It makes her wish this upright coffin of mirror and brushed steel was a closed casket. It's almost enough to make her stop the lift and head back out. Not just out of the building either, but out of Austin, out of America, far away from planet Earth. It's not her unbrushed hair, or the smudged mascara. It's not her lipstick that looks like it was done by the chimp they tested it on. It's not that she looks like a Halloween decoration still up in February. It's the guilt in her ice-blue eyes.

The doors open onto a huge glass wall with a fluorescent pink D8N App sign. Mae takes a deep breath and steps out into a sprawling open-plan office. Natural light streams in through the windows, bouncing off the white walls and giving all the staff an otherworldly glow. The furniture is a mix of modern and industrial, and several large free-standing whiteboards are scattered around the space, covered in diagrams, sketches and to-do lists. Even at this hour of the morning (whatever the hour was) the office is brimming and electric with activity. The sound of typing, talking, and laughter fills the air; the smell of coffee and fresh pastries wafting from the kitchen. The ever-growing teams of marketers, designers, sales staff and technicians are free flowing around the space, swapping seats and shouting across to other departments, asking for notes and validation on whatever they're working on. The office reflects the company's culture – young and dynamic, a breeding ground of creativity and innovation. It's an exact blueprint of the office they'd sketched out on napkins at college bars and talked about late into the night sharing the single bed in Rob's dorm room.

Mae keeps her head down as she skirts the perimeter of the office. This used to be hers, but it doesn't feel that way anymore. Rob has been very protective since the accident, insisting he can manage here himself. It feels strange to be so separate from it now, when she'd once believed in it so much she put all her life savings into it.

At the far end of the main space are the executive offices. These are spacious and more luxurious than the rest of the space, with polished wooden floors, leather furniture, and large teak desks. The executive offices are where the company's founders and senior management team work, and where she and Rob once shared an office, having midday sex on their desks with an executive level view.

Mae slips through the glass boundary into the muffled quiet of the executive offices, and treads swiftly along to the door at the very end. She pauses, composing herself. She must act normal, or he'll see it in her. She knocks and enters without waiting for a reply, though the room beyond is empty. A rush of anxiety floods through her, though she had no real reason to think he'd be here. She tries to squash it down inside her. He could be anywhere. In the bathroom, getting coffee.

The office is just as she remembered: two large desks at either side of the room, an L shaped sofa in the space between them, currently extended into a sofa bed. Mae's shoulders relax a little – so he did sleep here last night. She moves over to Rob's desk, running her hand over the leather back of his chair. The computer screen is lit on the password screen, the company logo and mantra spread behind the login box:

D8N App
because burning love doesn't wait...

Mae's eyes move to the mess of documents on the desk: blueprints of the app's new features, visualizing the user journey from first swipe to first date. This had always been her favorite part of the process – the ideation and testing. Constantly tweaking until the process was so seamless it felt like second nature even to a first-time user. Making love feel easy. She moves the top layer of papers to see the data tables printed on the sheet below – changes to the algorithm by the looks of things. A complicated looking chart at the bottom is labeled, *DarkStork demographics*. She leans in to see it closer. It appears to be mapping out potential matches between different demographics – that was always Rob's remit. She just was the one balls-deep in the technical coding, bringing Rob's vision to life. Mae scans down the axis on the left, scrutinizing the data segments: gender, age, sexuality, religion, location, education, income bracket, career score, SMR (social mobility rating), MB score (Myers-Briggs personality score), attachment type, love language. Then Mae pauses. The bottom two are new, labeled in red ink instead of black, the same color as the new DarkStork branding: fertility rate and GVP. What was GVP?

"Knock, knock!"

Mae jumps back from the desk as the office door swings inward and a pair of sleek-fitting black stilettos steps over the threshold.

"Oh." The woman stops, clearly unsure of what to say.

Feeling the need to highlight her position, Mae attempts to stand more upright. "I was just waiting for Rob," she says, moving around the desk and holding out a hand. "I'm Mae, his partner and co-creator of D8N App. I don't believe we've met. Though I apologize if we have."

The woman looks at Mae's hand for a second too long before taking it, a Barbie-esque smile spreading across her face.

"A pleasure to finally meet you," she says through her smile. "Rob speaks about you in such high reverence. You're a pretty poetic easter egg, so I hear. I'd love to crack you open."

"Sorry?" says Mae, narrowing her eyes. "Are you gaslighting me?"

"I mean, Rob is constantly telling me you smell of napalm, torture tabby cats and you're a climate change denier." Rose shakes her head and laughs. "But no, of course not! Genuinely, it's an honor. I'm Rose." She holds out a hand for Mae to shake.

"Um, and what do you do exactly?"

"Oh, well, I'm a geneticist and molecular engineer by trade. Made my name researching female fertility and looking at hormone levels in correlation to genetic markers." Her smile is slightly patronizing. She tilts her head, eyes lingering on the ugly scars across Mae's hairline.

"So, you analyze the algorithmic matches between genes? Guess that makes you the *real* matchmaker, huh?"

"Well actually right now I'm filling in the role of Chief Financial Officer and, I guess, Rob's intermediary second in command."

Mae takes Rose's hand. Her grip is firm and her posture oozes confidence. Her bronzed, cinnamon skin is flawless and her eyes bright but impenetrable. She has a tattoo of a rose on a cross inked onto her left wrist. She lets go of Mae's hand and smooths her slicked-back hair.

"Rob has been out doing a final sweep of tonight's venue, though he should be back any moment." Her eyes move to the sofa bed, its white sheets ruffled, unmade. "Would you give me a hand with this?"

Together they collect the duvet and cushions, then fold

the bed back inside itself. Rose lifts the cushions off the footstool to reveal a hidden compartment where the duvet and pillows slot neatly, transforming the room back into a professional space.

Rose straightens up and brushes herself down, smoothing the front of her baby-green pantsuit. "Perfect," she says. "Did you want me to give Rob a message? I doubt he'll have much time for anything before this evening, his schedule is pretty packed today I'm afraid. But I can pass something on."

Something about the finality in this statement makes Mae bristle. Who is this svelte humanoid woman who seems to think she can tell Mae when she can speak to her fiancé? This woman who seems to know more about Rob's wants and whereabouts than she does.

"No," says Mae, trying not to sound too defiant. "No, thanks. I think I'll wait. You can get me a coffee though, if you like. I've got some catching up to do." Mae strides away from the sofa and plops herself down behind her old desk, kicking her legs up onto its mahogany surface in a brazen display of nonchalance. She looks around the room, trying to regain that old sense of pride and ownership she once held for the place. Her office. Her business – she, the co-founder of this crazy idea she once spent nights sketching out on bar mats and on the back of essay papers, finetuning Rob's vision from rock to diamond. Her's and Rob's shared success.

Rose doesn't move, that sickly smile still plastered on

her face. "I'm afraid I've been using that desk recently," she says. "It's been more productive to stick close to Rob while working on this launch."

Mae looks down at the desk and sees that sure enough, the surface is littered with papers she doesn't recognize, all branded with that same red DarkStork stamp in the header. Mae feels put out. It's clear this woman is overstepping the mark: taking her desk, talking down to her this way. But what can she do? She opens her mouth to respond, but just as she does, the door opens again and Rob steps in already talking out loud, completely oblivious to Mae in the corner.

"Cor, it's perfect," he says, spreading his arms to Rose and placing them on her shoulders. "This launch is going to be mega. The biggest thing ever to come out of Austin. Hell! To come out of America." He lets go of her and moves toward his desk.

"You are the shepherd of a new world," Rose boasts.

Rob sheds his jacket revealing his broad shoulders and muscular back through his fitted shirt. He drapes the jacket over his chair and stands by the window, looking out over the city. "I feel like I'm a man up on the moon and I'm looking down at planet Earth. And you, Miss Cross—" Rob cuts off short, spotting Mae behind her desk. "Oh, Mae. What are you doing here?"

It stings Mae to hear the way his voice changes on seeing her. She suddenly feels very conscious of the foundation stain down her top.

"I just came in to see you," she says. "And to catch up

on things. I think it's about time I stepped back into the battlefield, don't you? I soldiered through a coma after all."

Rob looks to Rose, and though Mae can't be sure from behind, she's fairly certain they're exchanging some sort of silent communication.

"Could I speak to you alone, Rob?" Mae asks. She catches his eye and holds it. Rob sighs and nods at Rose, who turns and leaves the room without another word.

Now alone together, Mae feels her guards slipping down. She crosses out from behind her desk and comes to throw her arms around Rob's neck. "Hey, you." She leans in for a kiss, but Rob ducks away from her.

"Christ alive, Mae. You stink of cheap booze. Have you been on the lash?"

Mae freezes – caught already.

"Well? You sound really off-kilter."

Mae's mind races, clutching the air for excuses. "Yes," she says. "Yes, last night I did because I was mugged."

"What?" Rob's face changes to a look of confusion. "What do you mean you were mugged?"

Mae turns from him and throws herself down on the sofa. "I mean I went out to get a pizza because I'm sick to death of those doggone ready meals, but then I was jumped and they snatched my phone right out of my hand, and a load of cash from my purse too, and then legged it." She takes a deep breath, afraid to stop now she's gotten going. These lies have more twists than a pretzel factory. "And no, before you ask, I didn't get any defining details or anything like that, it all happened too fast, and you know I can't really focus on things that well anymore, so it was all very disorientating and—"

Mae can feel her face turning red, and luckily Rob seems to read this as a sign of her feeling emotional rather than simply out of breath. With three long strides he comes to sit next to her on the couch and pulls her into him. She breathes in the heady scent of his cologne – Tom Ford Tobacco Vanille de Parfum, his favorite, and the same one she's bought him every year for Christmas since they first met. The smokey notes were a nuanced nod to his penchant for lighting up a fag when in a tizzy. "I guess someone really is trying to kill me, huh?" Mae jokes into his shoulder.

"I'm sorry, Snugglebug. You should have called."

"How could I, without my phone?"

"Indeed."

They continue to sit there, Mae's ear pressed up against Rob's chest. After a couple of minutes listening to Rob's breathing, there's a knock at the door.

"Come in," he calls.

It's Rose.

"Sorry Rob, but this really can't wait."

"Yes, of course." He turns back to Mae, back in business mode. "Go home, Mae. Sort yourself out and get dressed up for tonight, if you still feel up to it."

"I feel up to it," says Mae with defiance. Like she's going to let this pompous Rose girl do her job a minute longer. She couldn't be more of a snotty cunt if someone blew their nose in her twat.

"Okay, fine. Well then, I'll pick you up at eight on the dot."

"Can't I stay and help? I mean it. I want back in, this is my business too, remember?"

"We'll talk about it later, Mae. Please. I really just need to get over tonight."

Mae nods but doesn't look at him as he stands and goes to sit behind his desk. Rose stays where she is, holding the door open as a clear invitation. Mae grits her teeth and wonders if it's a bad sign that she now doesn't feel any guilt for last night at all.

DB

He has no luck with women. Not that he really has time for a woman in his life. This is what DB is thinking as he puts his nieces' bedroom back together, steals a candy bar for breakfast and prepares for the walk of shame in last night's clothes.

There was a time when he thought he and Mae had a shot. Back when they first met, him just out of his five-year relationship with Wilma – a woman he should've said goodbye to after the first date – and Mae bashing that pretty little head of hers (not yet titanium-plated) against the bar, trying to figure out the moment she'd become the pawn rather than the partner to Rob's relentless ambition. He can remember the first time he saw her. It was the day of his interview, and she was trying to do her makeup in the elevator up to the 45th floor. He had spent hours preparing for the interview at D8N App, seeing it as his chance to really start over. Just as the elevator doors began to close though, a frazzled looking blonde darted in, bashing her funny bone as the doors caught her.

"Shit," she cursed as the elevator started its ascent. She was juggling a makeup bag and a mirror, her hair disheveled, her mascara wand waging war against her eyelids. But Jesus fuck was she attractive. "Sorry, running late," she mumbled.

"Which level of corporate hell you headed to?" DB asked, taking a wild stab at humor.

"45," she said, continuing her makeup.

"D8N App? Same here." DB grinned, but again, didn't get a reaction. He tapped his foot, trying not to look at her too much. She looked tired, he thought – the sort of tired that's down to more than just a lack of sleep. "It's a tough world out there, ain't it?" he asked. "Between gettin' that makeup on point, workin' that coffee maker to spit out something less grainy than beach-day pubes, and crushin' interviews on three hours of shut eye – the struggle's real out here."

Mae's hand made an unplanned detour, leaving an inky smudge below her eye. She snorted. "You have no idea," she replied. "Especially when those influencer YouTube makeup tutorials make it look so goddamn easy peasy."

"Yeah, I've been down the YouTube rabbit hole, too. I've watched more 'How to Tie a Perfect Windsor Knot' videos than I care to admit. And would you just look at this shit-show?" DB gestured to the poorly knotted tie stolen from his Pop's wardrobe that very morning.

"That is pretty shameful," said Mae, giving him the side-eye. "Though at least you didn't end up with a mascara monobrow like I just did. And lipstick like I head-bunted a clown."

"You're right." He grimaced. "I think I just had a flashback to seeing Times Square Elmo take his mask off." *Yo, did I really just say that out loud?* Not even into the office and he was already letting his true humor show. He wanted to trade barbs, but some verbal sparring lines shouldn't be crossed. To his surprise though, instead of looking horrified, Mae's eyes softened with spark of intrigue.

"We're almost to the top of the Notre-Dame tower where I'll be ringing the bell." DB hunchbacks over – such a bad impression that Disney might sue. "Well," he said, trying to skate over the misstep. "I hope it's safe to say that makeup skills are probably not a crucial part of the job at D8N App then? It would really work in my favor if you don't *have* to be dateable to work in dating."

Mae snapped her mirror closed and dropped her mascara wand into her bag. "If I'm anything to go by, I'd have to say being 'dateable' is most definitely not on the list of employee requirements." She met his eye for the first time and grinned, her crystal blue eyes flashing with mischief.

"Though I guess you could argue the term 'dateable' is somewhat subjective."

The elevator stopped and the doors opened.

"Nice to meet you, my undatable elevator amigo. Quasimodo."

DB offered a small bow. "Glad I could brighten your day with my makeup commentary. If all else fails, hopefully I get the bell-ringer job."

When Mae showed up later in the interview room he almost shat himself. Her make-up was still wonky, but she'd clearly had a coffee of three – or in hindsight, perhaps a sniff of coke – and she had the sexiest, smug grin on her face, pinching the dimples in her cheeks. For real. If she hadn't been his boss, he'd have taken her on the desk right there.

DB lets himself in his Pop's house and heads straight for the fridge. He uncaps the milk and gives it a sniff. "Aw, hell nah," he says, recoiling at the sour, eye-watering cloud of toxicity rising from the carton like morning-after breath. DB dumps the whole liter in the trash, then digs out a can of Modelo instead and cracks it open.

He looks around, his eyes tracing the cracks in the stucco ceiling, remnants of the devastating '98 floods. The house is plainly decorated, save for a few traditional African masks hung on the white walls. DB was born in Senegal, but his parents came to America when he was four. He grew up in New York, but his Pop moved to Texas after the divorce, buying himself a small but habitable home on the outskirts of Austin. DB visited when he was a kid, though less and less as he got older. The bedroom he sleeps in now still has his old Manga posters on the walls and faded DC bedsheets – the large desk, three computer screens and collection of half-coded motherboards not really doing much to make the room look any more grown up.

He takes a swig of beer. He should really do something with the place now that it's essentially his, but the idea of moving things around feels way too final. Miracles happen, after all. They could announce some crazy new experimental treatment tomorrow, that somehow has the power to un-mutate mutated DNA and give his dad back his mind, movement and memory. Miracles. He sighs. He really should visit his dad today – his one day off before working through the weekend. And he has the dumb DarkStork launch party to go to. Flashes of last night return to him. Mae's laugh, Mae's curves, the sweet warm taste of her coochie. She'll be with Rob though. She'll be with mother-fucking Rob.

*

DB showers and chooses a suit to take to the dry cleaners. His Pop's assisted living facility is about a half hour drive out in Georgetown. He loves visiting his dad, but the home itself makes his skin crawl with its faint antiseptic smell, drab magnolia walls and the Zombieland nurses with their fake-ass smiles and baby voices. Still, the nurses seem to have more rapport with his dad than DB these days.

An hour or so later, after dropping off his suit for the launch party, he pushes open the heavy glass doors of the care center. Each step feels like a step deeper and deeper toward his own fate as he heads further into the hellscape past residents in wheelchairs and nurses in scrubs offering their usual false platitudes: "Morning, Danny", "He's on good form today Danny", "I'll bring your favorite cookies by shall I, Danny?". He feels like an intruder in this sterile world.

His father's room is small and square. Every side is filled with photos of happier times – memory joggers, a sad attempt to help him retain a small sense of who he is. There's a picture of the two of them fishing back when DB was in high school, each holding a fishing rod, arms around each other with wide grins on their faces. There's one of DB even younger, riding a bike with the Batman logo on the front, Henry running by his side with arms out to stop him falling. Then there's the photo of the three of them – DB, his dad and his mom, before the morning he came home from school to find his dad's bags packed and his family fallen apart. It was a long time before he forgave his dad for leaving. Now he wishes he could get back some of that wasted time. Life's too short to hold grudges, especially with family.

"Hey, Pop," says DB, forcing a smile as he approaches his father's chair.

Henry's eyes, once bright and full of life, meet DB's gaze. Now they're cloudy, a window to a mind trapped within an increasingly uncooperative body as the Huntington's tightens its grip.

"Danny Boy…" Henry's voice is a mere whisper, an echo of the commanding bellow his lungs once held.

"How are you feeling today?" DB asks, perching on the edge of the bed. "Up for a smoke out the back?"

His father's response is a slow, painful series of movements and incoherent mumbles. On any other day DB would have put on a smile and coaxed his dad outside with him. But his patience is frayed today, his pulse still set to the rhythm of the panic he'd felt waking up in his niece's bedroom alone, just like the morning of the accident – the day his life was finally supposed to come together but disintegrated instead. Just like everything else in his life. Surely he has the shittiest weakass luck of any other miserable clump of mutated cells flummoxing around this dusty-ass rock.

"Alright, then," he says, making a show of standing up. "I'll be back in ten. Save me some cookies, eh?" DB heads for the door without looking back. If he doesn't look back, the guilt won't be so bad. If he just keeps moving, he might be able to outrun the inevitable.

5

Mae

Mae stands waiting outside her and Rob's loft. She's wearing a long silk dress she doesn't remember buying and has tamed her hair into a classy half-up, half-down style that makes her look like she's about to step into an advert for Pantene conditioner. She's done as Rob asked – she's 'pulled herself together', though perhaps in a different way than he's expecting. She's sick of being sick. She's never been the type to enjoy sitting around doing nothing and now that she's been discharged, there's no reason she can't return to her old life with full force, starting tonight. Mae smiles to herself. What is it about red lipstick that makes her feel 900% more like a boss?

Rob's Aston Martin Goldfinger pulls up at 8pm on the dot. He had it converted to a fully electrified powertrain sports car – the first authentic remastering of the original. Mae opens the door.

"Are you my Uber driver?"

Rob's eyes widen at seeing her all dressed up – the first time since the accident and Mae feels her cheeks glow. She forgot how much she likes it when he looks at her that way.

Rob gestures her in. "My lady."

"I'm so happy to see your sexy mug," says Mae, leaning over to kiss him. She strokes his patchy facial hair, lingering with the bridge of her nose pressed against his. "That beard doesn't get longer these days; it just gets more serious."

"Buckle up, kiddo and whack that air con up, would you? It's bollocks hot today. Texan oven heat burning the British right outta me. Hey—" He double takes. "That's the frock you wore that evening at The Shard, isn't it?"

"Oh, the night you proposed? Maybe it was. I don't remember. Sorry, I guess that's a memory gap. Sometimes I wonder if I dreamt you dropped the knee." She leans back and buckles in as Rob turns the ignition and ramps up the music.

Mae clears her throat and busts out a limerick to the beat. "There once was a British bloke called Rob, I'd slob on his knob like corn on the cob. But now he's grindin' just his job."

Rob laughs. "There once was a cheeky lass called Mae.

My dearest diabolical darling bae. She's wicked in a proper top-drawer way, come what may."

"Ha! Aw, you." Mae slaps him playfully. "I miss when we'd do limericks about each other. We used to do this all the time. Didn't we?"

"I've got something for you," Rob nods his head toward the back seats. "In the box."

Mae stretches an arm behind her and retrieves a white box. Inside is a brand-new phone. "Aw, shucks. Bless my soul. Thank you!" Guilt twinges in her chest as she tips the phone out into her hand and turns it over.

"No more getting mugged, alright? Or flushing it down the loo, or leaving it out in the scorching sun, or any of the other stupid things you do with your phones."

"I'll protect it like my baby."

Rob frowns. "I don't know how to respond to that."

"Wow." Mae stares him down in the mirror. "I can make fertility jokes about myself. Your only job is to laugh along. C'mon, don't leave me hanging."

"I didn't mean it like that. You're right, you've been trodden on enough in your life."

"Tread on? That's cold. Remember when I got hit by a car? I don't remember but my skull does."

"I just never know if you're joking when you say this stuff. Like are you wanting me to joke along, or do you want reassurance? It's just hard to tell sometimes. Especially since – you know. It's made you harder to read."

"Obviously, I'm joking about it. I can joke about my

fertility just like I can joke about being hit by cars, and my bionic skull. I don't want your reassurance. When have I ever asked for your reassurance? Disability, shit fertility, superhero skulls, c'mon, laugh it up."

Rob eyes her in the mirror. "It's not cricket. Alright, well. Maybe reign in the self-pity in front of the investors, yeah?"

"Marzipan dildodick." Mae stares out the window. She hadn't wanted a baby before the accident, not urgently – but Rob had. They'd started to try, Rob had told her, but they'd had no luck. Now, on the other side of a near-death experience, Mae has to admit she's starting to appreciate the importance of having something to leave behind. She wonders if Rob would be open to trying again?

"So, are you going to tell me about this DarkStork project then?"

"I can't babe. It's not announced yet. You'll just have to wait and see."

Mae blows at the air. "Come on. You can tell me. It's half my baby after all."

Rob ignores her. "New tech, new investors. Profound future implications. Will be a game changer. Please," he accentuates the plea, "don't drink too much or say anything off-color. I can't let anything taint this evening."

"I'm not going to drink at all," says Mae.

"Really? At a party?" Rob raises an eyebrow. "That's new. Is this you trying to be a better person? De-comafied Mae 2.0?"

Mae's not sure how to take that, so she doesn't say anything. Was she really so awful before the crash? Rob's a real saint for sticking by her through all that.

"Thanks for the phone," she says.

"My pleasure. Just a mere drop in the vast ocean of my sterling good deeds." Rob smiles and turns up the music.

The DarkStork launch party is being held at a rooftop nightclub in downtown Austin. Rob has hired out the entire venue for the occasion – Mae can only imagine what it must have cost him on a Friday evening in peak July. Rooftop clubs were becoming increasingly popular in downtown Austin, especially now that the summers seemed to scorch hotter and longer than Mae could recall from childhood – global warming really was no joke.

They arrive fashionably late, Mae in her silver dress and nude kitten heels, only marginally overshadowed by Rob in his tightly fitting, iridescent leather trousers, neatly pressed white shirt and high-top sneakers. Inside the club, the walls are covered in flashing D8N App signs, and the dance floor is packed with people: their guest list ranging from shareholders and potential new investors to tech influencers who look like they've taken a second mortgage to buy a digital racehorse, and celebrities hoping to become the face of the D8N App brand. Already Mae can see Matthew McConaughey, Mark Zuckerberg and Mark Cuban. Rob has his hand pressed against Mae's lower back as they enter. No one acknowledges Mae. She expected somewhat of a warm, open-arms arrival. "No welcome back?"

"Mae. You said not to celebrate your return. They don't want to intrude."

"So that's it? I was in a coma and got a titanium skull. I thought I was so metal when I lost my virginity in a mosh pit. Now I'm a literal metalhead. It's a pretty big deal!"

"Don't be daft." Rob strides ahead and Mae feels him transform into someone else – a socialite, a schmooze, oozing with an arrogance that feels displaced in him. Displaced at least for Mae's memory of him. Mae remembers when she was the vibrant one in the relationship – always brimming with big ideas, the life of the party, the social gladiator. But now, constrained by her own feeble limitations, she's become the sort of reserved, introverted, socially awkward person she always pitied, holding her mounting anxiety in contempt to a social world that leaves her feeling like an outsider.

"Badu. Snoop. Sheeran. Dolly." Rob nods to people as they pass, a path forming before them as they move through the space. Waiters appear on either side of them holding gold trays of champagne and appetizers. Rob takes a glass, and Mae takes a caviar blini – which turns out to be a lackluster triangle of damp toast with a spot of tiny herring roe on top. Christ, so tasteless even a bunch of cows grazing on barren land would be itching to eat something better. Presumably, this is part of Rob's endless effort to appear classy and sophisticated – a very British concern. To impress the guests with impeccable taste and refinement, even though his own fridge is bare save for a pot of BBQ sauce with a crusty lid and a yellowing lemon that sank to the bottom of the fruit bowl three weeks ago. Mae forces herself to swallow, her eyes still lingering on the champagne flutes.

"Just in time," comes a voice from behind them. They turn to find Rose, her dark curls caught up into a delicate bun at the nape of her neck, allowing the low-cut swoop of her dress to attract the fullest of her onlooker's attention. Rose sashays in, her red ruby heels clicking like a wicked witch who missed her cue to be under a house—where's deadly tornadoes when you need one? Undoubtedly, there's one wreaking annihilation somewhere right now. Mae tries not to feel too sickened as Rose swoops in and plants a lingering kiss on Rob's cheek. Rob's hand falls from Mae's back.

"You're just in time for your opening," says Rose, pulling back from Rob but leaving the deep, elegant floral scent of her perfume behind – that fancy-schmancy scent of a luminary strutting down the streets of Paris with a beret and a baguette under-arm. "Shall we?" She extends a hand in the direction of the stage at the far end of the club. She's no doubt deluded herself into thinking she pisses honey and rosewater. Hell, she must reckon her lady garden hoo-ha whiffs of fresh summer plum when it surely reeks of earring backs.

Rob nods, taking a long sip of his champagne. "We shall," he says, before turning back to Mae. "Would you be a dear and amuse yourself for a jiffy? I need to deliver my speech." He poses it like a question but doesn't wait for an answer before allowing Rose to lead him away. Mae feels like the dumpy girlfriend every athlete dumps the day he signs with an elite team.

Standing alone on the crowded dance floor without even a drink for company, Mae tries not to let the bitter taste of resentment tinge the character she's been trying so hard to uphold. Ever since last night, she's been trying to shake the sense of something stirring inside her. Something alive and hungry, familiar and dangerous. The person she was last night was a glimmer of her past self, she's sure of it. The person she really is deep inside. But is that the person she wants to be? Deceptive, lustful, spontaneous.

Mae's distorted vision makes it hard to see the room as a whole. She scans repeatedly, like she's spectating a Wimbledon match. Mae moves further into the club, smiling politely at anyone who catches her eye, until that is, she spots a DB bopping with a group of what must be colleagues only a few feet to her right. His smile is wide and mischievous as it was in the bedroom, mis-matched hazelly eyes sparkling in the dizzying lights. A sudden wave of nausea descends on Mae. She was always told, you gotta watch out for the smiley ones. Maybe they're smiling because they're picturing a guitar getting smashed over somebody's head. What if he sees her? What if he speaks to her? What if Rob sees something between them? Ducking her head, she diverts out to the edges of the room, bumping shoulders and tripping into people half-blindly as she goes.

When she reaches the bar along the side of the dancefloor, she stands close to a huddle of investors – close enough to look as though she might be a part of them.

"Mhmm," the man closest to Mae murmurs gravely. "Yes, the UN projects the worldwide population to hit 10 billion by 2050, over 11 billion by 2100." Mae tries to keep up, but the statistical conversation is giving her a headache. She used to be so quick at this stuff.

Another voice echoes the first's murmur of agreement. "Mm-ah. It's true, we're due a catastrophic carnage clusterfuck fuckageddon if we don't act now. This might just be the key we've all been looking for – and in such a simple package."

Mae tries to crack a joke. "Why is it called D8N App? So basic. If Rob got a tattoo it'd say *tattoo*." The investors stare at Mae. She opens her mouth to try and save it, but luckily at this moment, the lights on the stage go up and the music dulls, enforcing hush as layers of conversation are replaced by the D8N App jingle calling the room to attention. From every corner, eyes turn toward the stage, as Rob clears his throat.

"Hello! Thank *y'all* for coming," he says, waving down at his guests. Mae rolls her eyes. Rob's never said *y'all* before. "I'm proper buzzing to finally share our new algorithm update, DarkStork with you. This is the culmination of years of hard work, and I believe it is the most important innovation in the dating industry since the invention of online dating. It's an absolute corker!" The room cheers as raised eyebrows and looks of intrigue are exchanged amongst the guests.

"DarkStork uses artificial intelligence and ground-breaking data insights to match people based on their deepest desires," Rob says, pacing up and down the narrow stage, followed by a pink spotlight. "It's not just about finding a bird – or bloke – you fancy. It's about finding someone who shares your interests, your values and your dreams. Someone who sees the future the way you do and is deserving of yours. But what is it exactly that allows us to achieve this god-like feat? Well, I guess that's for us to know." He winks and the room laughs. Mae looks around at the audience, most of them holding flutes of champagne, dressed to the nines in Louis Vuitton, Hermes and Balenciaga. All of them wholly and earnestly enraptured by Rob's words. His dancing smile makes him look like he's having more fun than a commandeering packed-pew preacher. In spite of herself, she searches the room for DB but can't find him among the seduced sea of faces.

"What I can tell you though, is that we're pushing the boundaries further than ever before, analyzing millions of data points to learn about not only a person's social and personality-based attractions and interests such as food, music, and streaming behaviors, but also their biological desires. I know, I know, it's a wee bit Black Mirror-esque. AI-powered ultra-personalization with the ultimate built-in privacy protection safeguards. Forbes recognizes it as the ultimate matchmaker of the modern age, a true global behemoth and the undisputed king of the dating app landscape. Hell, the *app* landscape. Our reach now extends to rival the likes of Meta, X and other entrenched digital giants." He grins toothily at his audience, then suddenly turns serious, his eyebrows flattening and the chiseled outline of his cheekbones gaining shadow. "Let's face it. Some people just aren't meant for love. A like-for-like match, albeit, but one that fits so that they too can see out their days with another who is exactly deserving of them. And for the rest of us, there will be no more falling in love just to find out our mate is unable to carry our love into the future. It's a dating algorithm built with the greater good in mind. The greatest good! It's an algorithm for love that lasts, love that lives, love that spawns. DarkStork is going to help people find their soulmates and make the world a more fruitful place. Now, if you'll excuse me, I'm off to accept my knighthood. Tallyho." Rob takes a step back out of the spotlight and the crowd explodes into applause and wolf-whistles as the new D8N App advert starts to play in Rob's place on stage.

Mae, still hiding by the bar, tries to shake the goosebumps prickling up her arms, Rob's words, *make the world a more fruitful place,* echoing around her head, ricocheting between nerve endings. She watches Rob's shape move down the steps from the stage to dance-floor level, before the dark crowd absorbs him.

She cranes her neck. She should congratulate him. That's what the new Mae would do. The doting other half, the devoted partner, the simple, sane, loyal girlfriend. She clenches and unclenches her fists to quash the itchy sensation igniting in her fingertips, to stop it from spreading up her arms and into her chest, of taking hold of her completely. The constant fist clenching makes her think of clutching a gun – an invisible trigger being drawn. A silent battle within. She takes a deep breath and tries to calm herself. It was just words. Badly chosen words. But after their tiff in the car, it felt more pointed than it should. Fruitful. Is that what Rob wanted? The way Rob says *fruitful* makes Mae want to rip his tongue out through his dickhole. In her mind's eye she sees the curve of Rose's perfect hourglass hips and jealousy bubbles inside her.

"Hey trouble."

There's a voice in Mae's ear but her peripheral blindness stops her seeing immediately who it is. She casts around, feeling a little dizzy from all the movement, all the colors.

"Moving speech. Mic-drop bars right there, huh?" DB raises his eyebrows at her meaningfully.

"What is it with you and sneaking up on people?" she asks, glaring at him.

"Ayy, what a greeting. Almost as bussin' as your goodbyes. Oh wait." His eyes flash.

"Shut your yapper," Mae hisses, dragging DB away from the bar. There's no-one in life nosier than a bored bartender. "That didn't happen, okay? It won't happen again. And stay away from Rob. I can't let him find out what

I did. What *you* did! You got me drunk. And you never mentioned you're what, like married with a kid? Does fucking in your kid's tent get you your nut, you pervert?"

To Mae's disbelief, DB doesn't seem at all taken aback by her outburst. Instead, he throws his head back and laughs. "Dayum!"

"Are you really laughing right now? Mae tries to push past him, but he grabs her arm. "Yo! Let me go. You should walk away before I punch you in the ball sack."

"Mae, Jesus, would you chill. That was a kid's castle, for real. I'm not married, no kids. I'm also not gonna snitch to anyone, especially not Rob. I ain't gonna confess to the Pope of Apps. Okay? I value my life as much as you value a good night out on tequila."

Mae narrows her eyes at him. "Then who's kid is living at your place?"

Mae spasms in utter confusion. DB winks. "It was my cousin's crib. I crash there sometimes, but not in my niece's bed."

Mae rips her arm back out of his grasp but doesn't try to escape again. The truth is that she's finding it hard to be angry at DB. All the frustration and guilt she thought she held feels less insistent now that he's in front of her. "You really won't say anything?"

"I'm keepin' it low-key, Mae. I wouldn't put you in danger like that."

He meets her eyes and holds them, completely cold in their solemnity.

"Danger?" Mae asks, a lump rising in her throat. "What does that mean?"

But DB simply shakes his head. "I need a drink."

DB moves past Mae to lean on the bar. Mae watches as he orders himself two tequilas and a Manhattan. He downs the tequilas one after the other, then takes up the Manhattan and turns back to face Mae again, the same, lined expression on his face.

"What did you mean, DB? What danger?" Mae presses, unsure exactly why she can't just drop it. The goosebumps have returned to her arms, her fingertips now electric as high wire. Was this anxiety, or something else?

"Are you with him? Or are you *with* him, Mae? Why are you still sticking around?"

Mae shakes her head. "I don't understand. We've been together four years since college. We met in gamers coding club at Uni. He helped me escape from my parents. We built ourselves up from nothing and look." She gestures around the room. "Look at what we've created."

DB clicks his tongue. "Yeah, just look at it, eh? A pair of real-life cupids orchestrating true love."

Mae scowls at him. "And what exactly gives you the right to start telling me how my own relationship works, hey? Or my business for that matter."

"This business still in your lane, huh? Even after you got driven off the road and had your whole skull reconstructed in aluminum?"

"I was hit by a car not driven off the road, and my skull

is titanium. Triple-enforced titanium, you could run it over with a tank and it wouldn't break. At least get your facts straight before you come by insulting me. At least I don't look like I pay for sex with bitcoins."

"Mhmm. Ok Dollar Store Barbie. You look like you know how many calories a hand job burns."

Mae shamelessly smiles. "I do. It's fifty. That's six almonds. Aw, hellfire. Go ahead. Tell people, no one will believe you put your snake in my boot anyway," says Mae. "You've got the sex appeal of a school bus fire."

"Says the girl who kept moaning, *oh, you get me so wet!*"

"That was just our periods syncing."

They look at each other. The corner of DB's lip twitches, and they both dissolve into giggles. "Okay but listen. I've never cheated before, so I don't want you to think I'm loose with the cooch, drunk slut, piece of trash."

"I don't think *all* those things. Though you are loose. Your box is so stretched out it doesn't queef, it coughs."

"Fuck right off you fucker. You hit it on the first night."

"Touché."

"I mean, I definitely drink too much and make questionable choices. But I'm a good person. I think. I am clumsily inept, like a blind stray dog tap dancing through minefields."

"It's a vibe, may as well be as you are. You're good. We're golden."

DB opens an arm and pulls her into a hug. It's surprising, the intimacy of it. More intimate somehow than the hugs she used to get at home. When DB makes to pull away, Mae doesn't let go immediately. Tears leak from her eyes. She dabs them on the back of her hand.

"We should probably mingle with this super fun party," Mae says, righting herself. "God everyone's so boring, going on and on about D8N App. I need to ice my jaw from getting face-fucked by boredom all night."

DB shrugs. "None of these men get women wet, they just bore pussies to tears."

Mae looks around distastefully at their fellow guests, her eyes coming to settle on the back of a familiar curly head. "I have a question," Mae says, turning back to DB. "Do Rob and Rose hang out at work? Like private meetings? Go to the bathroom at the same time?"

"I don't know. I'm not the restroom attendant." DB hiccups, half his Manhattan now down the front of his suit jacket.

"Yeah. Alright." Mae sighs. "Now I need a drink." She grabs DB's drink and gulps the rest of it.

"There she is. Mother Terrorista."

"Ugh that whiskey is brutal. Prison toilet whiskey," Mae grimaces. "I need another." Damn, fuck it. Who is she kidding? All this testosterone in one room, of course she needs a hefty stiff drink. Mae orders a round of tequilas for the two of them, plus two Manhattans. It's only as she presses the cocktail glass into DB's hand that a realization comes to her. "Oh, last thing, this is random. But I don't suppose you've seen my phone? I think I must have left it at your cousins."

DB shakes his head, clearly amused. "You mean you don't remember hurling your phone into Lady Bird Lake?"

"That's a sick joke, right?"

DB doubles over laughing again.

"Why would I throw my phone into the lake?!" asks Mae in disbelief.

"Oh, far too many reasons to get into right now." DB hiccups, clutching a stitch in his side. "Maybe if you let me take you out again, we can get into it."

"Nice try," says Mae. "I'm serious, never again."

"You don't have to sleep with me just because we go out for tequila, even if it goes against your track record."

"*My* track record, you seemed to be pretty well practiced yourself."

"Well, I mean, I'm not the one who stole the roofies."

"The what, Dickbutt? Are you accusing me of date raping you?"

"Ha! No, to be fair I think you only stole them out of principle. It was actually kinda noble. And scary, you basically threatened those college kids. You asked them for gum and then turned into a *gimme 'em pills or I'll send your cock in a box to yo mom* kinda scenario."

"Course, out of principle. Women don't roofie dudes. We can get sex whenever we want. Just gotta decide if the dude is worth a week of cranberry juice, antibiotics and yogurt. It's usually not. You ever got a UTI?"

"No, I don't think so."

"Good, when men get 'em y'all go loco in the coco. President Lyndon Johnson got one, then launched Operation Rolling Thunder – a mass bombing campaign against North Vietnam. That said, if I could roofie a guy into texting me back fast, I would. If I slipped him something and an hour later, he's like, *oh girl I wanna take ya to dinner*, then I'd be drugging dudes all the time."

"You'd roofie a dude for relationship intimacy? That is sad."

"I miss cuddling, waking up next to someone – that morning touch."

"Don't you and Rob live together?"

"Yeah, but he sleeps at the office a lot. He's battling some demons cuz his hairlines receding or maybe because his fiancé is half robot. To be honest, I don't even know if he still counts as my fiancé." Mae twists her ring finger, tracing the space where an engagement ring should sit but where instead she has a single band tattooed into her skin. It felt romantic at the time, but hell, it'll be hard to give back to him. She swallows and lets her hand drop back to her side. She's let things get too personal again. "I think I'm broken inside in an unfixable way. We were talking about having kids before, well, all this, but haven't been able to. I think my pussy secretes disappointment. I am probs gonna die alone. Unless an apocalypse comes, and we all die together."

Mae looks up. DB's dark eyes are boring into her, but they're not filled with pity like she was expecting. It's more like a sad understanding. Like he can read all the subtext she didn't mean to write. "Mae," he says, eventually. "Do you even like Rob?"

Mae closes her eyes. She wishes she didn't. "No, I don't like him," she says, opening her eyes. "I love him. He makes my heart bust a nut. He could sodomize my Granmeemaw in front of me and I'd still love him. I used to sit and watch him program all day, then we'd order Thai food and stay up late playing video games. It was kinda simple and perfect. I miss it." DB widens his eyes to indicate something over Mae's shoulder and she trails off.

Turning, Mae finds Rob swimming through the crowd toward her, Rose half a step behind him, gliding like a serpentine mermaid. Mae looks back to DB but finds only the backs of other guests now dancing to Erykah Badu performing Out My Mind, Just In Time.

"So, how did I do?" Rob drapes his arm around her shoulders in the manner of an old school-friend, or an older sibling. "Weren't they just lapping it up? They're eating out my ass crack. We've had three potential offers of investment already." He pumps a victory fist. "I've been indoctrinated. I spoke cornbread—I said *y'all!* Blimey, when I said it, I swear I felt a tooth loosen." Rob chuckles, clearly impressed with himself and his attempt at southern slang.

"They lurveee him! I thought they were gonna carry you off on their shoulders." Rose croons over Rob's shoulder, stroking the arm of his suit. "You really are the savior of mankind."

Mae bristles. Who does this woman think she is, playing the slut card right in front of her? Swooning Rob with compliments. Mae always wondered if Rob's back hurt from sucking his own cock. Well, two can play at the game. "Well, that's my man. I'm the King's wench." says Mae loudly, slipping a hand down over his buttocks. "Someone might get lucky tonight. I never could resist a powerful Englishman." Mae runs her fingers round Rob's thigh and squeezes. Rob lets out a half-gasp as her fingertips graze his balls.

Mae catches Rose's eye and feigns embarrassment. "Oh sorry, Rose. I don't mean to make you uncomfortable." She withdraws her hand but leans into whisper loudly in Rob's ear, "We'll save this for the bedroom, hey baby?"

Mae doesn't see DB for the rest of the evening. Instead, she commits to her role of adoring girlfriend to the most highly influential man in the room, in-between solo shots of tequila. She can feel Rob's ego expanding, bloating to fill the entire dancefloor; she allows her own presence to grow alongside his. She laughs loudly at the right jokes in the right places, flirts just enough with the right investors and presses her body up against Rob at the climax of each song as it reverberates off the walls. By the end of the night, D8N App has secured five new investors at over $30 million apiece. Not bad work for a night of swooning. And to top it all off, Rose slunk away around eleven with not another word to either Rob or Mae. The chode-licker, it seems, she's finally learnt her place.

By 3am the room has all-but emptied out. Leaving only Mae, Rob, and a handful of their youngest employees dancing to Shania Twain's Whose Bed Have Your Boots Been Under. Mae pulls herself into Rob's back and runs her tongue down the length from his ear to his collar. "What say you and me head to bed?"

"I'm rather keen on it." Rob whispers back, and Mae can feel a fire lighting in her groin.

*

They catch a pedicab back, just like their ol' college days, and stumble into the loft already shredding their shoes and jackets. Rob presses Mae up against the large glass windows overlooking the city, his hand sliding up under her silk dress. "No, wait," Mae gasps as Rob bites her lip. She needs this to be done right. "Wait right here." She grabs his balls in his tight trousers and growls in his ear, then runs upstairs to the bedroom.

It's been months since they shared a bed. Longer since they got even close to having sex. Mae digs deep into her drawer of disused lingerie until she finds the shockingly-sexy black leather number she bought for Rob's birthday – back when they did that kind of thing. She slips out of her dress and steps into the bodice. It sits nicely on her, accentuating her tits and cutting her in at the waist. She can hear Rob moving downstairs as she struggles to hook the garter belt to the stocking, fumbling with the clasp. "Ugh, he's gonna think I'm taking a shit," she mumbles as it finally snaps in place. Then it's just a fresh paint of lipstick and she's ready – ready for a fierce make-up fuck. Mae walks out posing, pushing her chest and butt out as she struts down the stairs. Rob hasn't undressed at all. Irritation tugs in Mae's chest as she notes the Oculus Rift VR headset strapped over his eyes.

Mae coughs as she reaches the bottom of the stairs, holding her pose. "Babe, I'm ready."

In one swift movement, Rob turns, Kung-fu chops then kicks out in Mae's direction. She steps back out of his way, nearly tripping over herself.

"Rob? Can you – we were in the middle of something."

"One second, babe," he says, resetting his stance.

"Um, you're staying the night, right?"

"No, early morning and big day tomorrow. Hiya!" Rob kicks again.

"*Early morning*," Mae mocks. "Like hell. You start your days when 84-year-olds do. Please stay? It'd mean a lot to me."

Rob bends his knees and raises his hands in defense against an invisible opponent. "Don't do this," he says. "Don't make me feel bad. If a shark stops moving it dies. Just be thankful I'm here and you get to see me before I get swept up in launch day blips."

"You've barely stayed over in the past 5 months. I'm not asking you to smash a baby's skull with a rock. Just spend the night. Is that so much to ask?"

Rob stops fighting but doesn't take off the VR headset. He looks toward her, or to where he thinks she is, his sightline a good half a meter off. "Don't count the days. Make the days count. You need to chill."

Mae looks down at her outfit and tenses her jaw, trying hard not to lash out.

Rob sighs. He draws a hand down over his face, taking off the headset. "Mae, look." He moves toward the couch and beckons her closer, patting the space beside him. Mae sulks over, begrudging. Finally, he looks at her properly, eyes lingering on the lace now decorating Mae's bony body. "Are your knickers on backwards? The tag is in the front."

Mae rolls her eyes. "That's just a little charm. It's part of the trim."

"Right." Rob waves the blunder away. "Look," he says again. "We haven't slept together since the accident. And I'm not saying that's on you, but I'm not saying it's on me either. We're different people than we were, and I want to reconnect, of course I do. But I just don't think now is the best time." Finally, he looks up at her with those big, topaz eyes, lifts a hand and tucks a strand of hair behind her ear. "Let me get this launch done, okay? Then, when it all quietens down, we'll take some time just the two of us."

Mae stares him down and tries to believe him. Tries to conjure from memory, the last time he'd looked at her straight this way; the last time he'd kissed her without her kissing him first; the last time he'd stayed the night and she'd not woken up alone. But she can only conclude that either these memories no longer exist, or they never did in the first place. He was right, this was not the same Rob she fell in love with. But somehow, realizing this just makes her angrier. And God she's angry. Right to her shamefully untoned core. How dare he abandon her. How dare he not even try.

Mae closes her eyes to simmer her rage, breathes in through her nose and lets a single tear slide down her cheek. "At least stay for one nightcap," she whimpers quietly, resting her forehead on his shoulder. "And tuck me in? Please, Rob." She looks up at him, her bottom lip trembling in that way he never could resist. "You don't have to stay. I just want to *feel* you. I miss you."

Rob runs a thumb over Mae's quivering lip just as she knew he would, and she takes the opportunity to breathe in, inhaling his air. He tastes of whiskey and menthol. She breathes in deeper and lets out a low murmur. Rob shifts slightly, and Mae senses his dick hardening. Only she knows exactly how to get him going.

"Whiskey on the rocks with a twist?" she asks, faking a yawn. "I'll pour, if you go turn down my bed?"

She stands before he can answer, then watches him up the stairs as she pulls down two glasses from the drink's cabinet and his favorite bottle of Dalmore 25–year-old single malt Scotch whiskey. She takes the glasses to the kitchen and sets them on the center island as she searches the fridge for a lemon. It's then, in the light of the refrigerator, that she spots her bag on the floor. The bag she took out to the bar with DB. She scoops it up and feels around inside: sticks of gum, pens, lipsticks, candy bar wrappers, and a small bag of pills. Mae holds up the little plastic Ziploc and scrutinizes the contents. They could be anything. Aspirin, Prozac, Viagra. She tips one out into her hand and turns it over. Viagra would be good. She could do with a Viagra. Not that Prozac would do her any harm, though it does dampen libido to that of a sea sponge. Rob would do good with a Viagra.

Taking a pill from the bag she places it on the side and searches for something to crush it with. Settling for the heel of her shoe, she hums to herself as she crushes, then scoops the now white powder into one of the glasses. Forgetting she only has one shoe on, she loses her balance and stumbles backward, barely saving the whiskey from spilling all over her.

"Damn, girl. Yo wasted!" She laughs at herself, setting the glass back on the counter as she stumbles trying to unclasp her second shoe. Once her feet are stable, she goes back to the counter. She looks from one glass to the other, unable to remember which one she put the pill in. She crouches over, trying to tell which one is cloudier. "Ah, fuck it." She tips the bag out on the side and crushes the lot, then scoops it all into the second glass.

Upstairs, Rob is sitting on the edge of Mae's bed – their bed. He's dimmed the lights and drawn the curtains; even laid out the tee she likes to sleep in on the pillow.

"One whiskey with a twist," Mae hands over the drink. "You don't mind if I change in front of you?" she asks, already unclasping her garters.

Mae pings her bodice across the room as Rob takes a sharp sip of his twisted whiskey, downing half the glass in one. She leans over Rob's lap to reach for her tee, leaving her exposed neck free for his lips. He takes the bait, burying his face into her. Mae slides his hand inside her, then removes it. "Hey, let's finish our whiskey first."

She sits up and takes a sip from her glass, watching over the rim as Rob drinks his too. Once both glasses are empty, Mae crawls toward him and unzips his fly. "Dirty talk me like you used to. Code talk. Encrypt your payload inside me. Choke capitalism. Choke me." Mae takes him in her mouth and Rob groans.

"I forgot your dirty talk turns into anarcho-tech commentary," Rob manages as Mae chokes harder on him, ramming the back of her throat. Then she sucks hard and pulls him free.

"Tell me to shut my wench mouth." Mae reaches over to her nightstand and pulls out a set of handcuffs. She dangles them in front of him, then handcuffs his wrists to the bedpost.

"God, I forgot how rough you like to play," Rob growls as Mae sits on top of him, her thighs on either side of his hips.

"I'm so turned on, I could waterboard you in my *knickers* right now. I could Tsunami a daycare."

As he nuzzles deeper and deeper into her neck, Mae works his trousers free from his legs ready to slip him inside. By the time she reaches the goods though, Rob has already passed out. "Rob? Hey, you asleep? Not want me to glazzy yo glizzy? Grease yo griddle?"

Nothing. Mae sits back as Rob starts snoring.

6

Mae

Sunlight streams through a crack in the curtains, waking Mae up. She squints out at the sky. It's blue and blinding. She groans, rolling over, and is surprised to find another body in her bed. For a moment she panics, thinking perhaps she's found her way into another kid's bedroom. But then she blinks back the déjà vu and realizes it's only Rob, still in his dress shirt. She gazes at her sweet sleeping fiancé. She smiles and curls up to him. It's so unlike him to stay the night. She squeezes her eyes tight and breathes in his stale morning scent, trying to remember how they got to bed: she got dressed up and then she went down on him and sucked him so hard his stomach caved in like a Capri Sun, and then there was the handcuffs. She doesn't feel sore though. In fact, she still feels a little horny. A lot horned up, in fact. Did they not finish? Or did he finish in her mouth? Maybe it was one of *those* nights. She runs her hand over Rob's sleeping torso, down his abdomen toward his crotch, but stops when she realizes his arms are in an awkward position. Why would he still be handcuffed to the bed?

Mae's eyes snap open and she turns to the bedside table. Rob's glass from the night before is empty, save for a slice of lemon. Shit. What has she done? The alarm clock flashes 10:38. They've slept in way past Rob's usual start time.

Mae rolls back to Rob and strokes his chest. This is okay. He'll just think he fell asleep. He was exhausted after all. He doesn't have to know. She kisses his shoulder, then moves up to kiss his neck and then behind his ear. Back in college, he cited this as his favorite way to wake up. Mae would plant kisses the whole way up his left side until he stirred, then he'd roll her over and spoon her from behind. Back when the mornings were the best time of day. This morning though, Mae's kisses didn't rouse him.

Lifting herself up, Mae moves her hand down his trousers and whispers in his ear, "Wakey, wakey, my hand on your snaky."

Still nothing.

Mae reaches out and touches his cheek. He feels cold. "Rob," she says, a little louder. "It's nearly eleven, babe."

Nothing.

Mae shakes him gently. "Rob, come on," she says. "It's time to get up. Are you fooling me? You're always such a shit prankster."

Panic seizes Mae's gut. She shakes him harder. "This isn't funny, Rob!" she shouts. "Wake up! Wake up, Rob. If you're trying to frighten me, you're doing a first-rate job!"

But he continues to lie there, serene, and still.

Mae's heart is pounding now. She jumps out of bed and runs to the bathroom. She turns the tap and splashes cold water on her face, trying to calm down, but she can't shake the feeling of impending doom. This can't be happening. He's just asleep. Just very deeply asleep. Mae looks at herself in the mirror, her face now dripping with water, her eyes rimmed with the make-up she didn't take off before getting into bed. She turns from her reflection and tiptoes back to the bedroom. Rob is still lying there, completely motionless.

What the hell is she going to do now? Her mind runs through a list of possibilities: an ambulance, the office, his parents. Hell no. She needs someone impartial. Someone who will understand.

Mae takes the stairs two at a time then throws herself onto the floor where her jacket and clutch from last night were discarded. Her hands shake as she fumbles for her phone and dials.

The phone rings just three times.

"Mae? What's goodie?" DB's voice sounds uncertain over the speaker. "Also, hey, my bad for dipping out yesterday, y'know shit got a little funky, thought it'd be best to bounce.

"What?" Mae shakes her head confused. "That's not – it's not that, I…"

"Is everything alright? You're up early. I thought you were a nooner. You sound—"

"No, it's not okay. I'm not okay, please, DB I need you here now. Please." Mae can hear her voice shaking. It's all she can do to hold the phone to her face.

"Where are you?"

"I'm—I'm at the loft. Our loft. Mine and Rob's. It's—"

"I know where it's at," says DB. "Stay put, Mae. I'm on my way."

Mae drops the phone onto the polished wood and a strangled sob escapes her – the sound of a dying panther. Is this who she is underneath? Or is this what the accident made her into? Surely Rob would never have loved her if she'd been this way all along?

Mae scrambles to her feet and starts to pace up and down. If Rob wakes up, she'll start over. If Rob wakes up, she'll never drink again. If Rob wakes up, she'll confess to everything she's done and then she'll win him back and they'll be better than ever. And he will wake up.

Without conscious thought Mae goes to the kitchen and starts to prepare Rob's favorite breakfast, the one she made for him on their first morning together – breakfast churros with cinnamon sugar. It was her mother's recipe. Or is her mother's recipe, Mae supposes, though Mae hasn't spoken to her mother in years. Mae cracks the eggs into a bowl and whisks, then turns on the stovetop and digs some flour out of the cupboard. The doorbell goes, just as the pastry begins to sizzle.

"Coming," Mae calls, flipping each sausage of dough before running to the door. There's knocking. "Hold your horses," Mae shouts.

DB stands in the hallway looking frazzled, his hair ungelled and his shirt untucked. "Mae, Jesus, are you okay?" He pulls her into a rough hug from which Mae struggles free.

"Shit, get off I'm gonna burn the churros." Wriggling free, Mae runs back to the hob and saves Rob's breakfast just before it catches.

"Churros?" DB follows Mae to the kitchen and watches as she frantically plates up the churros, dusting it with cinnamon sugar. "Mae, what's the fuss all about? You sounded like someone had died."

"No!" Mae screams. "He's not dead, don't say that."

"Who's not dead, Mae? What's going on? I hope you clownin' – for real, hop off your unicycle and ditch the red nose."

Mae grabs DB by the hand and leads him up the stairs. "I didn't know it would do this, I thought it would just make him a little drowsy, a little out of it, so he wouldn't want to leave. It isn't what it looks like, I didn't date rape him."

"Date rape? You mean, you gave him those roofies?

Mae stands back from the bedroom door to let DB in

first. Rob is still exactly as she left him – not even the smell of fresh sticky sweet churros has made a difference.

DB approaches the bed like a criminal. He reaches out, and prods Rob's head with his foot.

"Don't kick him in the head!" Mae hisses, running to the bed and booting DB's leg away. "Don't hurt him."

"He's comatose Mae, I don't think he gives a shit about a little nudge in the noggin."

Mae bites her lip. "You really think he's comatose?"

"Maybe he's just resting his eyes. Have you not checked that he's breathing?"

Mae shakes her head.

DB leans over Rob's body. "I'm no doctor but I can't feel any breathing." DB checks his pulse. "Nothing. Dead, dead. Deadass dead."

Mae turns to DB, her eyes flashing, brain in overload. "Let's roofie ourselves. Then we won't remember what happened, can't be accused. I still have a few."

DB's eyes widen. "You only have a few left from that big ass bag? You fucking overdosed him!"

Mae casts about, frantically searching the room for a different way out. "Ok, let's call the cops. I'll tell the truth. It was an accident."

"*Sorry officer, she tripped and handfuls of roofies poofed into powder and plopped into his whiskey glass.* That's the move– roll the dice, hope for a decent prison, and don't drop the loofa."

"I can't go to prison. I'll be judging my jumpsuit's cheap

polyester fabric, stitched with shit seams the moment I get my first prison shanking. I'd rather go to hell than prison. Maybe hell is actually like a bangin' disco doozy, and that's why no one ever comes back from it."

"You'll go to hell either way. Why go to prison first?"

"You'd hate prison, dude. You'd get picked last for the prison dodgeball team. We are gonna burn for this."

"Excuse me. This isn't a *we*. I have nothing to do with this."

"I need your help, please! I gulped you. I gulped you up. That should mean something. If you know what my hoo-ha feels like I should have the right to ask for help in a life-or-death situation!" Mae begged, tears bubbling under her eyes. "I just wanted Rob to sleep over. I wanted to wake up with the sun coming through the window just catching a corner of his face like a sleeping angel and cuddle up to him like we used to before the world turned against us."

"Ok, stop talking. Let's get him on the floor and start chest pumps or something." DB moves over to the bed, as though to pull, then stops. "Damn, for real? He's cuffed up. Mae, please tell me you have the key."

Mae pushes past DB and starts to rummage through the nightstand. "I don't know where it is. I don't know! I don't know! I have a wine opener. Maybe that'll work."

"Hold up. What's that noise?" asks DB. "I think his phone is going off somewhere."

"But that's his phone there," says Mae, pointing to the iPhone on the bedside table.

DB places a finger over his lips and they both listen to the muffled ringtone. Mae looks down – something is vibrating near her foot. She stoops to pick his pants up off the floor and digs into the pocket, pulling out a second iPhone in a gold case – one Mae hasn't seen before. Mae stares at it. He has 18 missed calls and 56 texts.

"I don't understand. This isn't his phone."

"Ha, yeah cuz no man has ever had two phones." DB rolls his eyes. "Well, there's only one way to find out," says DB, nodding to Rob.

Mae crouches down and holds the phone over Rob's face. It unlocks just as the phone begins to ring again and Mae almost drops it in shock.

"It's Rose. Rose! What do I do?!"

"Don't answer it!" says DB. "I swear to God, I will murder you and bury you with that phone if you answer it."

Mae's finger hovers over Rose's name. "Like hell, you'd murder me."

"Two dead bodies are just as mental as one."

"Ok. First new rule, no more saying the words *dead*, *murder* or *comatose*. Those words are outlawed."

"Outlawed? How can you outlaw a word?"

"Well just say it then. Say it and see what happens."

"What ya gonna murder me too?"

"Don't push me. I'll show you how the cow ate the cabbage. From now on use code word…*huevos rancheros*."

"Ok let's figure out how to get rid of this *huevos rancheros* you *huevos ranchero'd*."

"Funny. Real knee-slapping funny." A distinct rumble ripples the air between them. Mae glares at DB. "Jesus, Dickbutt. Are you seriously hungry right now?"

DB shakes his head. "That's not my stomach, that's your loud-ass stomach."

"No, it's not." They frown at each other, then look at Rob.

"Shit. It's Rob!"

Rob groans, his head flip-flopping from side-to-side.

"I thought you checked his pulse?!"

DB checks his own neck on the left and right. "Which side? Left?"

"Either side!"

"Nothing. I've got no pulse, either. Sheeeit. I told you I'm not a doctor."

Mae looks at DB, then at Rob still handcuffed to the bed, then back at DB again. "Shit. You have to bounce." Mae shoos DB back out the door. "Quick, go! Scram! Skedaddle! Ándale esé!" Behind her Rob groans again, louder this time.

"Mae? Who's that– what's? Blimey, my head."

DB attempts to duck toward the door, but trips over his own ankles and sends himself stumbling.

Mae kneels down next to Rob and strokes his face. "Rob? Are you okay?"

Rob blinks up at her, looking dazed. Then his eyes slowly begin to harden. Ocean blue ripples frosting over and turning to blocks of ice.

"Hey, slowly!" Mae says, as Rob heaves himself up onto his elbows. Mae tries to wrap a hand around his back to help, but Rob shakes her off.

"For fuck's sake, I feel like my ribs are broken. What the bloody hell am I doing here?" He massages his temples, scowling at the floor. Mae bites her lip. He pulls his handcuffed wrist trying to rip it from the bedpost. "The arse-piss fuck?!"

"You, um– you fell asleep in the middle of sex, which kinda hurts my feelings," she says. "And now I can't find the key." The words float in front of her. They look as unconvincing as they sound.

"I feel like I've been hit by a sodding car," says Rob one-handedly rubbing his temples.

"Let's not forget I actually was hit by a *sodding* car." Mae says. "You ain't even getting a glimpse of a sliver of my pain."

"Did you drug me last night?"

"Not on purpose. I just wanted you to spend the night. You gotta allow for some human failings."

Rob violently tries to pull his wrist out of the handcuff. "Mae, unlock me."

"I don't know exactly where the key is. And you know what I'm sorry about this lil blip, but we probably need to have an overdue quiet calm chat anyways."

"Little blip? Proper chinwag?" Rob shouts.

DB's face peaks around the corner.

"And don't think I don't know you're here," Rob

growls. "What is this? You shagged again, did you? Over my unconscious body – real top-notch classy."

"What?" Mae looks up at DB, the accusation piercing her right through. "I—" Mae stammers, like a stork caught in headlights. She throws herself down next to Rob on the bed. "I didn't know who else to call, Rob. I thought you'd knocked yourself out."

"Don't give me that barmy bullshit." Rob tries to shift himself upright, meeting her face to face. He pushes his forehead against hers and snarls, "Don't you think I'd believe that load of bollocks again. Once a cheater, always a cheater Mae. Just didn't think you'd go for something so petty."

Mae's whole body is shaking now. The pressure of Rob's head against hers feels like burning metal, branding her with a scarlet letter. His breath is hot and sour, tainted with twisted alcohol.

"I don't know what you're talking about," Mae whispers. "Why would you think that? I love you. You know I love you."

"Cut the pantomime, Mae. You cheated on me before the accident and you're cheating on me now, only now I know the signs. Now I know what to chuffing well look for."

Mae draws back, stumbling away from the bed. "I don't believe you," she says, shaking her head. "I wouldn't cheat on you if you were here for me. All the memories I have of us before the accident are happy. I don't believe this is all on me. I won't." She casts around, looking for DB. But he's no longer in the doorway. Rage burns inside her. She doesn't care, she doesn't want him here. Had he fucked her before? Had they had an affair before the accident? What sort of sick cuck wouldn't admit something like that? Nausea ferments in Mae's stomach, burning up her esophagus. She buries her face in her hands. Why can't she remember?

Rob kicks out at Mae. "Sod off and get that goddamn key."

"Don't touch me cockface!" she screams. "After everything I helped you build. All my savings I put into fund your dream. I don't believe you." Mae's hands are shaking, and her heart is threatening to burst from her chest.

Mae sees a jewelry box Rob had given her on her last birthday. It was a pretty thing, shaped like a little temple with a dome up upon it. Mae opens it and then, a little tinkling tune begins to play. Blondie's *Heart of Glass.* Mae sees the key and takes it out of the box. She tosses it in front of Rob, just far enough from him that he can't reach it. Mae shakes her head at DB and storms out. DB starts to follow her.

"Let her go," Rob tells DB.

DB scoffs. "Yeah, cuz you need me to give you that key."

The sound of metal clanking against their wooden bed frame rattles through the loft as Mae's heart drums so violently she has to catch hold the banister. She feels her way down the stairs and out of the condo. Blood pounds against her ears, hearing buzzing. She can't see – her panic turning light to darkness, the world spinning in her peripherals.

Reaching the street, Mae crouches down on the curb and presses her eyes against her knees, rocking back and forth. Why can't she just remember?

A car rushes past, blaring its horns and in a flash, Mae is back there, lying in the street in a puddle of blood with glass around her, lungs punctured, leg broken, the black stork staring her down.

Mae wipes away the sweat pouring from her forehead, gets up and starts to walk. She can't see the people she barges through. She'll never adjust to bumping into things on her blind side. Her chest tenses like a heavy vice, constricting her breaths to short, ragged gasps. Her shit-blind vision and exploding anxiety consumes everything around her. There are children everywhere, or so it feels. Kids screaming, balls and bikes near missing her as she feels her way along the streets. Another day of school closures thanks to the extreme heat wave pounding a swath of the country with record breaking temperatures. Heat days are the new snow days. Lethal global warming. Hot enough to fry eggs on a gravestone if the hens weren't layin' them hard-boiled.

After what feels like a full lap of the burning hot city, Mae goes to her storage unit in the garage. She fumbles with the code then digs hungrily through a box, checking the labels of her many prescription bottles. She knocks back two pills to help her relax. *So much for barebacking reality.* Her doctors had prescribed Xanax to help her deal with the anxiety caused by exaggerated startle response PTSD due to her vision loss, but Mae had stopped taking it, fearful it would further affect her fertility. Today, she's as ready to pop them as a Pez dispenser. Mae leans back against the lockers and closes her eyes, as slowly her anxiety begins to melt away, replaced by a tingling sense of calm – a warm, buzzy feeling tickling through her body.

Mae walks back to the loft block and buzzes herself up. When she reaches the loft, the door is open, just slightly, and she can hear voices. Rob, now unhandcuffed it would seem, and DB. What the hell is DB still doing here? She shuffles closer, straining to make out their words.

"Aren't you the IT dildo called into my office when the printer is jammed?"

"I'm a cyber security engineer."

"It doesn't matter what your job title is, BD." Rob cuts in. "Just stay away from Mae."

Mae leans a little too heavily on the door and it squeaks inwards. The voices inside go quiet, giving her no choice but to announce herself.

Spotting her, Rob shakes his head. Mae's eyes find DB over Rob's shoulder. His face is red and contorted. He shakes himself, clenches and unclenches his jaw, then sets a solid pace past them and out the door without looking at Mae.

Maybe it's the wonderful numbing of the Xanax, but Mae finds she doesn't care. In fact, she's glad DB is gone. Glad she didn't have to look him in the eye and ask if he's been lying to her this whole time. If that wasn't the first time he'd fucked her in his nieces' bedroom. If he already knew her body and her positions and the ways to seduce her. If he'd done it all on purpose.

Rob walks over and pulls her into a hug. "I'm sorry," he whispers into her hair. "I thought I'd lost you after that accident. I guess I've just been scared to be vulnerable with you again."

"Where were you when I needed you?" Mae sniffs.

"I visited you in the hospital when I could. Visitors are given time limits."

"Thankfully. If you'd visit longer than a few minutes you would've pulled that life support plug to charge your phone."

"I made sure you got good care."

"Wow, thanks." Mae pulls away, separating herself from Rob's embrace. "No, you're right. I'm wrong. You deserve an award for that. Like fish should be applauded for swimming. Good job being a bare minimum decent human."

"Mae." Rob sighs, looking at his feet. "You can't imagine what it's like to cut your teeth on building a bloody global giant social network company from your college dorm, and have it take off and become seen as some sort of visionary tech titan mogul within a year. Yeah, first get the loose, freewheeling spirit - raising tons of money, huge amounts of hype and setting off on utopian-sound missions of changing the world. Get invited to fancy conferences, investors shower you with money, the media heralds you a disruptive innovator..."

Mae frowned, was this him trying to make her feel better? "Uh, boohoo? Where are you going with this?"

"Then you sit in boring meetings and fly in private jets around the world so investors can yell at you while sensitive data regulators are breathing down your neck and dripping poison into the big guy's ear. Sometimes with poison one drop is enough. And it's constant. It never stops. The incessant pressure from investors to boost growth of the fastest-growing company. They can be like wolves. Pissed wolves. And then you're constantly fretting about having to avoid catastrophic mistakes and mop up hurricanes of piss. I never know where on the fuckometer I am. It's the bollocks of the jungle out there. Creating an empire forced me to reckon with there's nothing more important in my lifetime to work on and nothing more enabling for people's future. What I'm working on will change people's futures, everywhere. I can't cock it up."

Mae rolls her eyes. "You make it sound like you are founding a new religion or a whole chocolate factory."

"I've seen the world for how it really is, and it has changed me. I've seen the bollocks fuckbag handy shandy truth. And God, Mae. I'm the most grateful you survived and are still here. The day of your accident was the worst day of my life. I made sure you've gotten the best care and was there when I could be. I was there for you. I've been there for you the whole time, because Christ alive you can be incapable of taking care of yourself. Like I dunno if you should run a bath without having Coast Guard standing by.

You are brazenly inept sometimes."

Mae moves away from him. Her brain feels tired and foggy – mental fatigue from all the mixed emotions, mixed messaging, mix of drugs and alcohol swimming around her body. "I don't understand what you're doing right now," she says, too exhausted to argue. "This feels like some sort of sordid personal attack. I was looking for reassurance."

"Mae, I've been trying. But when I'm trying with you it often feels like walking up an escalator that's broken. And I'm sorry for that."

Mae stops in front of the piano and stares at it. She used to play. Used to play a lot. She was good, too. And Rob used to be her audience. Her solo cheerleader in the crowd. The only cheerleader she needed, anyway.

"Mae, I'm sorry," Rob said again. Mae felt him move toward her, then his arms wrapped around her waist from behind, his square chin digging into that soft space between her neck and shoulder. He wouldn't be trying so hard now, if he didn't mean it. Even if he was doing a shit-ass job of getting the words out – right?

"I'm sorry too," she said, eventually. "I'm struggling. The brain doesn't fully mend itself like a cut or a bruise. This last year has been a fuck-ton cornucopia of trauma and confusion, and I miss you. I miss that oracular beard. Your voice. Dunno if hearing it makes me want to cry or cum. I just wanted you to spend the night. I want to write I miss you on a rock and throw it at your face, so you know how much it hurts to miss you. I even miss your snoring.

Sometimes I wish you'd send me audio of your snoring."

"Really my snoring?" Mae can hear the smile in Rob's voice. "The body's way of telling everyone you're an arsehole even when you're sleeping."

Mae giggles in spite of herself. "Yeah, your snore wanders all over the spectrum from 1980s gas powered chainsaw, to farting clown eating a pumpkin pie while driving a mack truck."

"Mae, I am your lighthouse in the rain, in stormy gale force wind, tornado and mortal shake earthquakes. I stay lit for you. I stay lit. I don't go dark. I gave you space for you, in your best interest. I love you. I've not been good to you recently, and what you did was melodramatic – and murderous. But I love you. That'll never change. Nothing, absolutely nothing supersedes love."

Mae nods and leans back into him, allowing him to absorb her weight.

"Mae, I miss us. The old us. Do you remember your toothpaste prank? The wasabi cream switcheroo, testing my claims that I can eat the spiciest food. Which, I can. I can take the heat. I can fare far better than you, my dear." Rob's smile holds a charming playful challenge. "You keep life interesting, my love, always full of surprises. That wasabi fire explosion in my mouth, like a kiss from the sun, a spicy, burning inferno. You, my dear, are the reason I can handle the heat in more ways than one." Rob leans in closer, his voice laced with loving excitement. "So, bring on the wasabi, or any fiery adventure you've got up your sleeve. I'm game, you cheeky, wild, unpredictable bugger."

Mae's smile completely widens.

"Let's put the kettle on and start again. Can I stay the night?" Rob pulls back to look at her face and Mae forces a smile. She nods, though can't quite bring herself to say it out loud. This is not the Rob she fell in love with. Not the Rob she remembers.

"Please. I miss sleeping next to you. Even though you toss and turn like a rotating hot dog on a gas station roller grill. Though, last night you didn't." Mae winks and grins devilishly.

Rob shakes his head. "Blimey Mae – too soon."

7

Mae

As soon as Rob leaves the next morning, Mae digs under her pillow. She lay awake all night with that mysterious phone gripped tight. She needs answers. Needs to understand who she was before, and who Rob is now – and what happened in the dark space between. Of course, she knows the phone might give her none of these answers. But it's something, at least. Something she knows didn't exist before the crash.

Mae lights up the lock-screen. The background is abstract – a screensaver that no doubt came with the phone – and the number of notifications has doubled. She must have silenced it by accident. Mae clicks, and the phone prompts her for a passcode – six digits. She tries Rob's birthday, then her own, then Rob's mom's. She tries spelling out the name of Rob's first dog – George. Rob thought it'd be funny to name his dog the same name as the uncle he resented. She tries the name of his college punk band, The Ticks, and finally D8N App. The password screen locks, informing her she has 15 minutes until she can try agai

"Damn," Mae curses. What hasn't she tried?

Chucking on one of Rob's old college tees, Mae goes down to the kitchen and digs out the Chinese leftovers to pass the time. Anxious eating. She can almost feel her mother's eyes burning through the back of her titanium skull. She knobgobbles a battered prawn ball the size of a golf ball down her gullet and grabs the phone. She wracks her brain but can't think of a logical passcode she hasn't already tried. It could be literally anything.

Mae swallows too early and feels the last globule of batter all the way down to her stomach. Maybe if she plugged the phone into a computer, she could bypass the passcode? Doubtful, but worth a try.

Mae sets her laptop up at the kitchen counter, then sets to untangling the knot of wires they keep in the kitchen drawer to find one with an end that fits.

"Hot-diggity-dog. Gotcha." The phone lights up, but the password screen doesn't disappear. "Goddamnit to hell," she groans, shaking the phone. "Gimme something." But the phone just stares blankly at her. She can see her reflection in the black mirror. Lifeless and void of personality like personality of room temperature water. Who would've thought phones choose their owners just like wands, hey?

Half an hour of Googling and three prawn balls later, Mae admits defeat. Full and frustrated, she yanks the wire free from the port with a little too much force and sends her laptop spinning across the central island to the floor. The crack echoes off all the hard surfaces in their minimalist loft. Mae doesn't even have it in her to check the damage.

She looks down at the phone in her hand – all those notifications taunting her. There's only one person she knows for certain calls on this phone. Rose.

Mae pulls her own sparkling new mobile from her pocket and scrolls through her contacts downloaded from The Cloud. Her thumb lingers over the number for D8N App offices. What would she even say to Rose if she did get through to her? *Hey, you know that secret number you have for Rob. Is that just to dip his pen in your company jizz lagoon, or is it something bigger?* She could just imagine Rose sat at the desk across from Rob's as she got the message, putting it on loudspeaker so they could laugh at her paranoia together. No. That will never work.

She puts the phone down – she'll need a better plan than that. Mae bites her lip, her eyes scanning the living space as though it might somehow present an answer. Perhaps – maybe, Rob has a personal number for Rose written down somewhere? If she could send Rose a message on a personal line, she might be able to trick her into meeting somewhere. Get her away from the office at least. Some sort of neutral territory.

Mae has always kept physical address books – an old force of habit that she'd trained Rob into adopting. She couldn't really believe Rob would be stupid enough to write Rose's number in their shared address book, but she was clean out of better ideas.

They keep the address book in a drawer under the coffee table. Kneeling on the wooden floor, Mae lays the book flat on the table and starts to flick through. A, B, C. Rothchilds. She traces an index finger down the page, and there right at the bottom is Rose. Astounded, Mae gawks at the page. Then, she frowns and looks closer at the handwriting – slightly slanted with looping ls and over-extended ts. Not Rob's rushed scrawl, but her flamboyant, try-hard hand. Why would *she* have Rose's number? Mae shakes her head. She must have written it down on his behalf. Surely?

She pulls her phone out again and goes back to her contacts. She flicks down, stopping at R. 'Rose the one and only gal-pal lady-bro Mae-bug will ever need'.

"What the dead dicks parade is going on here?" Mae blurts out loud. Her head is throbbing. She's friends with Rose? Mae gets up and paces the living room. She sits at the piano and strums a few off-key chords. She takes two Xanax. Then she clears up her broken laptop, puts the address book back and gets dressed. She pockets both her and Rob's phones, though not before shooting Rose a simple text with a time and the name of a café far enough from the office that they won't risk Rob or anyone else passing by. It's time to get some answers.

*

Café Pedrotti's is a family-run Italian spot just behind Possum Trot Path and Gun Fight Lane, the perfect distance from D8N App offices to be both accessible and a pain to get to on an hour's lunch break. Mae arrives a little before 3pm and settles herself in a corner table. There are only two other people still nursing their paninis, and the owner is cleaning tabletops with a checked tea-towel, preparing for the after-school rush. They have a radio station playing low in the background. Blondie's *Heart of Glass*. Damn that song is following her today.

Mae drums her fingers on the table, watching the café door. What if Rose doesn't come? She checks her watch. It's 3pm on the dot. The café door chimes.

Like something out of Suits, Rose steps in wearing another one of her pantsuits, this time in a shade of pastel pink, with her hair gripped back off her face. Despite the shifty hour and location, she holds the same presence as she seems to have around D8N App – assumed authority. Rose briefly surveys the small café, nods to Mae in the corner and waves over the owner, all in one scripted movement.

"One small matcha latte with oat milk, if you have it,

soy milk if you don't. And if you have neither, I'll just have mint tea," says Rose, sitting herself in front of Mae.

The owner nods, then looks at Mae. "Decaf cappuccino, please," she says. She can't handle caffeine these days – the first cup she had after the accident was like having a heavy Norwegian black metal band beating on the inside of her metal-plated head.

"So," says Rose, sitting back. "What's with all the cloaks and daggers?"

"I just have some questions," Mae says, slowly, "about us. Maybe, let's clear the air?"

Rose raises her eyebrows, though Mae could swear she faltered slightly. "Go on," she says. "Which air would you like to clear because all air is on fire these days. The Earth is a fire truck on fire."

"Well," says Mae, choosing her words carefully. "I just wondered, why you didn't tell me we were friends? You know, when we 'met' at the office the other day, you acted like I was some stranger in a raincoat. Like that was the first time we'd met. But it wasn't, right?" Mae studies Rose's face as she says this, watching for flickers of guilt or anger. But Rose keeps her expression impressively sterile. A blank, stony poker face devoid of emotion is so easy for her. So easy it must be her cum face.

At that moment, the owner returns with their orders, momentarily blocking Mae's eyeline. When he moves away again, Rose has rearranged her face into a look of shame. She cups her hands around her teacup and stares down into it with creases between her eyes.

"You're right," she says, her voice quivering. "We were friends. Really close friends, for about a year before the accident. We did yoga and took our lunch breaks together. Went out for dinner and cocktails every Wednesday." She sniffs.

Mae has to hand it to her. She can put on a masterclass show. Rose sips her cup of tea with her pinky extended like she snorts caviar off monocles.

"Right." Mae leans back and crosses her arms. "So, what happened then? I got hit by a goddamn car and you just couldn't bear to look at me anymore?"

"No, Mae. Of course not!" Rose looks up, her face a picture of hurt and anguish. "We'd fallen out before that. About a month before, to be exact. It was stressful, I didn't know what to do."

"So you pretended not to know me! Stress is forgetting where your keys are. Cognitive decline from a severe traumatic brain injury is forgetting what your keys are for! I just lost years of my life and you're telling *me* it was 'awkward'?!" Mae grips her hands into fists, digging her nails into her palms to contain her anger. "What the bush-whackin' hell did we fall out about, anyway?"

Rose rotates her coffee cup on the table, avoiding eye contact.

"Go on, tell me. And I want the truth. Dontcha go piss on my leg and tell me it's raining."

Rose closes her eyes and takes a deep breath. "You and

Rob were going through the break-up, and—"

"Wait, what?" Mae's whole body tenses. "Me and Rob were broken up?"

Rose looks up, meeting Mae's eyes properly for the first time. "Just listen, okay? You and Rob were broken up. You left him, you weren't happy and hadn't been happy the whole time I'd known you. Sure, you were full of all these romantic ideas of 'you and Rob were meant to be' yada yada blah blah. But then you started trying for a baby and it obviously didn't happen fast enough, and Rob was pining and blaming you, and it was starting to get—" Rose flashes a glance up at Mae and then back down at her latte. "Well, you know, it was starting to get nasty. You moved into mine for a couple of weeks, we thrashed it out, and you decided to leave him."

"Right," Mae whispers, trying to think objectively, but already her mind is spinning. She broke up with Rob. They were broken up at the time of the accident. They'd been growing apart. That doesn't make sense. Or does it?

"I still don't understand why *we* fell out?" she says eventually. Rose meets her eyes again.

"It wasn't planned or anything. And it only happened once, when Rob was between places, staying in the office. And Mae, I felt terrible about it, I did. But you know, I was going through my own stuff too and I obviously knew so much about your guys' situation-"

"So, you fucked Rob," Mae surmises.

Rose pauses. "Yes."

Mae can't tell whether the world makes more or less sense now. Her brain is still fighting to connect the dots, to put things into chronology. She and Rob broke up. Her best friend slept with her fiancé – ex-fiance? Ex at the time, or so she claims. They fell out. Rob moved out?

"But—" Mae falters. "But me and Rob, we're together now?"

"It was a drunken one-time slip-up. Stupid mistake. And then, okay, also while you were in the coma. But that was different. We didn't know if you were gonna make it. He was a mess. We were all a mess. I promise, Mae. Really."

"Yeah, I guess a coma can really put a relationship on the back burner." Mae mocks sarcastically. "But that's not what's—" Mae claws at the thoughts and feelings in her head. "I mean, why are we back together? If I left him, why are we together now?"

Rose pulls a face. "I don't know. That's none of my business."

"You watched us through a breakup and then when I lost my memory just let him claim me back? Isn't that like manipulation? Or—" She wracks her brains but can't think of a word awful enough to sum up just how disgusted she feels. "How could you?"

Rose reaches across the table and grips Mae's wrist. "I'm sorry, I know. I've been a dreadful friend, I just felt so embarrassed. You were so angry at me."

Mae looks down at Rose's hand. On the one side, it sounds like she'd been a good friend before the accident:

letting Mae stay through a breakup, giving her advice and wine and sofa to crash on. But then she still fucked her fiancé while Mae was unconscious hanging on for life. Then just sat and let the whole thing play out in front of her again. And yet even after all of that, she might be the only person who was being drop-dead honest. This was a mother-fucking catch-22.

Mae shakes Rose off and says again, "How could you?"

"I'm sorry," Rose says again. "I really am. And I've missed you. For what it's worth. Even fighting with you. In fact, fighting with you was always the best bit." Rose smiles, a dark glint in her eyes, and Mae finds herself smiling too. Despite everything, this is more honesty than she's had out of anyone in a long time. Whatever Rose did to her in the past, Mae needs a friend. She knows that much for certain.

Mae takes a sip of her decaf coffee. It tastes burnt and bitter. "This coffee is just—"

"Dog shit?"

"Hot-diggity-dogshit. Like I dug up your childhood dog, killed it again, nailed it to your front door then ate its shit."

Rose splutters halfway through a sip of her latte, blowing a spray of green droplets all over the table. Mae doubles over, and the two dissolved into easy, belly-aching laughter. When they finally recover, Rose has the hiccups, and Mae doubles over again.

"You used to never drink cow's milk, or even almond milk. Mega hardcore vegan before your head got blown in."

Rose looks at Mae, surveying her like an interesting new species of monkey at Dallas Zoo. "What do you say, I skip the rest of my working day and you and I go rekindle our abandoned sisterhood over something that tastes a hell of a lot better and more alcoholic than these?"

"I think that sounds like the best idea anyone has had this side of intensive care," says Mae, pushing her bitter coffee away. "After all, we have broken cornbread together. Let's get blitzed."

*

Twenty minutes later, Mae is following Rose down into the musty, cool air of the underground bar. The dim lights cast a soft glow on the exposed brick walls, contrasting with the throbbing drum and bass reverberating through the floor. She feels a twinge of excitement. How long has it been since she's had a good dance? Lord knows she deserves to let what's left of her hair loose.

"Come on, drinks first," Rose says, tugging Mae's arm. Mae grips Rose's wrist, allowing herself to be guided as her eyes adjust to the darkness. The bar is long and polished and already crowded with people – students mostly.

They slide in between two groups of students decked out in burnt orange Longhorn jerseys and leant against the bar.

"What can I get you ladies?" the bartender asks, leaning in slightly so they can hear him over the music.

"A couple of margaritas," says Rose, ordering for the both of them.

"And six shots," Mae adds with a grin. "Tequila. Double them up."

The bartender nods and sets to work. Mae watches him, mesmerized by the swift, practiced movements. She feels a strange sense of déjà vu. Like she's watched this exact guy do this exact thing before. She wonders if she came here as a student? She and Rob could've owned this dancefloor.

The margaritas arrive first, their glasses rimmed with coarse salt. Mae takes a sip and immediately feels more alive. "Hell yeah! Yeehaw!" She bangs her palm against the bar. "Now that's a margarita, good God, damn. If I hadn't watched him make them, I'd say he has a maestro marg magician locked up in the back."

The shots follow, lined up in neat rows with little wedges of lime.

"To tonight," Rose says, raising a miniature glass.

"To tonight," Mae echoes, clinking her first shot against Rose's. They throw back the shots, the liquid burning a warm path down Mae's throat. She feels the familiar buzz start to take hold, loosening her muscles and lifting her spirits.

"Let's dance with the devil tonight," she says, grabbing Rose's wrist again. They weave through the crowd, finding a spot on the dance floor where the music is loudest. The bass thumps through Mae's body, and she starts to move, letting the rhythm take over.

An old guy with a scruffy beard and a plaid shirt sidles up to them, trying to join in. He's uncoordinated, his movements janky and awkward.

"Ugh, he's gross," Rose mutters, rolling her eyes. "Goddamn tick."

Mae laughs, though she doesn't totally get the insult. "Watch this," she says, stepping closer to the old guy. She starts grinding against him, exaggerated and over-the-top. The guy looks confused but tries to keep up, his attempts making him look even more ridiculous.

Rose bursts out laughing, and Mae joins in, pulling away from the stranger. They stumble back to the bar, clutching each other for support.

"We need more shots after that," Mae declares, catching her breath.

They order another round, and this time, Mae takes her time savoring the tequila. It feels good to let go, to be in the moment without worrying about a past she still can't piece together.

"You know," Rose starts, her tone turning serious. "The last time I was here was with you, just after you had your miscarriage."

Mae looks at her, surprised. She had a miscarriage? "Really?" she asks, looking down at her stomach.

"Yeah," Rose continues. "Fuck me, it was the best night. We got absolutely wasted!" She grins putting an arm around Mae's shoulders, engulfing her in the smell of expensive perfume. "You were telling me how much you wanted to give up on the whole baby thing. You were so over how obsessed Rob had gotten with it. It was ruining your relationship, ruining your knockout bod, and your alcoholism." She winks.

"I don't remember any of that," says Mae. Rob would remember though. How much else did they go through that he hasn't talked to her about? Not that he's in the habit of reminiscing or even giving her a *good morning honey tits* these days. Feels like now her family portrait's down to just a mirror, and her emergency contact? 911, forever.

"Ah Mae," Rose's eyes glint with mischief in the neon lights. "We had wild blurry nights at all these underground raves. But when it got really good was when I started experimenting with biohacking CE6 extracted from certain deep-sea fish that see in the dark. It's this synthetic compound prototype that has potential for treating diseases and giving temporary night vision to soldiers. But you know me, I can't resist pushing boundaries and got a smidge carried away. I bio-hacked a concoction of psychedelic phenethylamine-laced 'Shine Job' eyedrops. Trust me, it was insane! An out-of-this-world visual effects party drug. We danced like absolute maniacs."

Mae is impressed. She can't pretend she isn't. This shit sounds like exactly the sort of thing she hoped her younger self would have gotten up to. Hallucinogenic party drugs brewed by her bio-gen wizard bestie. Son of a gun, they sound cool. "Girl," she says. "You really are a geneticist extraordinaire! You can come off as a homeschooled quirk with pet rats you'd CRISPR gene-edit to glow in the dark. I really wish I could remember those glory nights."

Rose digs into her purse and pulls out a tiny bottle. She wiggles it in Mae's face. "We could make new memories tonight, if you like. Hell, even my lab rats were tripping before they died." Rose winks.

Mae lets out a snorting laugh. Her eyes light up in devilish glee, making an eager gimme gesture.

As Rose applies the drops to Mae's eyes and immediately her vision starts to change. The dim room around them begins to blur and warp, colors bleeding into one another like a melting canvas. Mae blinks rapidly, her breath hitching with anticipation.

Suddenly, she finds herself transported to a vibrant discoteca rave. The walls pulse with electric energy, adorned with neon graffiti that shifts and morphs into mesmerizing patterns. The bass of the music reverberates through her body, syncing with her heartbeat, as she and Rose return to the dancefloor, twerking in unison to the pounding rhythm.

The room is a throng of flesh, moving together in a chaotic harmony. Flashes of strobe lights create a stop-motion effect, capturing moments of pure ecstasy on the faces of the ravers. Mae's senses are heightened; she can taste the sweet, metallic tang of the air, feel the vibrations of the music in her bones, and smell the mix of sweat and Rose's perfume. And as she dances, she feels the alcohol and drops turning her mood from free-wheeling, no-fucks-to-be-giving, out-for-herself rampant Mae, to pissed-off-at-the world titanium-plated, bitter-boyfriend-butchering murderous Mae.

"I fucking hate him," she screams, but her voice is swallowed by the sea of packed, nuts-to-butts bodies.

Rose guides Mae to the bar in the back. "I know," says Rose, draping one arm over Mae's shoulder and handing her a Cosmo. "He's a class A bastard who owes all his fame and success to the women around him. He's a freaking pawn in his own company. You should get out while you can." Rose squeezes Mae's shoulder and whispers in her ear, "I mean it, this company isn't what you built. It isn't what you think, not anymore. Your co-founder shares are a hefty company stake, they'll sure be worth a sum. Regain your independence and rid yourself."

Mae snorts and downs her Cosmo. "What are you blabbing about? Yo. You're drunk. And me. I'm drunk." Mae sways where she's stood and Rose grips tighter to hold her upright. Mae's thoughts were swirling around her like a tempestuous storm. The weight of her failing relationship with Rob finally bearing down on her, an oppressive force she can no longer ignore. It's as if she can physically see the rift that has grown between them, an unspoken chasm that's drowned all the intimacy they used to share. He's been avoiding her, avoiding them, avoiding the very essence of what a relationship should be. It's an agonizing dance; the way he sidesteps the issue every time she tries to confront him. He is nothing but a masterful manipulator, turning the tables and making her feel like the villain.

The room feels suffocating. Mae clenches her fists, frustration and anger welling up inside her again. And to think she could have been free. If it wasn't for the accident, she would be long gone by now. There must have been a solid reason for her to leave the first time around, some clarity she'd had in that moment. She couldn't ignore the glaring truth any longer. It was time to free herself from the web of deceit and evasion that Rob had woven around her heart. "Fuck him. Rose, you can have him here or there or anywhere. In a house with a mouse. In a box with a fox. In a boat with a goat. I don't give a fuck."

Rose takes the now empty Cosmo glass from her and replaces it with a glass of water. Mae chugs it gratefully.

"We take water for granted," says Rose. "Water wars are in our future."

"Yeah," says Mae. "We forget the benefits of water: flushes out toxins, improves skin, and if your man cheats you can always just drown him."

8

DB

DB arrives at the D8N App offices early the Saturday after the launch party, his head still buzzing. After that whole embarrassment with Rob, he straight ghosted the gym and went straight back out to get good and properly wasted. Three bars and two clubs later he woke in the alley next to his cousin's house with only one shoe and a bruise on his left temple in the shape of a fried egg. Luckily, his fellow Saturday-crew, all the young 20-somethings (poor fools), are also scattered around the office like casualties of a war against sleep. It looks like some of them even slept in the office, or else pulled all-nighters after whatever rave they'd been at. Some of the more familiar ones greet him with weary, but cheerful waves. Damn does he wish he could still bounce back like that.

Fuck me alive, I'm struggle-bustin'. Need that caffeine fix. Avoiding his desk for an extra ten minutes, DB shuffles through the cluttered kitchen, his movements reminiscent of a zombie in search of sustenance. He fumbles with the coffee machine and with the precision of a seasoned caffeine addict brews two double shot espressos. He downs one right there in front of the coffee machine and clutches the second with shaking fingers as he makes his way to his desk. *At least the coffee would wake me up faster if I spilled it on my crotch.*

The Sales team are the only other team forced to be in at the usual time, though they seem to have embraced the concept of 'rise and grind', having all bought themselves McDonald's breakfast on the way in. The smell of bacon, egg and cheese McGriddles and soggy hash browns has turned the air over their desks hot and thick. DB's stomach churns at the smell. He's never been much of a breakfast person. Not since his dad's famous chicken and waffles – the only breakfast ever worth getting up for.

Heading to the very back of the office where Tech and IT sit separate from the rest of the office chaos, DB stifles a yawn as he fires up his computer, fully intending to do as little-to-no work as he can possibly get away with, maybe even taking a nap under his desk if the boss doesn't show. *I'll straight drink three coffees, pour a cup on my balls and numb some prescription amphetamines, then take a nap. Nothing like a good desk nap. If sleep is the cousin of death, then naps are the uncle who sells weed out his van and always has donuts.* But what greets him on the screen sends a shot of adrenaline straight up his spine. Warning symbols blink like ominous beacons, filling his monitor with flashing red and orange lights. An attempted hack into their systems. Panic surges through DB's veins.

"Shit," he mutters under his breath, his mind racing. "Shit. Shit. Shitty. Shit."

DB snaps into a state of robotic efficiency. His fingers smashing on the keyboard at a frantic pace, locking down everything, changing passwords, dissecting lines of code. Who would want to hack a dating app? Jealous lovers? Bitter exes? God knows he's had a couple of those. But no, it's more calculated than that – waiting for the night the whole office is out at an event can't be a coincidence. It must have to do with the finances. Money. Hackers are always after money. Only once he's sure he's got the thing under control does he snatch up the phone and dial Rob's line. DB can feel the blood in his head pounding in sync with each ring. He'd been hoping to be able to dodge Rob for at least a week after the handcuffs sitch, but alas a voice crackles on the other end and DB tries not to imagine Rob waking up next to Mae.

"Rob," says DB, his voice a mixture of urgency and sleep-deprivation. "We've got a situation here."

When Rob enters the office twenty minutes later, all evidence of McDonald's and hangovers has been eradicated.

Three more technicians are now also at their posts, helping DB source the root of the near-hack and seal it off best they can.

"Do not let anyone into my office." Rob's voice booms across the office. "Except DB. Bring him to me."

Still reeling from his adrenaline-fueled efforts to secure the systems, DB brushes the creases from his Lil Wayne t-shirt and follows Rob through to his office. DB hasn't been to Rob's office before, it usually being out of bounds to the average employee. The spacious room holds two imposing desks on opposite sides and an L-shaped sofa in the center. A Sonos system is playing a soft background of synth-pop, a stark contrast to the tension infused in the air.

Rob, already sitting behind his desk, nods at DB and gestures for him to take the seat opposite him. DB does as he's told, feeling like a child in the headmaster's office. That is until the image of Rob half-naked and cufflinked to his Alaskan King bed resurfaces, and DB has to bite the inside of his cheek to stop himself from smirking.

"What you reckon? Did you manage to find out how the hacker shimmied so far into our systems? That's a sticky wicket." Rob cuts straight to the point.

DB exhales. "The break was cunning, that's for sure," he said, scratching at the stubble on his cheeks. "The hacker targeted a vulnerability in our firewall. It was a sophisticated phishing scheme, built to mimic the login page of one of our key servers. It was so convincing, even I had to do a double take."

Rob listens intently, his eyes fixed on DB.

"Our intrusion detection system flagged it, and I managed to isolate the breach before it could compromise any sensitive data. The hacker got through the outer defenses, but I contained them within a virtual labyrinth of decoy servers. I've also taken additional measures to strong-arm our defenses. The punks won't be getting back past us anytime soon. And, if they did ever come back stronger," he continues, his voice steady, "I crafted a DDoS hacktivist attack using a botnet as a contingency plan. It basically unleashes a viral torrent of traffic onto D8N App, overloading the servers. It acts like a temporary shutdown, a moment of system failure for a hot minute. We're golden."

Rob nods and leans back in his chair. His expression is hard to read: half-seductive, half-accusing. DB shifts in his seat and forces himself to think of Rob half-naked again to lighten his headspace.

"You know," says Rob, eventually. "I did some digging into your background."

Oh lord, here he comes, thinks DB. *This is going to be like getting raw dogged with a spiked dildo.* Of course, this was always gonna happen at some sad point. He might as well just pack up and leave the building now. Or maybe security was already chucking his things out the window, watching them combust into smithereens 45 floors below.

"Lo and behold, I had no idea you were such an infamous crook yourself." Rob stands and starts to pace up and down behind his desk as he works backward through

DB's CV. "Five years at CyberNet, building leading security systems for the likes of NASA and the Federal Government." He raises his eyebrows at DB who can practically feel the sweat patches growing under his armpits. Rob pauses and looks at DB square on, staring him down. "Weren't you thrown out of MIT for that infamous stunt, breaking into the FBI's mainframe just to prove a point. I had thought you were all mouth, no trousers, but turns out you're a proper G."

DB meets Rob's eyes. Yes, it's true he's lied on his CV for every job since being chucked off campus. 'Graduated with honors in Computer Science Engineering and Software Programming', which in fairness, would have been his grade if they hadn't blown that one little escapade completely out of proportion. It's not like he was going to *do* anything with the information he saw. He was just proving that he could. Jeez, surely that makes him the best hacker in the world – right?! Not that the prissy, money-grabbing board members at MIT could appreciate such misplaced genius.

"Yeah, well. My Pop taught me not to advertise my hacking skills. Ya don't stand in line at the bank shouting, *hey I know how to crack safes.*"

"Ah yes, your father, *the* Henry Dubois. I used to watch documentaries about his heists. Not that his involvement was ever proven, of course." The grin that spreads across Rob's face is manic, glinting in his eyes like a cartoon villain. It takes DB by surprise. But then, the grin is wiped, and replaced by a dark, somber expression. "DB, this hack was not a random attack. We've been receiving threats for weeks. Ever since we unveiled the first rumors of the DarkStork update. I need your help to secure our systems. And when I say secure, I mean so secure it would put a chastity belt to shame."

DB shakes his head, trying to brush off Rob's concern. "Stop and frisk. Honestly Rob, this wasn't nearly as bad as it sounds. It's probably just some kid pissing about. Today to be a hacker all you need is a few bucks, a mild dislike for humanity and an internet connection. The victims of cybercrime aren't hacked by mask wearing masterminds who drunk the Kool-Aid, there is no manifesto. These days they're just coming for some money. They'll even negotiate. Best just to pay them quick and be done with it."

But Rob's expression doesn't falter. His eyes bore into DBs as he says, "I am being cyberpunk fisted up the gallbladder. They don't want money. They want data. Personal data. And we have far too much of that. I'm no expert coder, but I do know there's no limit to how deep these breaches could go."

Now it's DB's turn to raise an eyebrow. What sort of personal data could Rob possibly have besides the usual social media bullshit you can pull off a Meta profile? "So, they want to know D8N App user's birthday or email? Hardly seems worth a fuss. It's such a nothing issue to get crucified over…"

Rob leans forward, his voice dropping to a hushed tone,

competing with their K-Pop backing music. "Data is the greatest transfer of wealth in history. Data is the new currency. Data is the most valuable asset on Earth. It has surpassed oil. The big tech companies are digital kleptocracies. Mankind's' digital traces are mined into a trillion-dollar-a-year industry. Hackers are always after data. You don't know the half of it. D8N App, we are the rare gem of good guys. We don't monetize users' personal data. Our unparalleled, unbreachable privacy fortress safeguards their safety. Thus, this leak is more toxic than a dog's shit in Chernobyl."

"So, what is it you need from me, exactly?" asks DB, shifting in his seat.

Rob rolls his shoulders and clicks his neck from side to side before saying, "I'm promoting you to Head of Cybersecurity. I want you as our frontline of defense."

DB hesitates. This was the man who only, what, 24-hours ago was threatening his job if he doesn't steer clear of his girlfriend. His girlfriend who's so dissatisfied with him that she actually goes to bars by herself and ends up sleeping with strangers. Or at least, people she thinks are strangers. Mae has always been too good for this dickhead.

"I can't say being your virtual bodyguard is my idea of a dream job," says DB, folding his arms in a manner he hopes will hide his agitation – isn't this exactly what Mae told him would happen before the crash erased her memory? "Look, no shade," he says, "but this role was a lot more enjoyable with Mae leading. At least she told me all the dirty under-the-surface truths to help me do the jobs properly. You throw me dumpster scraps and a mutton head, talking like I should cook up a Michelin-star banquet feast." DB holds his breath. Rob doesn't seem the type to fall for probing, but it's worth a shot. "What if I say no?"

"Don't. This isn't an offer, DB," says Rob, deadpan. "Either you take the job, or you get out. I can't have a prolific hacker sat here ready to be bought out by petty criminals. Don't pussyfoot around. Pick a side. Here, now."

DB's mind is working double time. Did Mae set all this up before the crash? And if she did, why has it taken so long for Rob to follow through? What if this is a trap. Rob might be a class A British *arsehole*, but he's a deadass smart arsehole. The sort of man you want on your side, rather than the alternative. And wouldn't it help Mae to have someone on the inside?

"Fine." DB relents. "Yes, option one. I'll take option one. I'll cook, bro."

"Smashing!" Rob exclaims, his demeanor shifting instantaneously, and DB is once again reminded of a cartoon character. Is there anything low-key human about this man?

"How about a drink?" Rob gestures to the couch. "Call it an official welcome to the belly of the beast."

DB eyes the bottles of amber liquid lining the cabinet behind his desk. He nods.

As Rob pours the drinks, DB settles onto the L-shaped couch and tries to squash the weight in the pit of his stomach telling him he's selling his soul. Rob hands DB a large glass of whiskey and sits beside him with an exaggerated sigh. "This'll help grease the wheels." The scent of Mae's perfume clings to Rob's clothes. DB turns his head ever so slightly away and chugs a huge gulp of alcohol. There are very few situations alcohol doesn't make better these days. He's taken to downing half a bottle of whiskey in the care home carpark before visits. Sometimes it's the only way he can bet himself inside.

"Let's crack on, DB," says Rob once they've each taken a couple of large, silent swigs. He sets his glass down on the low glass table in front of them and Rob turns to face DB more closely. "You asked for dirty truths, so this is me giving you a yellow card. You are not to breathe a word of this to anyone, not even with your dying breath. What I'm about to tell you must never leave these four walls."

All the hairs up DB's neck stand on end. *These four walls* evoke the image of a prison cell, where people are sent to be punished. *This is it*, he thinks. He puts his glass down and forces himself to meet Rob's eyes. Rob nods his approval, then takes a deep breath.

"D8N App is invasive. It aggregates your digital data, and not just the usual stuff. It collects everything from your social media, your web searches, your credit card swipes, locations history, your likes, online and cellular communications to your WhatsApp messages. Then it goes into your entire friend network and pulls out all your friends' data as well. You name it, your uncle's neighbor's friend of a friend's sister's goldfish's birthday, D8N App knows it. But that's not why it's the most successful dating app. No. That comes down to the genetic data."

"Genetic data?" DB narrows his eyes, waiting for the punchline. "How the hell would you collect genetic data without people knowing? And why?"

Rob holds up a hand to silence him. "Rose isn't just here for admin, she's a pioneering geneticist and molecular engineer. When she saw what we – I mean, what I was trying to build she came to me with this incredible mindfuck finding. The ability to match people based on genetics." Rob illustrates with his hands. "Turns out DNA is the holy grail recipe of a good relationship – bloody holy of holies. Here, let me show you." Rob jumps up to rummage through his desk, returning a moment later with a tablet. On the screen are various diagrams of different DNA strands, all labeled and color coded.

"See this," he points to a pair of patching genes in the top left diagram. "This is the region called rs3796863 on the gene CD38. It's related to the oxytocin system. Everyone has either a C or an A allele on each of their two DNA strands, which is how we get the three groups CC, CA, and AA. Here we can see that the CC genotype is linked with greater marital satisfaction. Specific genes are pronounced for bonding and attachment security. While here—" He points out another pair of matching genes. "Having two A alleles is far more likely to lead to conflict in a romantic relationship."

DB leans in over the screen. "Is this for real? A genetic dating app." He draws his hand over his eyes, then refocuses. Is this the reason for all his failed relationships? For his parents' divorce? Had it really been in the science all along? "This is a dream, right?"

Rob shuts off the screen and reaches for the whiskey bottle. "Science is the best wingman. I'm telling you, DB, what we have here is groundbreaking. I'll hook you up with Rose to go through the hows etc. in more detail, but for now what I need you to do is make sure there aren't any leaks. This. Can't. Get. Out. Okay? That's a marching order. If anything leaks I will make sure the culprit is forced to emigrate to a manky no-man's-land where there's no water or internet, where their only out is to drown in a bucket of their own piss."

"I'll bottoms up to that," says DB, raising his now full glass. Had Rob really just trusted him with company secrets? He wonders if there's any chance Mae will remember any of this – it was her company too, after all.

9

Mae

Mae is showered, dressed and sat calmly on the couch with a homemade dirty chai latte when Rob tries his key in the new lock. She listens to his confusion while looking out at the view. She's surprised by how calm she feels. Coiled. Ready. In controlled.

"Mae?" Rob is bashing on the door now. "Mae, are you in there? My key's not working."

Mae sets her mug on the coffee table, stands and slides her slackened overalls strap over her shoulder. Then she takes an extra moment to close her eyes. She inhales slowly, blowing her lungs up like a balloon animal at a kid's party—

held in a slaughterhouse. She clenches and unclenches her fist. She's ready. Time for a hell-raising showdown.

"Mae, are you in there? The door is bolted."

Mae takes three bold strides toward the door, checks that the chain is still in place, then lets it open the customary two inches. Rob is standing in the hallway looking haggard. His cheeks are sunken, and his eyes are bulging, probably from a combination of coffee, whiskey and valium. That $200 luxury moisturizer he uses has done fuck all to stop him aging.

"Are you taking the piss, Mae?" he says pushing hard against the chain. Then he sighs like the Oscar-winning actor he apparently is and rolls his frog-prince eyes. "C'mon. I'm too knackered for a muggy pantomime. Let me in and you can do whatever this is once I've slept. Alright?"

Mae smiles at him but doesn't move to lift the chain.

"Oi, I'm serious, Mae. I really can't be faffed to deal with one of your tantrums right now. So could you kindly stop being a melty toddler with a harpoon for five bastard minutes and let me put my head down."

"You know what, Thomas Robert Malthus," says Mae, her voice cool and steady. "You maybe should have thought about that before using my hospital bed as a singles bar to pre-grief bang your co-worker. Or co-partner as I guess you wanted her on the board with you of Suckin' and Fuckin' LLC. Is there something intensely erotic about seeing your girlfriend in a coma? I wonder how long into my coma you fucked her. Not a cool move for the king of dating apps, the savior of the modern-day romance. You lit my life on fire and act like you're the hero because you somehow show up first to put it out by spraying runny shit through the sprinklers."

Rob looks like he's been dropped into a bath of iced custard seething with great white sharks. Then he recovers his face, resetting with a nonchalant, smart-ass look of subdued innocence. "She told you that, did she? Because clearly Rose has no motive in this at all. Not like she's had eyes on my job from the get-go. Bloody hell, is your brain still cabbage, Mae?"

Mae crosses her arms. "So, you didn't fuck Rose, is what I'm hearing?"

Rob sighs and throws his hands up. "Maybe I haven't banged her, but maybe I've been dry humping her noggin. Her medulla oblongata is so smashing, I jizzed all over her frontal cortex. How's that? Does that fuel your self-righteous quest to drag me down into your rubbish gutter?"

"They say men like women for their minds, and you could've had mine. Literally. You could've brainfucked me. My skull had a gloryhole."

"And what if I did give it the old nut and bolt job, Mae? What would you do then? Not gonna leave me, are you. We both know that. So stop flapping your trap, get it out of your deranged, bollocks-for-brains, brain-damaged little system and let me take my nap. Open the sodding door!"

"Just want to be clear, for the record y'know. When I sue you for the company I helped you start, and all the public humility and the therapy I'm gonna need to recover from the shock that most dudes ain't so lil shrinky dink down there that we can do more than scissoring. Your dick is so whack you've basically been giving me pussy."

"Yeah, you know Mae, you know what, I did fuck her. I did fuck another woman while you were comafied and I thought you were gunna die. So, shoot me. I had a moment of weakness, and she had all the right, warm, wet bits for me to slip and slide right on into to make myself feel better. A bash and dash. It wasn't cheating, it was a bohemian whim. You happy?"

Mae shivers. She hadn't realized part of her was still hoping. She bites down on her tongue, letting anger consume her. "Mhmm. Except, I actually shouldn't even really care. Cuz, we were broken up then, right?"

Confusion ripples over Rob's face before settling on what Mae is getting at. She watches the tell-tale reddening around his neck – a fattened goose staring at the roasting oven. Lord pisshead.

"That's right," says Mae, smiling with malice and triumph. *Not so smart now, is he.* "Strange thing to forget unless of course you've been victim of a near-fatal car accident, had your skull shattered, spent six months in a coma and had five brain surgeries to rectify the damage."

"Mae, wait!"

"What? Got an explanation for that too, do ya Mr. Wolf of Who Gives a Fuck Street?" Rob opens his mouth to say something, but Mae holds up a hand to shush him.

"That'll be all thanks, my latte's getting cold. My attorney will be in touch about the loft, though seeing as the down payment was all mine – well. Fuck you and your lil' limp-ass carbon dickprint. I hope your cock falls off." Mae flings the door shut and collapses against it.

"Fuck," she says to herself. "FUCK," she yells across the loft at the top of her lungs – so loud, a child would've pissed on the rug. She can hardly believe how good it feels. She could be high, or at the height of an orgasm – no it's better than that. At least better than Rob could ever manage, that's for sure. Mae laughs out loud. She has so much energy she doesn't know what to do with it. She gets to her feet and heads for the floating stairs up to their bedroom, taking them two, three at a time. Without a single conscious thought in her head, she begins to yank all of Rob's drawer open, emptying their contents all over the floor – his socks, boxers, watches, cufflinks. Then she makes for the wardrobe and starts dragging his shirts one by one from their hangers, then his trousers, then his jackets, before launching his pristine, mirror-ball-shined shoes at the walls. It's a massacre. A massacre of all the many costumes Rob wore.

After creating a piece of interpretive art with all Rob's belongings strewn around the flat, Mae throws on her sunnies and grabs her handbag. She has no idea where she wants to go, or what she wants to do. All she knows is she's determined to celebrate her newfound independence in every way the good city of Austin will allow.

*

Sunday has always been Mae's favorite day of the week. Partly because Sunday is the only day she's ever allowed herself not to work – this she gets from her mother and grandmother. Her whole family are deeply catholic, and so was she until she got to college. But even after tucking her religion in a bedside drawer, Mae kept the no-work rule, and somehow managed to instill it in Rob too. This later made Sunday's their day for couple-time and her favorite day of the week took on a whole new purpose. Being best friends, roommates, study partners and business partners all wrapping up in one was tough. Sharing an office with the same person you share a bed with is missed out of the relationship guides for good reason: it's bad for romance, it's bad for boundaries and it's bad for sex. Just an all-round blood bath. Mae can't recall the moment when she stopped enjoying working with Rob. Maybe she never did. She can't be sure. Too much time has passed between those days coding into the night in Rob's dorm room and viewing offices on the 45th floor of the tallest skyscraper in Texas. She'd never had any particular desire herself to start a business. Sure, she didn't really have a plan to do anything else, but that's not to say she'd have done nothing if it weren't for Rob and his big idea. And it definitely wouldn't have been anything more than an idea if she hadn't got on board. They both knew that. Rob was great at the social engineering side, but he couldn't code a game of Snakes if you threatened to blast him in the eyeballs. This Sunday though, is fresh. Not a Sunday for God. Not a Sunday for housework. Not a Sunday for Rob. This is a Sunday for Mae. And from here on out—every Sunday is mine.

Mae buys herself an iced latte and strolls aimlessly through the city, stopping to admire the street art on South Congress Avenue, each vibrant mural painting its own picture of freedom. She takes her time, snapping photos of the colorful graffiti. Once she's had her fill she uploads the best ones to her Instagram with the caption: *Life is too short to live without freedom.*

Her next stop is Barton Spring Pools, a natural oasis in the heart of the city. She's always loved swimming, but Rob was never a fan of outdoor activities – Brits roast in Texas heat. As a kid, she spent every weekend in summer competing with her brothers to see who could hold their breath underwater the longest, or else who dared jump from the higher branch into the lake behind their house.

She didn't bring a swimsuit, so strips down to her underwear and takes a dive in her favorite cyan blue lace set. The water is crystal clear and refreshing, makes her actual skin feel energized. She floats on her back, basking in her own liberation. She should do this more often – swimming that is. And she would, now that she didn't have to think about the possibility of getting a brain infection. And she didn't have to think about someone else. Didn't have to do someone else's chores, or dress the way someone else liked, or turn up to the office in just the right mood. Why did anyone ever complain about being single? She'd quite happily never date again.

As lunchtime approaches, Mae chooses one of the food trucks parked nearby the pools and treats herself to a fish taco. She relaxes out on the grass to eat, watching children splash in the pools while their mother's read and chatter. A book would be nice. She's never been into reading but thinks that now might be the time to try. She makes a vow to buy herself a book next time she passes a bookstore. A nice trashy, female-empowerment novel that shits all over relationships and reduces men to squalid, petty stereotypes.

The rest of her first single Sunday, she spends like this. Laid back, soaking in the sun, not caring. That's the best bit – not giving a flying pig's backside what the world wants. When the sun begins to dip below the horizon, Mae's stomach begins to rumble again, and she decides to wrap up with just one last act of self-celebration. Dinner at the roof-top restaurant she'd booked and later been asked to cancel for their anniversary last month – maybe a work emergency, or maybe Rob was just banging her replacement on Mae's desk. Not her problem now.

The Sky Bar is an extravagant place – even on a Sunday, every guest is donning either an evening gown or bow tie. Mae's overalls and matted hair don't quite fit the aesthetic, not that she gives a dingleberry about dress codes. There was this one time back in college, one of hers and Rob's first dates in fact, when he invited her to a black-tie dinner party to meet his aunt and cousins (rich kids fam), and she turned up as one of those tuxedo bunnies you see in Playboy, fake tits and everything. Should've seen their faces – his aunt looked like she was trying to hold in explosive sharts the whole evening she was trying so hard not to call it out. Mae had to admit she kinda respected her for that.

"Do you have a reservation, Ma'am?" asks the maître d' in a pompous fake British accent. *Ma'am?* Ugh, do I look like I should be filling out a 'Do Not Resuscitate' form? Wouldn't put it past him if Rob did that.

"Um…yes." Mae lies.

"And what name would that be under?"

"Mae Day."

He briefly looks down his list. "I'm afraid I don't have you on here, and we're fully booked this evening." He looks her up and down and she notes the way his nose scrunches at her scuffed high-tops. "There's a Wendy's down the road. How about trying there?"

Smarmy dickhead. The muscles in Mae's jaw clench. *Keep your cool gal, keep your cool.* She forces a sickly smile. "Oh," she says in polite surprise. The name Christof swims to the surface of her mind – a nugget of memory that's apparently more important than her big life events. "Well, the owner, Christof that is, said he'd put me down. I'll give him a call." Mae takes out her phone. "What's your name?"

The maître d's eyes widen behind his little Harry Potter glasses. Probably fake, just like his stupid-ass accent. Mae guffaws inside watching the panic flicker through every muscle in his face. "Actually. You know–if that's the case." He looks down at the book again. "I'm sure we can squeeze in just one more."

Mae holds her smile. "I'll have that spot by the window over there." She indicates an intimate booth right up against the floor to ceiling windows.

"Absolutely. Right this way."

Mae settles into the window table and fixes her eyes on the cityscape stretched out before her. The twinkling lights of a sleepy Austin wink as though whispering *hang in there, girlfriend.*

"Are you ready to order?" asks the floppy haired waiter.

Mae looks round, startled. She hasn't even looked at the menu, so she flips it open and picks the most expensive thing she sees.

"Sure thing. I'll start with the seafood platter," she says. Then, feeling suddenly flirty adds, "But waiter, I do have one condition."

"A dietary restriction?" the waiter asks.

Mae leans closer, drawing him in with a sly smile. "Promise me the lobster won't fight back?"

The waiter chuckles, his posture relaxing. "I promise, Miss. Our lobsters are well-behaved and won't be likely to challenge you to a duel. Anything else?"

Mae pretends to think for a moment, tapping her chin. "Hmm, maybe a cocktail? But only if it's as fancy as this hella view out here. Can you make a cocktail that shimmers like these city lights?"

The waiter grins. "One 'City Lights' cocktail coming right up, and I'll be sure to make it sparkle like your smile."

Still got it, Mae thinks as she watches the waiter and his tight little ass walk away to make her cocktail. Maybe she should take him home, put that king sized bed of hers to good use? She's a free woman now, after all. She can have all the casual sex she likes. And she will. Okay, well she might. She hasn't decided yet. Mae rubs the tattoo on her finger and wishes her cocktail would arrive faster.

Three midnight blue City Lights cocktails later, Mae has eaten half a lobster, three oysters, a handful of prawns and a succulent crab, savoring every last bite to herself. Food – another thing she'll never have to share again.

"I see someone enjoyed their platter," says the waiter, appearing at her elbow.

"Nothing but the memories left, I'm afraid."

"Well, that's what we aim for. I'll take your empty plate now. Can I get you anything else?"

Mae shakes her head. "No, just the bill and a round of applause for the chef. Oh, and maybe a doggie bag for any leftovers in the kitchen. Wouldn't want the lobster's friends to feel lonely."

Mae digs through her bag for her purse and looks out again at the city while she waits for her bill. She could shoot her shot with this waiter, but right now a walk sounds better. A night starlit walk back home and a whole bed to herself with zero dreams of Rob and his fucktardary. She smiles to herself.

"Here you are, that's $165. Would you like to pay by cash or card?"

Mae filters through her remaining notes. "Card, if you would, maestro."

The waiter obliges, offering out a card machine for her to add the tip and tap her Amex.

"Perfect," he says, turning away. But then– "Oh, actually. I'm terribly sorry, Miss, but it's been declined. Would you like to try a different card?"

The word 'declined' hangs in the air like an ex-lover. "Whoops, that's odd," she says. "Let me try another." She whips out her Platinum and taps it on the reader.

The waiter shakes his head. "I'm sorry."

An awful, sinister feeling creeps over Mae's skin like a rash. "Right," she says, feeling embarrassment burning up her cheeks. "Would you just give me a moment to check my banking apps?"

The waiter nods, no longer smiling, and moves away from the table.

Fumbling with her phone, Mae gets up her banking apps and enters her passcodes.

Wrong password.

She must have pressed a wrong digit. She tries again.

Wrong password.

Cold dread is now pulsing through Mae's bloodstream, her heart racing. Out the corner of her eye, she can feel the waiting staff watching her. She tries to maintain composure.

Looking up the number for Amex customer service, she dials, drumming her fingers on the table as she works through the identity questions.

"Thank you for calling American Express. My name is Irma, how can I assist you today?"

Mae takes a rattling breath and can feel her voice shaking as she says, "Hi there, I'm having trouble with my credit card. It's being declined and I can't access my banking apps. I think maybe I've been hacked?"

On other side of the line, Irma's tone shifts to a more professional one as she puts Mae through all the identity questions a second time. "Alright," she says, after having Mae successfully count the second, fifth and eighth letters in her elementary school, "I'll take a look into this now, just give me a moment."

The hold music is jolly. Like something from a kid's TV show – the ones where the colors are bright like acid and normal people smile when giving bad news. The phone clicks.

"I found the issue," says Irma, speaking slowly and clearly, as though speaking to someone very old. "It seems that your credit card–well–isn't registered under your name anymore. It's under…Thomas Robert Malthus. Had it changed. Legal reasons. Your partner. Health-related. Does that make sense, Mae?"

The revelation strikes Mae like a sledgehammer and the restaurant around her slides out of focus. Rob put her under a conservatorship. A year ago. Was that why he'd been so weird about giving her allowances in cash as a way to 'help her memory' and 'make things seem more real'? Surely he should have signed it back once they discharged her, right? Surely that's a thing?

"Hello? Mae, are you there?"

"I… I'm here. I just can't believe this," Mae replies, her voice cracking. "I need money now, to pay for my dinner. Can't you just transfer some? You know it's me, right? You did all the questions."

"I'm really sorry, Mae. It doesn't work like that. I suggest you call Mr. Malthus your partner and get him to transfer some money for you. Is there anything else I can help you with?"

Mae hangs up the phone but can still hear Irma's words echoing around her titanium skull. *Had it changed. Legal reasons. Your Partner. Health-related.* She peers over her shoulder, but it seems the waiters have stopped watching her, all too busy counting out their tips from other customers. She's the only person still at a table.

The waiter comes back. "Mam, Manager Christof just called and said you'd been banned as you previously grabbed a lobster out the tank on the way out. And another time you pulled a mixed-menus prank, swapping all the world-class steak dishes for cauliflower and tofu. I've been asked to make sure you wait here till security comes back."

"Tofu?" Mae asks, buying herself time. "I don't eat tofu. What sort of tree-hugging activist do you think I am? You must have me mistaken for someone else. I'm allergic to lobster."

The waiter grimaces. "Sorry, Ma'am. That's what I've been told. And you just ate lobster."

Mae sighs audibly, her mind working in double time. She briefly considers faking a severe allergic reaction. But, nah, they'd see thru that overkill. Mae remembered the name Christof but none of the details—typical she can barely unearth the insipid memories, while the important ones remain firmly buried. "Okay. Well, then can I at least use the restroom? I'm only gonna have to piss on your freshly polished oak if you say no."

The waiter nods and steps aside. Then, without another backward glance, Mae walks fast, head high–performance mode. But the second the exit door clicks shut behind her, she breaks into a run. Like prey.

Mae doesn't stop until she's five blocks from The Sky Bar. She feels like she's suffocating. Her chest tightens and her breaths turn shallow and erratic. She leans back against a cold, bricked wall, gasping for air, her heart pounding. Her cards. All her cards blocked. What in holy hell is she gonna do now? The world crumbles around her, leaving her alone, helpless and exposed–like she's back on that operating table, skull cracked open, everyone deciding what's best for her. God, she's never felt so fucking alone. Mae squeezes her eyes tight, trying to regain control, but is instead met with a familiar flash of images: glaring headlights, the screech of breaks, the smell of rubber on tarmac and the fatal crunch of bone on metal and she feels her non-existent skull cracking.

10

Mae

She's been searching for hours, turning the already chaotic loft upside down in search of any clue that might help her regain control of her life.

"There must be something, you son of rabid raccoon." Mae roars in frustration hurling the file she's been looking through at the wall of Rob's home office, knocking his degree certificate to the floor. She's rifled through every file in their filing cabinet, torn apart old letters and bills, and even flicked through Rob's favorite books and photograph albums. But each step led to a dead end. Mae slumps onto the floor. This is godforsaken hopeless. What's she gonna do without any money? What if Rob cancels payments for the condo and all their bills? She'll be thrown out on the street. The richest homeless person ever to live because Lord have mercy she's earned every penny in those accounts. How could he do this? Why would he? After everything. After she funded his great idea and stood by him through the investment pitches, the long nights, the setbacks. After all of that, he'd just let her curdle up and die. He really is an S-Tier selfish cuntbag. That dickless suckfuck would steal the nickels off a dead man's eyes.

Mae glares at the desk opposite her with all its drawers hanging out, its contents in a pathetic puddle on the floor. And it's then that she spots an irregular lump on the underside of the desk. Jumping away from the wall Mae scrambles across the floor to inspect it closer. She runs her fingers over the wood, then knocks on it three times, hearing hollow. Her heart races. A hollow compartment.

Mae runs out to the kitchen, grabs a screwdriver from their handy drawer then dives back onto the office floor. She grips her tongue between her teeth as she works the screws loose and pries the wooden slat free. A black A4 binder falls from the space, landing with a thump in her lap.

"Gotcha, yo bastard," Mae mutters, her hands shaking as she lifts the binder, weighing it. "I damn-well knew you couldn't resist playing CIA in your own home, you were always such a scrappy gumshoe."

Mae can hardly keep the manic grin from her face as she carries the binder out to the living room and lays it out on the couch.

"What have you really been up to?"

She flips open the cover and stares at the first page. Confusion swirls around her like a commode-hugging hangover. She turns the next page. And then the next. The binder is filled with crazed handwritten scrawl, broken up by complex charts and diagrams. There are references to algorithms, DNA, and climate change. But that's not the confusing bit – the handwriting isn't Rob's, it's unmistakably her own.

"What the—"

Mae leans in closer, her finger pausing on a page with detailed flowchart, highlighting various interconnected elements, like pieces of a thousand-piece puzzle she can't put together. She turns to a page that's been bookmarked by a random photo of her and her younger brother William Byron "Billy" – the two of them out on the ranch, stupid matching grins across their faces. A slip of paper flutters free, swooping dramatically side to side until it settles on the floor. Mae grabs it and turns it over. It's a profile, detailed and extensive with a black and white photo in the top right. DB. Mae's rattled brain is in overdrive. She scans the page, picking out the words her past self-highlighted in yellow: *seasoned hacker, best in the business, self-educated, off-the-grid. Son of Henry Dubois.* Then her eyes focus on the sticky note attached to the page, a reminder in her own handwriting reading: *Hire this guy to help.*

A chill runs down Mae's spine. She hired DB on

purpose. But why? To hack D8N App? Why would she need to hack the company she worked for? And why had she needed to hide all this stuff so carefully in her own home?

Mae's thoughts race as she tries to connect the dots. There's only one way to get answers to this. And for that, she's going to need to trust someone.

*

It's nearly seven by the time the door buzzer rings. Mae was starting to think he wouldn't show.

"Hello?" she calls into the speaker.

"Yes, Mae. It's me." DB's voice is low and rushed on the other side of the line. Mae buzzes him in and unlatches the door, then paces up and down biting her nails and clenching her fists. DB lets himself in just as Mae reaches her wall of windows. The city is still bright, though the sun had dipped low enough to give in an otherworldly glimmer, like being stuck on Mars. The joys of living in what is fundamentally a desert.

DB closes the door and dumps his laptop bag on the floor. "What's popping?" he asks, eyeing her from across the room. "You sounded kinda sketched out in your message."

Mae turns to face him, locking those hazelly brown eyes into a rigid, truth-bound glare. "No. Not okay," she says very seriously. "But also, don't know exactly what or why or who, or fuck—" Mae shakes herself. "Look. I called you because I need your help, but I also need to know I can trust you.

Like on the life of your sister's first-born mutant sort of trust. Ya get me, punkass? No games. I'm done with playing other people's games."

"You really do sound deranged," says DB, smirking. "However, I do love an anti-hero."

"Did you not just hear me say no games?" Mae glares, folding her arms. "Is that a yes, or what?"

"Without telling me the first thing about what's going on? Yeah, why the hell not. I mean," he pauses, bouncing slightly on the balls of his feet. "I kinda have something I wanna talk to you about too. I've had the maddest damn day."

"Alright then." Mae lets her guard fall and holds out a hand. "Then nothing you or I say or do in here tonight leave these walls. Yeah?"

"Nothing, you say?" DB winks, crossing the room to take Mae's hand. "That's a dangerous deal you're bargaining there, Miss Day."

"Yeah, whatever. Now shut up and tell me how we met, or I'll saw your teeth out. Not this time around, before the accident."

DB shakes his head, then steps back. "Um, weird opener, but sure?" He recounts the story of meeting Mae in the elevator on the day of his interview while Mae clears space for them on the couch and pours them each a large glass of whiskey from Rob's special collection.

"Mhmm." She nods as he finishes recounting the story. "Mhmm."

"Why are you asking?" DB looks around at all the scrawled notes, graphs and diagrams littered around them. "Looks like you've been plotting to rob a bank. This a murder board?"

"No," says Mae. "Way harder to crack than that." She coughs to clear her throat. "I think," she says, slowly, monitoring DB's expression. "I think that before the accident, I was trying to hack D8N App."

DB nods but doesn't show any sign of shock or surprise. He picks up his whiskey and takes a swig before asking very calmly, "And why do you think you'd have wanted to do that?"

"I think I hired you for a reason. Apparently I had a headhunter track you down." She reaches into her back pocket and pulls out the folded profile of DB she came across earlier. She hands it over and watches as DB unfolds it slowly. He scans it with little interest until reaching the highlighted section. Here he pauses, tracing a finger over his father's name – or at least that's what it looks like from Mae's seat on the couch.

DB nods slowly. "Yeah, this seems about right."

Mae narrows her eyes. "You knew?"

DB shakes his head. "No, not exactly. You had me double encrypt a load of files you'd coded in your own pig Latin-Norwegian language or something. I dunno what they were. But I did it – set you up with a black-level personal access code. That was the last I saw you, actually, before the accident. I've thought about it a lot, trying to tell myself it had nothing to do with anything. But now…"

"What did I say?" Mae shifts forward on the couch, her knees bouncing.

DB scratches his head. "You said you were gonna set up a job for Head of Cybersecurity and get Rob to promote me – you wanted to make sure I took it despite not liking Rob as a human being. You said it was why you hired me, and that you'd explain everything once you and Rob were over for good. Then you left."

Their eyes meet again. An unsettling sense of clarity passing between them.

"So, are you over now? You and Rob?"

Mae nods, subconsciously rubbing her <3 Rob finger tat. "He's making it that obvious, huh?"

DB shrugs. "Nah, just being even more of a self-righteous prick than normal." He looks at her finger. "Guess that tat's a bit harder to break up with."

"This Rob isn't even for him. It's for my favorite poet, Robert Frost."

"What your fav RoFro?"

"The road not taken. Two roads diverged and I took the one less traveled by and that's made all the difference."

"The one less traveled– don't ladies know that's how ya get murked?

Mae mock-scowls and chucks a couch cushion at him. "Whatever, DickButt."

DB grins. "So then, what is it you actually called me for? Not to go tit-for-tat with Robert Frost, right? I can't straight-up stand poetry."

"Consider yourself saved then." Mae smirks. "I got you over to help me finish whatever I started. Not that I know what that was exactly. I just can't shift this sense that I was onto something really big before the accident, and whatever it is, Rob is at the center. All these papers—" she motions at the floor, "this is all stuff I was taking notes on and data I was stealing from company files. I don't know why. I can't even make sense of half of it. It's just a random shitstorm of numbers that I can't read anymore. Half of it looks like DNA code and genetics. Maybe I was tryin' to get preggers or something and it got mixed up, dunno. And then there's this." Mae digs deep in her pocket and pulls out the phone she stole from Rob.

"Uhuh. Okay. Well, I can tell you for sure that you weren't trying to get up the duff." DB bends and picks up a load of papers from the floors. He started flicking through them, turning them every way up to take in all Mae's scrawls. "This is what I was gonna tell you – Lord, this is gonna sound mad Freaky Friday. Right. Okay." He sits up straight and looks at Mae with such a serious expression that Mae almost laughs. "So, Rob actually did make me Head of Cybersecurity today—"

Mae gasped. "Woah, for real?! But he was literally threatening you the other night. He hates the scrotum off your dick. That blimey limey."

DB shakes his head to quiet her. "That's not all. He also told me how D8N App matches people. Well, not in any detail, not yet. But all this stuff is bang on. He's matching people using their DNA. Like matching certain gene types to other gene types. Apparently, biology is more behind love than we think." DB shifts in his seat, his eyeline dropping.

"Uh. Mm-hmm. Ah. Umm. Huh. Uh-huh. Wha-"

"Are you having a stroke? Did you know about this?"

"The fuck? No, obviously not. What are you trying to say? That I'm the megalomaniac mastermind behind all Rob's Evil Knievel bullshit? This might be one of those rumors you get after disasters. Like, no one with an Apple Mac died on 9/11. Fuck. But how – how did I not know about this?" Mae puts her head in her hands, trying to compute this piece of the puzzle – to figure out how it connects to everything else. "But how is he getting people's DNA?"

DB grimaces. "Mae, it's real. They have people's DNA. They're genetically matching people. The *how* – now that's the worrying part. Though I also get the feeling this is just the surface of it." He scratches his head again. "I dunno, some of the shit he says. I just can't believe this is all just to help people find their soulmates."

Mae breathes out and slumps back against the cushions. Not that it's comfortable – Rob chose this couch because it looks like an extended version of The Captain's chair in Star Trek, but Mae has always maintained it's less comfortable than acupuncture to the vag. "Okay. Okay. Okay."

"Okay?" DB raises an eyebrow.

"Okay. Saddle up, gameplan time." Mae slaps her hands on her thighs. "I'm gonna take this bull by the horns, go through all these papers and try to make some sort of sense of where I was getting to. And you—" Mae digs into the pocket of her overalls and pulls out the mystery phone she stole from Rob. "You are going to hack into this phone and pull everything you can. I want passwords, messages, files, anything. Time to blow this thing wide open."

"Uhuh." DB takes the phone and turns it over in his hand. "And what about work? I'm Head of Cybersecurity now, remember? I'm supposed to be stopping people like you hacking the system."

Mae fixes him with a long, hard stare. "And there's me thinking you were the best hacker in the whole freaking country. If you ain't gonna giddy up, then giddy out my way."

DB grins. "Alrighty *Buckaroo* let's mark this beast before we throw it on the grill and see if it's juicy enough. Where does your boyfriend keep the branding irons?"

A sudden, overwhelming wash of relief crashes over Mae like a California wave, and she throws her arms around DB, pulling him into a hug. He rubs her back and waits for her breathing to calm. How had she gotten so lucky to have a friend like DB? A friend who would literally help her dispose of a body without a third ask.

Mae wipes the tears from her eyes, embarrassed. "Thanks, Dickbutt." She hiccups. "Christ, I'm such a loser."

"Nah you're not," says DB, patting her knee. "You're

the victim."

"Kiss my grits." Mae screws her nose up in disgust. "I ain't pulling no victim cards. Do wish I had a lick of cash though."

DB frowns. "What do you mean?"

Mae sighs. "He got a conservatorship on me, didn't he. Twat-ball-and-bag. Got control of all my cards, bank accounts, everything. Can't get a dime without going and begging the bastard. And I ain't stooping that low. I would rather learn what dog food tastes like. Who needs a pot to piss in? Okay, I do wish I had a lick of bus-stop bench money."

"Damn. GODDAMN." DB turns and punches the arm of the couch, making Mae squeal. "He's such a—"

"A Satan of financial trickitude?"

"That exactly." Now it's DB's turn to pull Mae into a hug. He grips her tight, whispering into her hair, "It's okay Maebug. I'm gonna hack the dickhead to shit. We're gonna take him down for every goddamn cent."

II

DB

DB has never been to the basement. He hadn't even known D8N App owned another floor until Rob escorted him down there in a covert lift at the back of his office. Even now he's not totally convinced that Rob hasn't somehow transported him into an alternate dimension where the D8N App office has no windows, the room lit only by the sinister neon signs mounted on every wall: the company's fluorescent pink logo burning itself into his retinas. Instead of desks, the room is a maze of what DB can only describe as high-tech smartboards, their screens independently flashing between long streams of code, 3D models of DNA and what seems to be real people's profile pictures. He trains his eyes on the screen closest to the lift and watches in real time as a young-ish guy with a goatee and vibrant green eyes has his profile (and his DNA) torn apart and put back together by Rob's digital army of code, potential matches flash up one by one on the right, before being discarded. After about fifty pictures, the screen settles, a goatee guy matched with an East Asian looking girl with a copper streak in her fringe. The D8N symbol flashes up between them. *Mae's gonna shit a skyscraper when I tell her about this.*

"This is a hermetically sealed bunker facility with heavy duty submarine doors," says Rob, walking ahead. "We've rerouted all drain lines away from the server racks and put on splash shields. We've installed waterproof equipment and watertight vault rooms. A ductless split unit keeps the server rooms a constant 68 degrees F. It's secured from the inside, and you need a unique code to operate the lift which changes daily. This way, buddy." Rob beckons him to follow. DB obliges though can't help whipping his head back and forth like a tennis spectator, trying to take in all the different matches happening around him. The room had felt claustrophobic when they first stepped in, but the further in they moved the larger it seemed to become, hundreds if not thousands of screens all working independently. The sheer magnitude of it is so overwhelming DB has to remind himself to breathe. In the furthest corner of the room, DB notes the huge, whirring server, nestled like a giant alien beehive with million red and blue eyes blinking down at them.

Rob guides him over to a huddle of desktop screens and motions to a wheelie stool. DB snaps a quick shot of the room and sends it to Mae while Rob loads the program.

"So first off, the very existence of this room is classified." Rob starts off as DB slips his phone back into the pocket of his jeans. "And this little stool right here, is the most important seat in the whole damn building." Rob claps a hand on DB's shoulder and grins over him. "In a nutshell, your job is to monitor the system, assess it for weaknesses, fix bugs, and spot hackers before they become hackers. It runs 24/7 and I won't trust another soul with it, so this is all on you, a'right mate?"

"When you say 24/7—"

Rob holds up a finger to silence him, then puts a hand inside his jacket and pulls out what looks like an ordinary smartwatch. "This," he says, handing it over, "will help you stay alert even when you're not in the office. Which in fairness won't be all that often." He raises a wicked eyebrow and DB forces a laugh.

The watch comes to life as DB puts it on his wrist and a bright pink welcome message appears on the screen: *Hello, Daniel.*

"You programmed it already?" asks DB, clicking each of the little app icons in turn – speed-dial contacts, a dashboard view of the backend of the server, D8N App itself and a live camera seemingly somewhere in that very room. DB squints at the tiny screen and his miniature double mimics from behind.

"All set up so we can be in constant contact whenever necessary," says Rob, clapping DB on the back again. "So, I guess I'll leave you to suss out the system then. Unless you have any last questions?"

"Err." DB looks around at all the screens with their flashing DNA profiles, trying to calculate how many there might be. One hundred? Two hundred? The thought sends a shiver down his spine, like a trickle of ice-cold water. How many people had Rob managed to get DNA profiles of – and without them knowing? "Actually, yeah."

Rob looks almost surprised, then rearranges his face into an expression of bemused concern. "Have at it."

DB swallows just as his phone buzzes against his leg – Mae's reply. "I just wondered how exactly you're getting people's DNA?"

"It's voluntary." Rob shrugs.

DB frowns. This isn't what it sounded like the first time Rob mentioned it. "Oh. I thought you said – I mean. How is it voluntary?"

Rob scratches his head. "Well voluntary, sort of. Genome sequencing is like the internet in the 1980s, it was there but no-one was using it. It's voluntary, like IVF."

Huh. Sort of. "How many people?"

"It's early stages—" Rob starts, but then the sound of heels on linoleum interrupts, and a new, female voice echoes through the room.

"Oh, nowhere near as many people as we'd like!"

Rose emerges from the maze of screens wearing one of her famous pantsuits in a shimmering ivory color, her curls are tight and precise, lips painted the color a seductive magenta. She smiles as she comes to stand on DB's other side. *It's like being flanked by Jessie and James, or Harley Quinn and The Joker.*

"People so sensitive these days, always worrying about stuff being personal and private. But nothing's ever private. And why should it be, when giving up your personal data could lead to something as invaluable as true love?" Her lips twitch upward into a gooney smile – the look of a love-struck teenager. "All Americans have had their data compromised at one time or another."

"Uhuh. But you're not really answering my question."

"Oh, DB." Rose sighs. "Sometimes getting what you want means giving up a bit of yourself. Have you never been in love? I – sorry, I mean *we* – are giving people what they want. I know it's not completely like, cool, or whatever. But what people don't know, can't hurt them, right babe? It's for the greater good."

DB looks up in time to catch the shooting look of warning in Rob's eyes, before he composes himself. "Right. How we get the DNA is beside the point. It's what we're doing with it that matters."

"Have you never heard the phrase: ask for forgiveness, not permission?" Rose croons, her fingertips stroking the collar of DB's shirt. "Well, anyway. I think you have everything you need down here for now. Rob, you're needed upstairs."

Rob makes to follow her, then pauses to say: "Oh, and DB. I only need to be contacted in emergencies. That speed dial on your wrist is only for use in catastrophic and unavoidable situations. Which, of course, won't happen now, with you on the case. Alright, crack on." And with that, he turns and strides back toward the lifts, following Rose.

DB waits until the lift doors have closed and the number above it has risen to level 45, then stuffs a hand in his jeans and pulls out his phone. Mae picks up on the first ring.

"Dude what's the deal with this secret floor?" she blurts.

"I can get you in," says DB. "But there are cameras."

"Hmm." He can almost hear her thinking. "What if I dress up as you?"

"Huh. Nice. You should join the CIA with ideas like that."

"Yeah, that's my Plan C career, after illegal dating app destroyer and ex-boyfriend assassin.

"Aight."

"When we doing this then?"

"We pull up tonight."

12

Mae

Mae adjusts the oversized Yankees hoodie she took from DB's apartment that afternoon. The sky is dark, and it's well after closing hours for Frost Tower's resident businesses. Even Rob is probably licking whipped cream off some prozzie by now.

She checks her phone again. 22.29. One minute.

The back alley she's hiding in smells of cat piss and garlic bread. Holy hell could she eat some garlic bread right now. Mae's stomach rumbles. She ran out of pocket change yesterday. *Gonna have to start selling stuff to eat at this rate. Imagine living in one of the nicest lofts in the goddamn state and not being able to afford a cup of instant noodles.*

A little further down the alley, a single door opens, and

a rectangle of light expands out over the tarmac.

"Psst. Twatface."

Mae takes one last cautious look toward the street, then scurries to meet DB at the service door.

"Ready to break into your boyfriend's empire?"

"Ex-boyfriend you goochface," says Mae, ducking inside.

The service corridor is cold, and their feet echo as they delve further in, trying to keep their pace casual, unflustered. They reach the elevator and DB jabs the button. Mae taps her foot while they wait, scrutinizing her own reflection in the polished metal doors.

"You have shit dress," she says, trying to break the tension. "Imagine supporting The Yankees and then actually advertising it to the whole of Texas, where fans bust their nuts for the Astros. How many times has this shit gotten you beat up?"

"Fuck you and your shaggy Taliban Barbie eyebrows," mutters DB as the lift doors slide open.

"Woah, did I touch a nerve there? For realskies? Fuck you and your bootleg-lookin' creased-ass Jordans."

"Yo, don't do that. Don't critique my sneakers – these are courtside kicks. You OD'ing right now. Mae, stop playin', take this serious."

"Yeah, yeah. Sorry, or whatever," says Mae, joining DB in the lift. "Guess my natural humor fails me when I'm nervous."

"You're not tellin' me you actually think you're being

funny, right?"

Mae catches his eyes and DB grins. "Dickweed," she says.

DB punches *basement* into the touch pad on his right, and the service lift rumbles to life.

"Tell me the plan," says Mae.

DB draws a sharp breath. "Aight, so basically, I spent all afternoon tweaking the screens so that if one of us is behind them, they're outta sight. That way, if one of us is at the desk and one of us on the floor, we good – Rob won't catch us slipping if he decides to peek in on the cam."

"Wow. High-tech." Mae raises an eyebrow.

"Y'bet your cute lil booty, baby."

"You lookin' at my ass in these jeans? Tsk, tsk. Gross."

The lift dings. Basement. DB nods as the doors slide open. Mae nods, pulls up her hood and claps her hands to her backside, her fingers splaying wide to form an improvised butt-shield. With a cautious waddle, she shuffles onto the linoleum, glancing over her shoulder, ensuring that DB's eyes cannot penetrate past her makeshift butt-staring barrier.

The glow of the screens washes over her like a cool pink bath. The soft hum of the equipment is almost hypnotic – the pulsing heartbeat of D8N App, for good or evil. Rows upon rows of screens flicker like digital fireflies, each one containing a different array of virtual connections and potential love stories. She half walks, half runs the length of the room. The sheer magnitude of it making her dizzy.

"It's like Disneyland for horny, virgin technophiles, whose virginity's fueled by remote control cars," Mae shouts.

"Keep it together," DB hisses, still waiting out of sight against the back wall. "We need to be discreet. I'm going now, alright? Stay hidden."

Mae, gulps back the whirlwind of excitement churning in her stomach. It's like standing on the precipice of a digital abyss, knowing that every click and every keystroke from this point on could get them closer to the truth behind the lovefuckfest.

DB settles himself into his desk chair – a master strategist surveying his battlefield. "Ready to blow up this hot bed of conspiracy?" he calls out to her.

Mae rolls up the sleeves of her oversized hoodie. "Let's bum-rush this metal clunker."

The buzz of the server becomes their soundtrack as they work, Mae marveling at the intricate sequences on the screens, her eyes scanning for patterns linking the matches. Meanwhile DB, stationed at the desk, delves into the backend of the server, his fingers dancing across the keyboard in quest for clues. Every half hour or so they swap positions: the person at the desk stands and yawns, as though innocently needing to stretch their legs. Then they disappear into the maze of screens so 'the other DB' can take their place.

Nearly five hours slips away, by which time Mae feels

like she's watched thousands of couples get matched with their so-called genetic soulmates. *Goddamn depressing or what?* She checks the clock on her phone, 03:22. The weight of time is pressing in on them now. The cleaners start at six. Mae needs to be gone by then. She squeezes her eyes shut, opens them, and refocuses on the algorithm's unfolding before her. Somewhere. Somewhere here there's a pattern. A pattern or an anomaly. A mistake, even. There has to be. Something, anything to expose the app's hidden agenda. No-one is this hell-forsaken good.

And then she spots it.

"Shit. Shit. Smear it all over a wall. Shitty. SHIT!"

"What?" DB calls from the desk.

Mae moves along the rows, waiting to see it again – the little icons beside certain people's names, an 'I' in a red circle, or an 'I' in a pink heart. Then, yes, there was another. A middle-aged man with carroty ginger curls and a red circle next to his name, matching with – Mae holds her breath as the potential matches flash up on the right, finally settling on a woman with buckteeth and a pink heart icon. She grabs her phone and quickly snaps the screen. "Hot dang! Fuck, man. I found something!" she shrieks, reeling, the blood bouncing against her eardrums like a motel mattress on Valentines. "I found something!"

The sound of wheels on linoleum as DB came rushing to see.

"What?" he asks, staring at a photo Mae is shoving in his face.

"Look. Look at the icons. It always matches people with the icons. Always a red circle with a pink heart." She watches his face, waiting for his excitement to match hers.

DB frowns, looking up at the screens along their row. "But not everyone has one?"

No, I'd say maybe like four or five in every hundred. I saw it earlier but just thought I imagined it. But it's real. And whatever it is, I bet'ya it ain't good." Mae's mind is lit up like a Christmas tree on nitrous oxide, already siphoning through potential meanings for the symbols. "Maybe it's matching billionaire sex traffickers exclusively with easy women who won't be missed. Or maybe you have to pay for one of these symbols, so you get matched with people from richer backgrounds, or with the best genetics. Or worse genetics. There's probably no demand for ginger sperm at sperm banks. Annie was a pretty unrealistic musical. Nobody really wants to adopt a ginger. I don't know. But we've got to find out what those symbols mean."

"You know– I think…" DB turns and stares straight at Mae, his chocolate eyes wider than she's ever seen them.

"What? I mean, it's about time an' all. But you think what?"

"Chill here." DB pushes past, disappearing back to his desk. A second later she hears his chair wheels rattle, then the frantic click of a keyboard.

"You can't leave me with that, dickprick," she yells from her hiding spot. "That's like slashing a Netflix series on the penultimate episode. Convicts on death row have suffered less."

Thirty seconds of tortured silence passes. Mae is about to yell at him again when–

"Yes. Mae, I have it!" DB's voice echoes off the tinted window, ricocheting around the room like a pinball at an arcade. "I knew I'd seen those symbols before. There's a file on the server collecting all the matches with those symbols next to them."

"What the lintlicker?! I need to see. DB, swap with me now. NOW! PRONTO."

DB is barely safe behind the screen before Mae makes a dash for the desk, throwing herself at the chair. DB was right. All the matches in the file are couples by those exact symbols. A red circle matched with a pink heart, each with cryptic letter 'I' in their center. Mae tries clicking on the match at the top to read further into their pairing, but a yellow sharp-legged bug icon flashes on screen, followed quickly by an error message. She clicks on the one below. And the one below that.

"Goddamnit to hell. They're encrypted."

"What? Girl, run that back?"

"Dickbutt, I can't open any of them. I can only see their names. Why the fuckity fuck would they have locked files on here? You're the head of cyber security!" she shouts in frustration. "Reckon you can hack it?"

"Err," DB's voice wavers. "I dunno. If they've locked it out even to me, I'm getting they've got some triggers behind me tryin' to get in. Swap back, lemme see."

Frustrated, Mae obliges, returning to her hiding place. Disinterested in watching more robot rom coms, she lies down on the floor and closes her eyes. "Tell me when you got something will ya, babe. I'm gonna get some shut eye."

"Bitch-hag," says DB.

"Scrote-scum." Mae smirks.

But Mae can't sleep. Not with the buzzing in her ears and the flashing screens imprinting pink and red across the back of her eyelids.

"Ugh, hell's bells," she groans, after what could be ten minutes or two hours. "Have you found anything yet?" she complains at the ceiling.

"No, I mean, not about that anyway. But…" DB's voice trails off.

Mae props herself up on her elbows. "But?"

"Have you ever heard of BioGenTechCross? I think they're the investors. They're named on all the confidential internal paperwork."

Mae digs into her broken memories. It does ring a bell. But then, she's lost so much of herself at this point, she doesn't really trust even her own intuition anymore. "I dunno," she says, giving up and throwing herself back on the floor. "Maybe. Maybe not. I'm shart-for-brains brain damaged, remember?"

DB continues clicking on the keyboard and Mae's stomach rumbles. She wonders how long it'll take her to starve to death. *24 hours or 24 days?*

"Wait. Mae, aren't they the company that does all the

genealogy testing for ancestry sites? Ancestry, MyHeritage, 23andMe – all that lot. I'm almost certain it's them. You send off a saliva swab."

Mae's eyes flit open, like a floodlight has gone on inside her. She clambered to her feet, suppressing the urge to squeal. "What if that's it?!" she shouts over the screens. "DB, what if that's how they're getting the DNA? Lots of people have taken them. Doesn't that make sense? This must have been what's on the files I had you encrypt!"

Finally, it feels like the pieces of the puzzle are slotting into place.

"Bet… actually, it does make sense."

"No need to sound so golly gee surprised!" Mae laughs.

"Hold up, hold up."

Chair wheels. Jordans. And a second later DB appears in front of her looking as exhausted and wired as she feels.

"You know what this means?" he asks, his voice flat and eyes serious. "This means we can prove they're stealing DNA. It's not voluntary at all." He grabs her forearms and shakes her. "We might even have enough to call in journalists, or even big guns. Take Rob down. Yes? Say yes, Mae?"

Mae's mind is spinning, all the imaginary puzzle pieces falling before her like autumn leaves, almost but not quite fitting together. "No, dude," she says firmly, pushing him away. "Let's not rush into anything. There's still something off about those symbols. Believe me, Rob is the least romantic person I know, there's no way he's risking something so illegal just for matchmaking. It doesn't add up." She locks his gaze, willing him to understand the conviction seizing her. "There's more to this."

DB sighs, his shoulders deflating. "Mae, you underestimate Rob. He's not a hoodie in front of a computer behind the screen hacker but the social engineering kind. People think hacker, they think computer hacker. We're great at breaking into systems and securing systems and have our own language, but this goes beyond coding and things like that. This is social engineering. This is real hacking. They're the extrovert social kind you have to worry about most. They also analyze weak points, but human error, like if you talk to one briefly they'll have already looked over your shoulder and know your phone passcode. They hack into humans thru human interaction, focus on behaviors and patterns and manipulation playing human emotions like a piano as they use sympathy principle to exploit trusting people. It's the art of misdirection. It's the legendary Trojan War in which the Greeks were able to sneak into the city of Troy and win the war by hiding inside a giant wooden horse that was presented as a symbol of peace. It's not technology, it's human error and that's only as secure as who is holding the key. He's The Condor."

They look around at the screens, still flashing. A digital tapestry of connections and deceit. DB yawns.

"We should probs get a shifty on," says Mae, stifling a yawn herself. She checks her phone – only forty minutes till cleaner o'clock. "Can I crash at yours? And buy me waffles on the way?"

DB narrows his eyes. "Well, guess I'd much rather you with me than have another showdown with Rob – or hell, next time maybe you'll take him out – shank him with a stiletto."

"Not used to being the front man, eh? Man up, DB— or at least lady down a bit. Were you raised by a single mom?"

"Actually, yeah, briefly. Mae, do you want breakfast or what? I'm finna dip."

"Yes. Yes I do. But I also want to know what this BioGen-Mc-Tech-whatever has to hide. They're Cali-based, right?"

DB hesitates. "Yeah, I think so. Why, what you thinking?"

"I'm thinking, let's go meet the Valley clowns. Real casual, like we could pretend we're there to update them on the project. Or invite them to some fancy palm tree shindig. I dunno, we can make something up when we get there."

"I'm sorry, *we?* Mae, I have to be here like 24/7, or Rob'll hang me up by my dick and eat my balls with beans on toast."

Mae rolls her eyes, though he has a point. She needs him here on the ground, just in case. Just to keep an eye on Rob. "Alright, gotcha. I'll go, you stay."

"Hey, no. That's not what I'm say—"

"Simmer down." Mae hushes him. "I'm not going to drive Diana speed. I'm a big girl with respectable tits, a titanium skull and I almost completed my rehabilitation exercises. Though, what happened to the days tits could get you anything? Anyway, I'm going. And while I'm gone, you try and get into those files. And I don't care who you have to sleep with to do it either, you dirty puppy."

"So, rewind that, you saying you care who I sleep with now?"

"Ok, I don't care whose wild peen you have to suck." Mae secures her hood, shooting him a playful wink. "But don't get any ideas, I'm taking the couch. No way we're ever having another go, Dickbutt."

"Girl, you trippin'. Don't flatter yourself."

13

Mae

Technically speaking, Mae shouldn't be behind the wheel. But having driven these roads back and forth for nearly three years in college – before she stopped speaking to her parents entirely – she feels confident that even half blind, she can get at least to the edge of California. From there, things may get dodgy, but what else is automatic stop for?

She reaches for the cup holder to take another sip of her chai latte. The spices are calming on her tongue though she misses the burn from the rum she usually adds to it at home. She sets the cup back in its holder and turns on the radio. Fifteen hours, or so she reckons. Plenty of time to come up with a plan.

Mae drums her fingernails on the steering wheel as she merges onto the I-20 Highway and the radio station settles on Bob Seger's *I Feel Like a Number*.

Mae sings it the best she can remember. "I feel like… just 'nother sp… spoke in a… huge ol' wh-wheel. I'm just a num… number."

Edging into the right-hand lane, Mae sets a steady speed and relaxes back. She woke before rush hour despite how late she and DB got to bed. Her dreams had been vibrant and disturbed – her usual nightmare now heightened by flashing faces, the screech of tires decorated with the persistent beeping of machines, and her own shriek of skull-shattering pain. She woke on DB's sofa with her head pounding, her t-shirt soaked with sweat. It was all connected. She knew that. Her accident, D8N App, the DNA stealing from ancestry research sites, the conservatorship. If only she could figure out how.

What do I know? She asks herself now. *What do I know so far?* Eyes narrowed on the taillights ahead of her, Mae builds a mental pinboard in her head, of the sorts Derek Morgan loves to swoon over in Criminal Minds before cracking a case. She must have gone through every box set of that show three times over in the ward – the only box set available when the hospital WiFi cut out, which it did a lot. Though her mental "murder board" is more akin to Charlie's in It's Always Sunny – a wild, chaotic tangle mess of conspiracy strings. A masterpiece of mental mayhem. At the center of the board, she places Rob – the mastermind, apparently. This doesn't sit quite right with her. Rob has never really embodied the strategic ringleader puppeteer sort. He was always a techy at heart, obsessed by detail, nerding out on tiniest intricacies of the code that allows people to reach across space to find each other. It had sounded romantic at the time, which is probably what led Mae to bankrolling him in the first place. The only reason he'd pushed forward with D8N App was because of Mae. He wasn't a big ideas guy. The thought of him coming up with something as architectural as genetic pairing feels at best farfetched and at worst like a futuristic conspiracy. It seems far more DB than Rob. Didn't DB say something about genetic engineering that first night at the bar? Then he mentioned double-encrypting files and claimed she hired him to establish a Head of Cybersecurity for Rob's promotion. Was any of that true, or was it all just a well-crafted lie? One thing's for sure: DB hasn't been transparent. He even kept their previous hook-up a secret, not mentioning it until she found out for herself. What if he had been hacking the company all along, using the hiring process as a cover? It's an internal tactic companies often overlook, assuming attacks come from external sources. DB could have remained undetected. Mae tacks a gray string. Shaking these disturbing thoughts. She needs to push on.

Branching off from Rob she pins D8N App itself – originally an innocent dating app that allows people to connect based on their life ambitions, personality traits and private model of what they think would make their 'ideal partner'. Revolutionary enough to breach the market, but not quite enough to change the world. Plausible as a Rob idea. Then off D8N App she pins two new red strings, one for DarkStork and one for BioGenTechCross, connecting them by a third to form an ominous triangle. Project DarkStork is being backed by this global biotech firm, which presumably means they have more of a stake than just simply supplying the genetic data. But what ulterior benefit could they possibly be getting?

Mae reaches for her latte again and takes two large gulps of now lukewarm chai. She and DB dug as far as they could into BioGenTechCross over triple stack waffles in the early hours, scrolling through CNN reports that named them the sole-biggest provider of DNA tests for ancestral genealogy sites, right back to their humble roots as a bio-medical testing and research center with no particularly outstanding breakthroughs besides one study into the inheritance model for genetic diseases back in the seventies. The company, as far as they could tell, had always been owned by the same family, having been originally founded in Ireland sometime in the thirties by a Cullen Rothchilds. Although he was not of Jewish descent, he changed the family name to 'Rothchilds' in 1944 as an act of anti-Nazi solidarity. It's now owned by his great-grandson, Cullen Rothchilds Junior. Mae draws to mind the picture of Cullen Rothchilds they'd found on the Forbes 30 Under 30 list from 2020, the year BioGenTechCross first became a billion-dollar company. He had the look of a man who could lure a fleet of ships to shore, with sun-kissed copper hair and the sort of silvery gray eyes that could cut through granite. There was an aura about him, even on paper – something both magnetic and dangerous – that made it impossible for Mae to look away, yet terrified of getting closer.

There are delays on Interstate 10, an earlier accident exacerbated by rush hour traffic. It adds over an hour to Mae's drive, and she quietly curses herself for her extended lunch stop at Wendy's. By the time she crosses into California it's already past sunset, and the route her GPS is taking her seems to be growing darker and darker – the desert landscape holding silence like a nuclear weapon.

Mae drives slowly. She hasn't seen another car since turning off the Interstate, and the desert dunes are looming higher with every mile. Above her, the night sky is a canvas of stars, her only source of illumination in the vast darkness. Mae couldn't say how far down that single winding road the map takes her, before suddenly out of the sand, grows a sign:

BioGenTechCross

International DNA-testing facility

Heart accelerating, Mae takes the turning and the terrain changes beneath her – the crunch of gravel echoing in the quiet desert air. Mae kills her headlights and coasts in the darkness. The only discernible features of the compound are the faint glow of security lights outlining the perimeter and the distant silhouette of industrial structure against the starry sky. The air feels close and charged with tension as she slows to a stop, parking what she hopes to be a safe distance away, hidden in the shadows of the dunes.

Mae cuts the engine and takes in her surroundings, her senses on high alert. She winds down the driver's window, welcoming the scent of desert sage and the whisper of the cool night through Joshua trees. She sits with the quiet, trying to stretch her hearing further out across the sand, tuning into the almost indiscernible hum of machinery adding an ominous undertone to the otherwise innocent landscape. And it's then that the clouds shift.

Mae swallows her gasp.

A partial moon casts a streak of light across the scene before her: chain-link fences topped with razor wire; the compound's building standing like silent sentinels, broad and foreboding; security cameras, their lenses catching the moon's glow, seem to stare out at her through the night. But the sight really punches the air from Mae's lungs is the graffiti. The messages are bold and angry, clearly drawn by the hands of impassioned protestors. Mae recoils in the driver's seat. Even through the night, even from a distance, the words painted in vibrant hues defy the darkness: DEATH TO THE NEW WORLD ORDER, SATANISM, COVID HOAX, HAARP, CHEMTRAILS.

"Fuck, Rob. What in the world of Voldemort-shagging psychopaths have you gotten yourself into?"

BioGenTechCross does sound like a cartel. But the Irish have no Mafia, because the Mafia don't kneecap you and tie a burning car tire around your head. The Irish have the Irish.

Mae sits frozen, staring at the hand-painted accusations until the sky rearranges itself and swallows up the moonlight. In her head, getting into the facility at night had felt like the logical option. But now, looking at the sheer levels of security, Mae can see that she'll likely arouse even more suspicion. She'll be better off coming by daylight, introducing herself as a D8N App founder – which, after all, wasn't a lie – and call it a perfunctory check-in. Yes. That feels better. Less likely to arouse suspicion. Mae shivers. Fuck the desert is freezing. She rolls up the window and pulls her knees to her chin, wrapping her arms around her legs. She wishes she'd bought an extra Wendy's Baconator to ward off the cold.

14

DB

The waffles Mae insisted they devour at three in the morning prevented DB from sleeping. Pumped full of sugar, he tossed and turned under his summer sheets, his mind going over what they'd found.

Eventually he must have drowned in his own exhaustion, waking to his alarm and sound of construction outside. Staggering from his bedroom, he's relieved to find Mae has already gone. He makes himself a double espresso and takes a cold shower to wash the night from his skin. Going back to D8N App now feels dirty. Like having found out how the app works makes him somehow complicit. Of course, he's not always been an angel when it comes to data. His dad was a master hacker, after all. But still, he likes to think of himself as a sort of Robin Hood in the hacking world. Taking from big corporations to even out the playing field for those on their way up. Thing is, DB had kinda thought D8N App was one of the good guys. A computer geek in his college dorm starting something groundbreaking. Maybe everything gets corrupt once it goes corporate. Maybe that's just the nature of modern business.

He needs to do a load of washing. The only clothes he can find are the jeans he was wearing yesterday and his Wu-Tang t-shirt with toothpaste down the front. DB rubs at the stain with warm water before pulling it on and brushing out the creases. His phone buzzes on the kitchen counter. It's Mae.

Skedaddled early. Lemme know if Rob lets anything slip.

Fuck. Of course, she made him promise to confront Rob about the source of the DNA. He unlocks his phone and checks his calendar. Yep, there it is. The meeting he locked down for 11am, already greenlit by Rob's assistant. He groans. Aight, guess it's go time. But first, one more espresso to set it off.

*

Everything in the basement's just how they left it in the early hours. No windows, so it's like time doesn't even exist down here. Could be day, could be night – doesn't matter.

Got that casino vibe, like it's built to mess with your head. The low hum of the AC and the buzz of the lights are the only clues time's moving somewhere else.

DB slides into his desk chair and boots up the computer. No major warning lights, just a couple of bugs to squash. He's on it, his fingers dancing over the keys like a piano prodigy, ironing out glitches, making the system flow smoother than Busta Rhymes' Break Ya Neck. At 10:45 his phone vibrates on the table – it's time to roll up to the viper's pit.

DB's nerves are whacked as he steps out of the elevator into the main D8N App offices. It feels like stepping into a festival compared to his isolated dungeon – radio bumpin', coffee machine huffing, folks buzzing around with laptops and board markers in hand. He navigates the sea of desks quickly, not really wanting to be stopped but also lowkey salty that nobody seems to have missed him up here. Like, sheesh, has no one even noticed that he's not been at his desk? Did no one miss his dreadfully sexist jokes or hip-hop tees, or generous lunchtime donut orders? He takes a glance over at his old desk and is gut-punched to see that someone new is already sat in it – a faceless ginger man staring into his old computer screen. He always thought gingers are God's way of giving everyone else a boost of self-esteem, but he feels the opposite now. And suddenly DB is back in school, when he had to take a month of sick to have his dick emergency circumcised thanks to the foreskin deciding not to grow with it, and when he got back not only had he lost his spot as first trumpet in the brass band, he'd also lost his then girlfriend, Sandy Dunmore, and spot on the oh-so coveted 'cool kids' table – a spot he only had because of Sandy, and never had again. Swallowing the bitter taste of these memories he turns away and pushes through to the executive offices at the back. No time for stupid childhood insecurities and office playground politics. Time to handle business and find out what all this shit is really about.

Tuning out the noise of the open plan office, DB raises a fist ready to knock on Rob's door – not giving himself the chance to think or back out. But then he hears Rose's voice coming from inside. Noting it's raised tone, DB pauses and edges closer, trying to listen in without making his lurking known.

"–I can't just make things move faster than the speed of bloody light overnight, Rose. That's not how it works."

"Cullen doubled the money. That means double the pace."

"Double the output, technically."

"No, Rob. Double fucking everything. The pace, the identification, the inferiors, the matches. Everything. I don't think you're quite grasping how huge this is. We need to move onto the next stage. Cullen's ready, but he can't get going until you fulfill your end of the bargain."

The room goes dead silent, and DB is suddenly very aware of the sound of his own breathing. He holds his breath, palms sweaty as hell.

"Right. Well, you think on it then, Rob. But I need an answer for Cullen by tomorrow."

The sound of footsteps on the other side of the door. DB jumps back, trying to play it cool like he's just stepped in from the office floor. The door swings open and Rose steps out, the length of her orange pants licking the doorframe.

"Woah." DB holds up his hands like he's dodging them crashing into each other. "My bad, Rose. In my own world." He flashes a grin. "Just got a meeting with Rob."

"Um. Cool?" Rose raises an eyebrow. "So, you gonna let me pass or what?"

DB bows out the way for her to stalk past, leaving nothing but the rich smell of bergamot and amber. *Now there's a mood that could wake a dormant volcano.*

Catching Rob's office door with his left arm, DB pushes in without waiting for permission. "Rob," he says, trying to make his voice firm. "We gotta talk."

"Christ on a Charlie-crack bender." Rob groans. "For fuck's sake. What is with you wankers today? I take this bloody shackle job home, which is this office, it fuckin chains me to the bed, fucks me raw from arsehole to dawn. Then, come sunrise, it greets me with a cuppa piss to the face, followed by a jolly good slappin' to ensure I'm awake enough to kick me in the bollocks. This ruddy job has invaded every blasted orifice, riding me harder than the Thames on high tide." He draws a hand down his face and gestures towards the plush chair in front of his desk. "Sure thing, DB. Whatever. Take a seat. Crack on."

That sounded personal. DB slams the door for show and takes the offered chair, his eyes never leaving Rob's face. Maybe his little confrontation with Rose will have worn Rob down enough to give DB a chance of answers? "I've been digging into the source of the genetic data we're using for the matchmaking algorithm. Care to explain why our investors are a biomedical company specializing specifically in DNA for ancestry testing?"

"Sniffing around, are we? No one called in a bomb, guv." Rob leans back in his chair, a sigh escaping his lips. "Look, DB, it's not as sinister as it seems. So yeah, they're developing the world's largest bio-database. But they're just backing us because they see the potential in what we're doing."

DB crosses his arms. "Potential for what, exactly? Genetic manipulation? Identity theft? Stealing people's DNA from ancestry tests is straight-up lightyears beyond next level sinister. Is this why you employed a freaking master-hacker for your cyber team?"

Rob hesitates, the pattern of his thoughts sending ripples across his forehead like a heart monitor. He shakes his head. "No, about hiring you because you're a master hacker though I will be sure to keep that on file. Duly noted: The whizzkid can do more than right click a mouse." He winks, that schoolboy cheek lighting up his eyes.

"Uhuh. So, by your omission, the DNA is not voluntary. So that's straight-up theft, right??"

Rob rolls his eyes in the manner of someone trying to explain one plus one to a toddler. "No. Wrong again DB. The DNA is not stolen – users consent when they accept terms and conditions. But—" He holds up a cautionary hand, "if that's not enough to stop you running to the FEDs you should know that this is more than just a dating app."

"Spit it, I got my ears open," says DB with as much forced sarcasm as he can muster.

"This isn't just about helping people find love. It's about preventing the spread of genetic diseases."

DB falters. "Genetic diseases? Hold up, what you sayin'?"

Rob nods solemnly. "Exactly what I said, mate. We match people not only based on their compatibility emotionally, but also on their genetic compatibility in terms of their ability to procreate or the risk of passing on genetic diseases. We call it Genetic Variation Probability, or GVP. We're not just in the business of matchmaking; we're in the business of improving lives – and without people even knowing about it."

DB sits back, trying to process. "So, what exactly are you doing with the people who have genetic diseases? Who are you matching them with?"

"Well," Rob hesitates again. "Well, I guess that's where things get a little murky. But you have to understand that it's all for a good cause. The greater good, as it were – Rose loves that phrase, though personally I think it makes me sounds like some sort of evil mastermind. Like something is rotten in the state of Denmark."

"Go on."

Rob leans forwards, resting his forearms on the desk. "Well – there's two routes, depending on whether your disease is recessive or dominant. With recessive conditions like Tay-Sachs, which essentially destroys a person's brain and spinal cord nerves, or cystic fibrosis which causes chronic lung infection, kids develop the disease if they inherit two risk genes – one from each parent. The genetic matchmaking software prevents two people from matching if they had similar genetic mutations that could result in hereditary diseases, stopping parents passing them on."

"And with the dominant diseases?" asks DB, a lump forming in his throat.

"Yes, well this is going to sound a bit extreme. But with the dominant diseases, we essentially use the DNA comparisons to make sure people who carry a genetic mutation, like those that cause brittle bones disease or Huntington's never find their true match, or even one close. You see, we have this category for people who are infertile, so by matching inferior with infertile. Come on, surely you've figured it out now, lad? At the end of the day my work is all about making progress on eradicating life altering genetic diseases, not only releasing the strain on our health services, but also making sure that every human being brought into this world has the best chance of a full and high-quality life." Rob sits back, letting his words settle in the air between them.

DB feels frozen to his seat, the weight of the revelation holding him down. His mind drifts to his Pop in the care home, too young to be there, too far gone not to be. But did Huntington's make his life in totality unbearable? Irrelevant even? Nah, no way. Obviously not. But then, that's not what Rob is saying. He's not suggesting culling the people who have it. Only proposing a world without Huntington's. Where such a disease wouldn't exist. Where someone like himself wouldn't have to live in fear. After a silence, DB speaks, his voice quiet. "You should have been real from the jump, more transparent about this from the beginning, Rob. People deserve to know what they're signing up for."

Rob shakes his head. "Come on DB. You're a smart enough bloke. You know I can't do that. The world would riot. They'd accuse me of playing God without permission."

"And aren't you?"

Rob shrugs. "Maybe a skosh. Maybe making God obsolete. But I know that you of all people, will appreciate the good that this could do." DB meets Rob's eyes, and sees there – despite disliking the guy, despite every bone in his body screaming at the subject immorality of it – that Rob is right. "DB, I know about your dad. I'm sorry, man. It's a grim disease. My aunt actually beat Huntington's – she shot herself in the head. Very competitive woman. I'd say that's where I get it, but we weren't blood."

"Lucky you, not having to live in fear of it."

Rob nods. "True enough, mate."

*

Back down in the basement. DB downloads D8N App onto his phone. He enters his details like a robot and lets his thumb hover over the sign-up button. Could it know already? Did D8N App already know his fate?

15

Mae

The sun struggles to claw its way above the horizon, casting a pale glow across the barren desert. Mae wakes with a start at the sound of heavy vehicles growling past the car. Stiff and groggy, her neck protests the makeshift bed as she leans forward to peer through the dust-caked windows.

Three conspicuously labeled delivery vans have just rolled into the facility, each marked with hazard signs and the warning: 'medical waste'.

"Medical waste my ass," Mae mutters. She watches intently, her eyes tracing the path of the vans as they disappear behind the imposing walls.

She leans back, feeling the stiffness in her limbs. Dust hangs in the air like a spectral haze. Mae grabs a water bottle and downs the whole thing in one. The decision to wait until morning feels like both a blessing and a curse – undetectable but also unfindable. If anything goes wrong for her here, she really would be on her own. Gathering her wits, Mae climbs out of the car and starts to clean the dust off the windows with a rag. The car has blended completely with the sandy surroundings, a mirage amid emptiness. Once the car is as presentable as she can get it, Mae buckles up and sets pace toward the facility's main entrance.

The security gates loom out of the sand, and Mae tries to set her face into an expression of ballsy innocence, ready to lie through her whitened teeth. But when she rolls down the window, she finds a young girl stationed at the desk – freckled with hair in two long braids, no older than eighteen.

"Hey!" says Mae, relaxing. "I'm here to see Cullen Rothchilds."

The girl nods and glances at the computer screen, her fingers clacking across the keyboard. "I'm sorry, ma'am," she says, frowning. "There's no record of a meeting with Mr. Rothchilds on my system. Are you sure you've got the right day?"

Mae laughs and rolls her eyes. "Yeah, I mean, it's a bit impromptu, you know? I thought I'd surprise him. He's been having a bit of a rough time, you know, health wise," she lowers her voice, gesturing down to her crotch. "Thought I'd cheer him up. Do you need me to give him a call to confirm? I mean, it would kinda ruin the surprise, I had a whole song prepared – but I get it. Rules are rules, I guess."

The girl hesitates, clearly torn. "I really should confirm this. Can I see some ID, please?"

"Oh sure, sure." Mae digs into her purse and pulls her old D8N App ID card, handing it to the girl. She scans it, her eyes flicking between the card and the computer screen.

"Been working with you guys for a good few years now. Course, my business partner's known Cullen a long while longer than that. That's how I know him, see, through my business partner. Now my ex, as well. Awkward situ. They do say never to shit where you sleep. I guess the same goes for fucking where you work."

Finally, the girl hands the ID back and clicks to open the barriers. "Alright, you're good to go. Just head on in and park to your left."

"You angel," says Mae. "My good deed is saved."

Passing through the gates, a mix of relief and fresh anxiety washes over her. *First hurdle complete.* She steals a glance at the graffiti she noticed the night before. It's still there, ominous messages sprayed across the walls. A shiver runs down her spine, that awful sense of foreboding curdling in her gut. She can't shake the feeling that she's just stepped into the lion's den, and the hunt for truth has only just begun.

The reception area is eerily silent as Mae pushes through the heavy frosted doors, just an empty desk with a clipboard inviting visitors to sign in. Mae smirks. *Nice try. You've got enough of my personal data.*

Dismissing the registration process, Mae scans her surroundings. Spying a faded sign to her right marked 'genetics', she starts toward it, pulling her shoulders back in an effort to look like she belongs. The corridor is narrow, the walls corrugated iron, and the chill in the air comes as an unexpected contrast to the desert heat outside. She glides swiftly past the unmarked doors on either side, a phantom in the sterile environment, careful not to linger. The lights above are vibrant and insincere. Too white. Too piercing.

About five minutes into her walk, a man appears from an office to her right and strides ahead of her. Mae hangs back. What will she say if he questions her? His white coat flaps against his calves, the signs above his head still pointing them down the hall. She has no choice but to follow.

Holding her breath, Mae keeps her distance while still trying to make her pace feel intentional. After another minute or so, the corridor meets an end, concluding at a quite ordinary looking door – no different from those they've passed so far. Mae pauses as the man leans in. A facial recognition system, perhaps? A piercing bleep echoes through the wall and the door swishes inward. Mae seizes the opportunity, catching it with her hand just before the latch seals and slipping inside.

The atmosphere is clinical, the hum of machinery echoing through the air. Mae glances around, her eyes darting from one workstation to another. People wearing goggles, leaning over microscopes. Petri dishes and syringes. Computers with 3D diagrams, just like those on the D8N App screens. A chill runs the length of her spine. She spots a lab coat, and a pair of goggles hung on a hook to the right of the door and swiftly slips into the disguise. *Alright. Hold it together, now. Act freaking natural.*

Mae saunters round the fringes of the corrugate space, trying to make her movements confident. Superior even. She could be an inspector, if anyone asks – or a new manager sent to observe. The room is a labyrinth of futuristic equipment, monitors displaying complex data, and glass cabinets containing mysterious vials. The urgency inside her mounts with each person who almost, but not quite, locks onto her presence. She walks with purpose, mimicking the casual stride of the scientists engrossed in their work. At each workstation, she attempts to glance at the computer screens, scanning for any other similarities between these and those in the basement at D8N App. But the technical jargon is incomprehensible. The screens far too intricate to interpret at a passing glance. It could all be completely separate, completely innocent – or it could all be connected. She has no way of telling.

A scientist across the room catches her gaze, his glance a little too direct, before leaning down to share a hushed word with the researcher next to him. Mae quickens her pace. The clicking and whirring in the air seems to be closing in, and suddenly it feels like the whole room is aware of her presence. She's walking too fast, tripping over her own feet. Then, straight ahead, her eyes are drawn to a man in a sharp suit, conspicuous and corporate-looking against the sea of lab coats. He leans in and the door in front of him swings inward – a door labeled Unit 9. Just before he disappears inside, he glances back over his shoulder, and a pair of striking, steel ash eyes stare straight into her. Instinctively, Mae knows this is Cullen. Knows too, that he's been waiting for her. Has probably been watching her this whole time. The genetics lab pulls away as Mae moves toward the door and closes it behind her.

The room pulsates with a dim ominous glow. Like a darkroom, the lighting is slightly red, the walls an all-consuming black. It appears to be a meeting room of sorts, a long table filling up most of the space, a huge, cinematic screen on the far wall with the BioGenTechCross logo glistening in the center.

Cullen turns to look at her. His eyes are deep, but empty. Like a psychopath. It makes Mae shiver.

"Top o' the mornin'. I wondered where you'd been hiding," he says, his voice sultry and hushed. Quieter than Mae would have expected – velvety like a smooth chocolate. "Security told me ye' were about. What brings ye' to my wee sovereign kingdom? Come for a bit of craic, did ye?"

It feels like a trap. This is all Mae can think. She needs to keep him talking, keep him occupied while she figures a way out. But then – it's not like he could *do* anything to her, right? She needs to keep the upper hand. Keep him thinking she knows more than she does. Yes. That's the way. Mae swallows and sets her face in an expression she hopes makes her seem aloof and unflustered. "Curiosity, Cullen," she says, moving carefully around the table, tracing her fingers along the backs of chairs. "The same thing that got the cat killed."

Cullen arches an eyebrow. "Curiosity, huh? And what is it yer curious about Dorothy Mae?"

Mae bristles at the sound of her Christian name. A name no-one, not even Rob would use for her. Who the fuck is this sumbitch? "Oh, you know," she bluffs, forcing a smile. "Just interested to know how our main investor is utilizing our partnership. I've been a bit out of the loop you see, so Rob suggested I pop on down to see all the great work you're doing for myself."

Cullen smirks and lets out a coy laugh. "Oh, Mae," he says, sauntering around the table toward her. "I know yer no longer employed by D8N App, and I'd wager yer not even a shareholder at this point. Where are ye' crashing these days? I hope that car isn't yer only refuge at night. Ye' do look like ye' sleep on a pile of leaves."

His words hit like a back-handed slap across her face. So, he really has been lurking. Mae's stomach clenches tight. "I know you're stealing genetic data, Cullen," she says, holding her voice clear and steady. "And Rob might be too visionary to question it, but I'm not Rob. You're using D8N App as a vehicle for something, I can feel it. And I'm not leaving until I find out what it is."

Cullen nods though doesn't look surprised by the depth of her knowledge. "Stealing genetic data, ye' say? My, my. The genetic data people send to us willingly you mean? Voluntarily when taking a PCR test?"

Mae freezes. Did he just say PCR tests? Her mind works furiously. That would make sense, of course. Billions of people took PCR tests, far more than those who take ancestry tests, never thinking that the little swab they put in the plastic baggie might be used against them. Mae shivers, but not from cold. Her blood has near-reached boiling point. Her distress surpassing an active-shooter-in-the-building frenzy. "They take them to test for a fatal disease, you potato-head. Not for the purpose of storage and analysis." Mae glares right at him now, standing her ground as he reaches her side of the room. "What are you up to, Rothchilds? and don't give me the same bullshit as Rob. I'm old and metal-boned enough to know men like you don't care about fairy tales."

Cullen lets out a little gasp and makes a face of mock hurt. "Mae, how could ye'? I believe in fairy tales. I've seen the pot of gold at the end of the rainbow. It's not my fault people don't read the small print. Did ye' read the small print on your Covid tests? No, no. Silly me. I know ye' didn't."

Cullen's lip curls. He's inches from her now, eyes glowing in the dark. Mae can't move, rooted to the spot by adrenaline. She never has been good in a fight or flight scenario, freeze is her response, has been since she was a little girl – her own body working against her. Cullen steps closer, his shoulder brushing hers as he breathes down her neck. His cologne engulfs her, and he whispers in her ear, "Watch yerself, Mae. Ye' might uncover more than ye' bargained for."

"Are you threatening me?" Mae asks, barely daring to breathe, silently cursing her own useless muscles.

"I'm enlightening yeh, love." Cullen draws a line with his nose from her ear down her neck and she imagines she can feel him hardening against her. "Such a shame," he says, "that people as sexy as yerself have to come into the firing line. Such a pity that yer genetics have failed ye' so." Mae whips around, coming to face him nose-to-nose. Cullen laughs. "Oh, hunny," he says, reaching up and stroking her hair. "Ah, ye' beautiful catastrophe. I can see what Rob saw in ye. And you're right, it would have been so much kinder if it had been him and not ye. But the world isn't fair – ye' of all people know that." His fingertips graze over the scars in her hairline, where the metal plates had been welded into her skull. "Yer far too clever for yer own good, Mae. But there's naught ye' can do now. Yer fate's been sealed." He leans in, his lips almost touching hers. "Just let it go," he whispers.

Mae's pulse is throbbing in her ears, threatening to burst blood vessels in her head. She can taste toothpaste and coffee on his breath. Vomit rises in her throat. Without a second thought, Mae leans in and bites Cullen's lip so hard that the metallic taste of blood fills her mouth. Cullen yells through his mouthful of blood, his eyes wide, shock delaying his reaction. Mae takes her chance – a swift knee to his groin. He doubles over, gasping for air, and Mae runs. Bolting from the room she barrels out into the vivid medical light of the labs. The researchers scramble as she crashes through them, shoving people out of her way.

"Stop her!" someone shouts, their voice drowned by the blaring of an alarm, reverberating like a power plant siren against the iron walls. Papers fly like confetti in a storm as Mae grabs for anything loose on the desks. Anything she might be able to use later. Someone grabs at the back of her lab coat, slowing her. She yanks her arm and feels the fabric rip as she launches herself toward the door back into the hallway, throwing a hand out to hit the door's release button. The shouts behind her fade, but the sirens in the hall are even louder, relentlessly pounding against her eardrums, setting the beat to her sprint back down the sterile corridor and out through reception.

The desert heat hits her square in the face, but the sirens don't ease. Stolen papers in one hand, she digs into her pocket for the car key.

"Come on you shitbox. COME ON!"

Finding them, she throws the car door open, shoves the papers into the passenger footwell and starts the engine before even closing the door. The exit barriers are closed, and Mae can sense people emerging from the building behind her, white blobs in her rear-view mirror. Mae holds her breath and puts her foot down. "ARGHHHHH!" She screams, gripping the steering wheel as the car bursts through the barriers with an unyielding crash, sending shockwaves through the vehicle. Mae's heart pounds, the taste of blood still lingering on her lips. And as the desert landscape stretches out before her, she peers back one last time to see the facility diminish on the horizon, swallowed by the vastness of the desert.

16

Mae

Mae pulls into her designated parking space, adrenaline still vibrating through her bones. The relentless drive from California to Texas echoes in the thrum of the cooling engine as she sits there, the dimly lit garage casting shadows on her anxious exhaustion.

She reaches for her phone, fingers fumbling as she dials DB's number again. It rings, as it has done each time she's tried it, but nothing. The voicemail's robotic voice underscores her solitude. She hangs up. She can't risk leaving a message – recorded evidence that could be hacked into as easily as DNA could apparently be extracted from plastic sticks. She draws a hand over her eyes and shakes herself. *Come on gal. Get it together.*

Mae drags herself from the car. She needs a shower and a coffee. No, she needs a scream into a pillow, then wet her throat with something with a kick. Something to make her feel normal. Then, perhaps, she'll be able to make sense of everything that's happened in the last 24 hours. She takes the elevator up to her and Rob's floor in a kind of trance, digs in her jacket pocket for her keys and shakes them loose. She presses her key into the door, but it refuses to turn. She frowns, draws out the key and inserts it again. But the lock remains steady. Confusion dances with panic in her mind and the air in the hallway seems to thicken. *He changed the locks. That arrogant egotistical delusional bastard. His head's so big that had he been riding shotgun with JFK the man would still be alive.*

"BASTARD!" Mae yells and kicks the door as hard as she can. "COWARDLY, PIECE OF HORSESHIT BASTARD." Each subsequent kick is fueled by an anger Mae hardly knew she had inside of her and the metal hinges clang in battle cry, refusing to let go. Mae falls back against the wall as the truth settles around her. She has no home. Her bank accounts are frozen. She can't even get in for a change of clothes. She has nothing but the car and the clothes on her back. *Holy hell.* How did life fall apart so fast? All she wants now is to punch a dry wall or dive headfirst into a frosty river and chug a bottle of whiskey.

Back at the car, Mae collapses behind the steering wheel and tries to figure out where to go. She can't return to D8N App – Cullen has surely already been in touch with Rob and told him what she's been up to – he'd definitely have told Rose, at least. Mae is a security threat now. A fugitive. DB is the only person she can trust. Her only beacon of hope in the spiraling chaos. If he'd only answer his goddamn phone. Mae eyes the security camera at the corner of the garage, it's red light blinking ominously. She shivers as cold dread washes over her like an ice bucket, and she starts the engine.

*

Mae is sat on the front porch steps when DB finally pulls in. She springs up, launching herself at the car.

"Why the hell haven't you been answering your phone?" She growls, her agitation turning to venom in her voice. "I've been calling you and calling you."

DB's eyes dart nervously as he steps out of the car and gestures for her to lower her voice. "Hold up. Not here, Mae. Inside." His tone is hushed, his eyes alert, like a wild dog.

"Fuck you, DB," Mae hisses, turning and stomping up to the front door.

Once inside, DB takes one last glance out the front before double-bolting the door.

"Gimme your phone," he says, holding out a hand.

"What? Are you shitting me?"

"Give it to me, Mae." His voice is firm.

Mae thrusts a hand into her pocket and slaps her phone into his palm.

"Thank you."

Mae watches, uneasy, as DB powers the phone down, and his own, then puts both devices in the freezer. She raises her eyebrows. DB exhales.

"This isn't a great time," he says. "There's a party tonight. A celebration to mark the ninety million DarkStork users." He meets her eye, the weight of his words hanging in the air. "But we do have to talk."

"You bet we do." Mae moves toward the sofa then stops. "But not without a drink. Clear, brown, rubbing, I'll drink it all up."

A flicker of amusement darts across DB's face. "Word," he agrees, then turns back to the kitchen, and pours them each a large tumbler of tequila.

They settle on the couch, the weight of unspoken truths suspended between them. Mae takes a deep swig, allowing liquid courage to warm her insides. "Start talking, DB."

DB shakes his head. "You first."

Mae nods with relief as the events of the past 24-hours spill from her like levees breached by a hurricane. She goes right back to the beginning, re-living in as much detail as she can everything from the ominous graffiti daubed across on the outside of the testing facility, to the masked scientists and petri dishes, the diagrams on the screens and the papers she stole. She recounts her conversation with Cullen with her eyes closed, though misses out the intimate details of his advances, skating over the warmth of his breath down her neck and the taste of blood now fused to the roof of her mouth. When Mae opens her eyes she finds DB frowning, a gentle crease pulling his eyes a little closer, though nothing of the horror she's feeling. Frustration pulses in her fingertips, she grips them into her palms. "What's up? That story not Hollywood enough for you?" She scowls, folding her arms.

"It was one thing when we thought BioGenTechCross was getting genetic data from genealogy sites but collecting DNA from PCR tests – that's a grotesque aberration of trust. And worse still, D8N App literally uses its so called 'superior data' as a marketing tactic to get more users! It's not linking people based on personality or biometrics, it's genetics. Stolen genetics. How motherfucking sinister is that? Maybe this is what I was investigating before the crash. Maybe this is what was in those files I had you encrypt? PCR tests. They pioneered PCR tests and now they're stealing DNA data of billions globally. Are they what comes out when you rub an empty bottle of napalm?!"

"I know what they're testing for," says DB, finally. "Rob told me."

Mae stares at him, but he refuses to meet her eyes.

Damn. Rob's got to you, hasn't he? He's a social engineering human hacker. "Well, go on then? Land the bombshell if you got it."

DB sighs and runs a hand through his hair, still looking anywhere but directly at her. "It's– they're matching people to avoid genetic diseases being passed on. Tay-Sachs, cystic fibrosis, sickle cell anemia, MD – the whole cocktail. So, if you have a recessive gene then you won't match with someone else who has one. And if you have a dominant one, then—"

"Then you don't match at all." Mae finishes his sentence for him.

DB looks down into his hands, then seeming not to know what else to do with them, he picks up his glass and downs the rest of his tequila in one. Mae watches, trying to gauge what his silence is hiding.

"So it's like genetic cleansing," Mae prompts. "But for the whole population. Fuck me. I'm fixin' to load my six-shooter and haul on up to the 45th floor. That's sick."

DB sniffs, puts down his empty glass and finally looks at her. "Is it though?"

"Is what though?"

"Is it really that sick?" DB pushes himself up off the sofa and starts pacing the room. "I just don't know anymore, Mae. My Pop – my Pop has Huntington's, got it real early too. Way before he was ready, and I– Well. I don't know if I have it too. And I don't know, I guess part of me thinks that maybe if something like D8N App can stop these diseases and even wipe them out entirely, can make sure that everyone can live a good, full life. Maybe not passing this down is more important than having the perfect relationship. What's harder than having a sick child? Many parents go to great lengths to spare their children from suffering, few realize the only guaranteed way to prevent it is not to bring them into existence. Maybe this is all a good thing after all?" He stops his pacing to look directly at her. But now it's Mae who can't stand to look at him.

"A good thing? You fucking what? At what cost, DB? They're playing God with people's lives! This isn't about preventing diseases, it's about free will. You can't motherfucking decide who procreates with who. You've bashed that part of my brain trauma that doesn't allow good to exist without condition."

"They ain't though! They ain't forcing certain people to have sex, they're just stopping certain people from meeting for their health. How is that a bad thing?"

"Right." Mae is on her feet now, crossing the room to stand in front of him. "Tell me this then, DB. If this whole God act is so moral, then why are they hiding it? Why aren't they plastering your genetic status across your profile so people can see their compatibility for themselves?"

"To protect them from prosecution. It's a *I don't know what data is on our servers* defense. And people don't want to confront our own susceptibilities, horrific lack of privacy, and hopeless dependency on tech. And for marketing, like isn't it far more romantic to believe you've found your soulmate than you've people matched with someone to avoid one of your botched genes being passed on? To quote Charles Darwin: *If you had an idea that was going to outrage society, would you keep it to yourself?*"

"Grow up, DB. There're no such thing as stupid-ass soulmates. A *soulmate* is just someone geographically accessible who's up for a shag and who also puts chips on their sandwich. And ideally with a kitchen island, high ceilings and exposed brick." Mae is shaking, partly from adrenaline, partly anger, and partly from lack of sleep. Her eyes are crossing over and her vision is blurry. "I can't believe you're defending them when you act like the type of guy who'd make a citizen's arrest," she says quietly. "I thought you were better than this."

"Nah. You don't understand," says DB, moving back toward the kitchen and reaching for tequila. "If I have Huntington's, it's a death sentence. It's a cruel disease that'll rob me of everything. And if D8N App can prevent even one person from going through what my Pop is going through right now, isn't that worth something?"

"And what about the people who are denied the chance to love and have a family, to live the rest of their days alone because of some algorithm? Is that fair?" Mae grabs her jacket off the sofa and makes toward the door. Just before she reaches it though, she turns back to see DB swigging straight from the tequila bottle. She feels a twist of guilt in her stomach. She hadn't known about the Huntington's. He'd never spoken about his dad like that before, and she'd brushed over it like it was nothing. But this wasn't the time. There was more to this, and she knew it. How could he be so weak? How could he be so susceptible? He was part of the problem. Maybe he is behind it all. "Where does it end, DB? If genetic diseases are stage one, what's stage two? Who will they be wiping out next?" And with that she turns and leaves.

17

DB

DB is sat alone on the couch surrounded by the low hum of the refrigerator. The air is heavy. Mae's infuriated departure has left an almost physical void in the room. He sits trying to contend with the whirlpool of feelings in his chest – the sense of pride at standing his ground, the conviction that morality is not always fair, and the ever-expanding welt of self-disgust spawning under his skin. He needs fresh air.

DB pours himself another whiskey and moves to the double patio-doors. He steps out onto the decking, slides the doors closed and leans back against them, taking in the arid wasteland stretching out before him. The land had been set aside for housing, but the investor went bankrupt, leaving it barren and desolate. He takes a sip of whiskey and tries to enjoy the numbing sensation as it trickles down his throat. He can't seem to shake Mae's words from his mind. *Where does it end?* The question echoes in his thoughts. Where does the pain and suffering end? *They're playing God with people's lives.*

Playing God.

DB swirls his glass – liquid the same color as the desert. Surely, with all the advancements in technology, it seems inevitable that man would eventually become godlike. And if man was always going to be God, then surely it makes sense to strive for a world where humans are perfect machines, free from disease and decay. Where they won't wither or go moldy. Where their brains won't turn against them and leave them trapped inside themselves. The worst kind of suffering.

DB can still remember the moment when the first signs of his Pop's disease became apparent. He was fifteen, still in high school but not really going as much as he should, and his dad had invited him down for a week-long fishing trip. It was early spring, the air still crisp with memories of winter. DB didn't particularly enjoy fishing, but that was the year his mother started dating Thibault, a Frenchman. She'd always had a soft spot for men with French roots, something DB suspected had drawn her to Pop in the first place, and the prospect of spending term break with his Pop had suddenly gained in appeal. He's grateful now, for that week spent learning to use a rod and listening to his father's stories, for it was on this trip that Henry had finally opened up about his past.

They were sitting by the lake on the second night of the trip, the sun setting in the distance, casting a warm glow over the water. Henry was trying to light a fire, striking and striking over and over, his hands shaking so hard that he couldn't get the pressure right to ignite a spark. Young DB watched from the mouth of the tent. He'd been trying to catch a phone signal to answer the messages from his girlfriend back home, but this change in his Pop had shocked him.

"You aight, Pop? D'you need a hand?"

Henry threw the box of matches at the ground and crumpled where he stood, his body folding like a house of cards.

"Don't take youth for granted son."

DB moved out from his canvas cover, leaving his useless phone on the ground. He bent down for the matches, struck one and lit the fire first time.

"Where are the fish?" he'd asked and followed his dad's nod to the freezer box. He set up the grate and speared two large trout to smoke. He'd never liked trout until that trip.

"Got my first real job when I was about your age," Henry said, watching his son. DB looked up in surprise. His dad had never talked about his job before, though he knew from his mother's snarky comments that it was something she didn't approve of – something outside the law. As a boy he'd always imagined his dad was some sort of secret agent, working in international espionage. If his dad hadn't been the un-coolest in the whole of New York, he might still believe it. "I'd always been good at puzzles see. 'Bit of a nerd' I guess you kids would call me these days. I could solve any algebra problem in under a minute. Could complete a Rubik's Cube in less than that. I was chess champion for the whole of Massachusetts. Wasn't any wonder really that locks and alarms and eventually computers were also easy to manipulate, easy to hack." Henry met his son's eyes across the smoking fish, the fire flickering in his eyes.

"A hacker?"

Henry nodded. "Started off as a white hat on the right side, then crossed over to the black hat. But it'll put you through college alright, and some."

"Nah, nah, hold up, Pop. You gotta hit me with more than that."

Henry reached forward and turned each trout over onto its second side, his hands still quivering. The scales underneath were charred and flaking, silver snowflakes fluttering off them into the flames. Henry sat back and placed his hands on his legs. "Can't do it anymore, see," he said, looking down into his lap. "Not with these hands. Not with the memory loss, not with the confusion. Losing myself, I am son. Not even sixty and my brain is giving up. Worked too hard for too many years, so I reckon. I was always wired different – I was quicker, smarter. Could see answers where others couldn't see nothing. And now it's all gone. All of it fading to nothing, and I don't think I'm ready to be nothing. Not ready to give it up, but don't have a choice, do I? None of us can choose when our brains decide to die."

Henry was shaking all over, but DB didn't move. Didn't know what to do. He had always seen his father as strong and independent, had never been allowed to see any other side of him. More than that though, he hadn't really had the chance to. Even when his parents were together, his dad was away for work so much that they didn't really have the usual father-son relationship. And since they'd divorced, DB had separated himself. Not really caring to start building the relationship in hindsight. But however stupid it sounded, he was now realizing for the first time that his father was a real person, with big experiences and stories to tell. More surprisingly still was that he wanted to hear them. Wanted to know him. "Lay it out for me, Pop," DB said eventually. "Start from the jump – I wanna hear everything."

*

Dressed and ready to go, DB scours the room for his phone before remembering he put it in the freezer. He opens the drawer and finds that Mae's is still in there too. *She'll be missing that.* Pocketing Mae's iPhone, he takes out his burner phone and brings up D8N App. Three matches. DBs eyes widen. Three matches, already? He flicks through the women, all young, all fairly attractive if not overwhelmingly good looking. He moves down their profiles one by one, assessing for compatibility. All well-educated, two American and one Canadian, all romantics and all into action movies. One has a dog, and the others want them. All three say they can cook and are looking for a long-term thing, but none want children. None want children. Alarm bells sound in the back of DBs head. Does this mean – it must. He's being matched with people he can't procreate with. People who won't pass on the disease his father passed on to him. As he stands there staring at his phone, a new match comes in – that little pink heart icon dropping down from the top of his screen. His fingers hover over the notification. *This is it*, he thinks. *This match will confirm everything. Huntington's, or no Huntington's. My fate.* He clicks.

*

That night's celebration was, exactly as DB has said to Mae, a celebration of DarkStork's first ninety million active users. The update was being rolled out slowly, but this was none-the-less a huge milestone. Almost 900,000 couples had already been successfully matched worldwide.

The party was being hosted at a wine bar just along the street from Frost Tower. It was invite-only with a guest list of just 50. This felt small for Rob, who's style had always been a bit less red carpet and a little more YOLO – renting out pavilions, hosting club nights or setting up bespoke company raves was the more Rob's usual vibe. But then, maybe it was just that DB had never been invited to one of the more intimate soirees.

"ID."

The security guy at the door is a mountain of muscle, like he stepped out of a WWE ring —broad and bald, with arms that could rival the size of a small car's tires. DB hands over his ID and watches the guy check it twice with intense gaze before granting him entry, like a skinhead Santa Claus, assessing if he's naughty or nice. DB nods in thanks as the guy hands back his license. New to this circle, DB knows he needs to be on his best behavior.

"Nice one," he says as the security guy eyes follow him through the blacked-out doors.

Inside, DB is greeted by a scene that can only be described as heathen. The air is thick with the scent of expensive perfume and cigars, and the sound of laughter and chatter oozes from the walls. There are lines of snow-white cocaine on every surface and waitresses dressed in garters, lingerie, and high heels flit around the room, serving drinks and hors d'oeuvres on golden-plated trays. *Sweet Jesus. So, this is how the other side rolls.*

DB slips through to the bar and orders a Tito's martini from a girl with blood red lips and a deep, seductive cleavage. It comes in a wide glass with a juicy green olive which he eats off the stick. This is it, he thinks. Time to put all that shit with Mae behind him. Rob was right. She is paranoid. The accident changed her, messed her up inside. Or maybe she was always this way, and the accident just made it more apparent. That seems more likely, looking back on it. After all, hadn't her whole reason for hiring him in the first place been to spy on her husband. What sort of twisted shit is that?

DB leans back against the bar and surveys the room. Over in the far corner, beneath an art deco print of a lady with curvaceous hips, he spots Rob. He lifts a hand in greeting and to his surprise, Rob's face lights up and he waves him over.

"DB, my latest convert!" Rob exclaims, spreading his arms and welcoming DB like an old friend. "How are you doing, guv?"

"Out here living, considering." DB grins, raising his glass.

Rob laughs, throwing his head back to the ceiling and clapping DB on the back. "Oh my giddy fuck. That's my man! Hey, everyone," Rob addresses the group around him, all male, all sleekly dressed in satin-suits and collarless shirts. "This is the duke of cyberspace and minister of propaganda – my head of cybersecurity, Danny. But, even cooler than that, he's also the best hacker in the whole of the USA. Son of The Jester, would you believe it? I nicked him right out from federal investigation." Rob throws and arms around DB and lowers his voice conspiratorially. "This guy hacked the behemoth Pentagon. He could shut up the internet if he wanted to. Lock down countries. Create his own warzone – or clear one entirely."

An uncomfortable heat creeps up from under DB's Oxford collar. *The first rule of being a master hacker is to be known by no-one.* That's what his father had said that night as the smell of burning trout swam around them. *The first rule of a master hacker is to be a ghost. You don't go around flexing, hey I can fingerblast a dead man's switch.*

"Woah, buddy. You're like the American James Bond, huh?" The tailored collarless guy to his left nudges him jovially.

"Or the American Blofeld." A second guy grins.

DB forces a toothy grin and chugs down his martini. "Ha, yeah. I'm a straight freak of nature. A cyber nuclear bomb. An agent of chaos. I could destabilize all our lives just because I feel like it. Don't get on the bad side of a hacker." The group laughs then segways back into the conversation they were having before his introduction. DB slips his phone out of his pocket to check for new matches. He just needs a couple more for confirmation. Of course, he could just log into the backend and check manually which category he's in – if he had the little pink mark beside his name. But that feels too close somehow. Too decisive. Like his asking to know, when really, he doesn't want to know at all.

Luckily for DB, this is the moment when conversation pauses, and they all turn to watch the holographic numbers ticking on the wall. The energy in the room is intoxicating as the countdown nears its climax. 89,999,999. Then, boom, in a flash, the numbers flip, rolling over to ninety million users globally. Ninety fucking million. The crowd erupts, a cacophony of applause and clinking glasses. A celebration of epic proportions, a testament to the power of D8N App. All around him, glasses are raised and the cheers ring out like battle cries.

"Well, hello there, boys!" A glamorous hand appears on Rob's shoulder, and Rose forces her way into the men's circle. She's clearly half-lit already, her eyes out of focus and cheeks flushed. She's wearing a vibrant turquoise dress with huge sections cut out of the fabric to show off the most alluring part of her figure – supple, bronzed skin setting a ruthless test for anyone who dares place an arm around her. "Ah, Danny. The Man. The Dan Man." She raises an empty martini glass in DB's direction. "We're on the same sauce, DB. Take a girl to the bar, wouldn't ya doll?" She steps across the circle and loops an arm through DB's. Too surprised to argue DB allows himself to be steered back toward the cocktails and stands silently as Rose orders them two martinis a piece.

"So." Rose lays her forearms across the gilded bar top. "I hear you're part of the inner circle. Quite a change of allegiance, no? What with your partner in crime being wanted for breaking and entering." She raises an eyebrow at DB, clearly watching his expression.

DB tries to keep his face blank. "I don't believe in partners. My father taught me to always work alone."

A wide, glossy smile spreads across Roses' face. "Your

father was a smart man."

"Is." DB corrects.

Rose holds up her hands. "Apologies – *is* a smart man. Such a shame, the way things end sometimes, isn't it? All that suffering." She sighs and drums her fingernails on the bar. "But then again, it's not like your dad was a saint or anything, right? He'd probably have been inferior anyway. Yeah, he'd have been a tick, alright."

Their drinks appear on the bar, distracting Rose and preventing DB from fully digesting the comment, though for whatever reason, it flares something deep inside him. Anger. Indignation. *What the smokes was that supposed to mean?*

Rose lifts her glass, raising a toast. "To a better planet."

DB meets her with a clink. "To a better planet."

As they each take a drink, DB stumbles through his thoughts, trying to come up with an innocent explanation for what she was trying to infer. Was she simply being racist? But then, she's Native American herself. Would that even make sense? Was she some sort of extreme libertarian, perhaps? Looking down on his father as you might a petty criminal? Whatever she'd meant though, why would that make his Pop inferior in the digital eyes of D8N App?

"You're not bad looking, when you put a shirt on." She's looking him up and down like a cow dragged to market, groping him with her eyes. "Cully calls you the handsome one, you know. *That babygirl fella*, he was calling you at the launch night. Had a thing for that grey hat you were wearing."

"Cully? As in, Cullen Rothchilds? The investor?"

Rose bats him down with her right hand as she takes another drink with her left. "Yeah, investor Cullen Rothchilds, whatever, whatever. My little brother, Cully."

DB narrows his eyes at her, unable to tell now how much of what she's saying can be trusted. Is she a Native American adopted by an Irish family? Or, then again, maybe this is the most honest state he'll ever get her in.

"It's all happening, DB! All happening. We did it. Me and my wee bro – we fucking did it. Pulled it off. The big one. Straight and narrow now. Straight and narrow, so long as your little friend behaves herself. That one's pure trouble. God." She groans, throwing her head back. "God she was always such trouble. Brilliantly smart, sure. But holy moly, what an emotional drainpipe. That accident changed her."

DB shakes himself. They're getting off-topic. "Hey, hey. Can I ask you something?" He slides a full martini glass toward her, thinking on the spot. "When you said earlier that my Pop would have been inferior either way. Well see, this is super nerdy of me, but like I just *love* science shit. So, how exactly do those rankings work? And, what's a tick?"

"Yes." Rose grabs DB's forearm, gripping it tight. "This is what I want. People like you, DB. People like you who *get it*. Because slap me with a sage bundle, this world. It's game over. Isn't it?!" She gestures around them, crazed eyes alive and her grin more manic than ever. Crazed eyes can really flip a pretty smile. "It's so raw-dogged fucked, but now we have it. We have the key to fix it – the ranking system. Ranking has always been the key. Life, liberty and equality are beacons of hope, entitlements decreed by one of the greatest manifestos ever. But fact is, it's all fiction – noble lies designed to make you think you're better than everyone else by virtue of being born on certain soil. But no. We're conceived already cuffed to forces beyond our control that will keep our ability to fulfill those unalienable rights beyond our grasp. We're not born equal. No one ever pretended we were, either. Not until recently. Now the world's hell-bent mad for it. But they're going about it all wrong. All wrong." She picks up her glass and tips it back, finishing her second martini in the space of fifteen minutes. "You get it. And you know what the best thing is? I'm not even an employee, I'm just a user. So if it all finally starts to snowball, I'll get to quietly slip into the sunset and just watch the magic happen. Bon voyage."

DB meets her glass for a second time, throwing back his drink, still ain't got the slightest damn idea what bitch is spitting on about. She's trashed. Completely lit. Gone like a newborn breastfeeding sippin' absinth, attempting a one-woman show. But the things she's saying and the way she's saying them are unhinged. DB pinches the back of his hand to make sure this ain't all a trippy dream. *Damn.* Maybe Mae was right after all.

"So, the inferior rankings aren't just about eradicating diseases then?"

For a moment, DB thinks she's clued in to how deep

his ignorance runs. Her glazed eyes flit from left to right as they try to fix on him again. Trying to read him. Then she hiccups and lifts a hand, pinching his cheek the way his grandmother used to do.

"Oh, baby. Robert's given you the dumb version, huh?" She tuts, crooning. "No, hunny. No. It's about so much more than that. People with genetic diseases are inferior, but *ticks* are even lower than that. Ticks are the scum of this Earth. The ticks *made themselves* inferior. We don't owe them anything. And then of course we get people like Mae. Oh, our darling little Mae, a criminal tick and unable to carry a child. I wonder what sort of malignant she'll end up with."

DB's stomach churns – his fears confirmed. Mae is infertile. He opens his mouth to probe further, to ask if Mae knows. But Rose's eyes have strayed, drawn by something over DB's shoulder. "And here he is – Cully, my right-hand man with the big red button, ready to cleanse us all!" Rose shimmies around DB, bouncing to meet the man who must be Cullen – broad, but not tall, draped in a fresh white linen suit. If he'd caught him on the block, he'd peg him for a Punk Prince, not a genetic scientist. He watches Rose greet him like they've just won the Super Bowl, and that's when DB spots her – the too-familiar champagne girl. A champagne girl who ain't really a champagne girl, and the last match he got through D8N app. It's Mae, rocking a sleek cocktail dress. If it wasn't for the subdued hue, the satin A-line fitted garment would be screaming S&M role play. DB's heart is caught between shock and panic. *How the hell?* Mae lifts a finger to her lips then vanishes into the crowd of tipsy bodies.

18

Mae

Mae hops as she runs, trying to kick off her stiletto heels as she wraps a stolen leather jacket around her shoulders. Shoving her heels in a dumpster, she shoves her feet into a pair of Nike's – also stolen and a size too small. Her slutty get up is earning her some sideways glances. She ducks her head and makes a b-line for the ivory Frost Tower.

She knew it. She knew this whole charade was about more than just genetic diseases. This was genetic cleansing. Genetic cleansing in the most sinister, underhanded way. Cold fury rises in her chest. How long would it have taken before people realized? Years? Decades? Rose didn't let slip who exactly is being cleansed or for why, but Mae doesn't need to hear the psychopathic reasoning. With everyone who matters drunk and drugged up down the street, this could be her best clean shot at shutting down the whole thing. *Time to take a swan dive on a live grenade you motherfucking neo-Nazis.*

A herd of football bros in oversized jerseys wolf-whistle from across the street. Mae blows them a kiss before ducking down the side alley to the security elevator. After checking left and right, Mae stuffs a hand inside her bra for the ID card she swiped from DB's kitchen counter on her way out. She raises the card to pass it through the reader, but the door is already open. "What the fuck?" Mae mutters, her confusion turning into suspicion. Who the hell would've left the door ajar? The servers are never left unguarded, and the bunker is always secured from the inside. She hesitates as the elevator opens its jaws – but she's come too far now.

Reaching basement level, Mae steps out into the familiar, pink-tainted light. The room is about ten degrees hotter than it is outside. The server fans whir like jet engines as the rows of screens flick through profiles so fast Mae fears she might have an epileptic fit. Mae scans the room, half-expecting to find a second intruder. But she's alone. Relief penetrates her veins. *Right*, she thinks. *I need something brick-ass heavy.* To her right, on the wall that houses the huge humming towers, Mae spots a fire extinguisher.

Mae strides across the room, her heart pounding. She

can feel the adrenaline coursing through her veins, a wild energy propelling her forward. The screens are her first target, her enemy, and she is determined to destroy them. She reaches the fire extinguisher and wrenches it from its holder. It's heavier than she expected, but she doesn't let that deter her. She swings it around, feeling the satisfying weight of it in her hands. Then, with a primal scream, she lifts it high above her head, takes three long strides and brings it down on the nearest screen.

The glass shatters with a satisfying crunch, breaking the picture into a kaleidoscope of colors and stealing the Barbie-pink light from its big square eye. Mae moves on to the next one, then the next one. The sound of breaking glass pings off every surface, a symphony of destruction that is music to her ears. She smashes and smashes, each blow sending a new thrill through her.

Finally, when the screens are nothing but a pile of shattered glass and twisted metal, she turns to the desk where DB sat that first night scrolling through profiles. She raises the fire extinguisher, ready to strike, but then pauses. She has time for a quick background check, doesn't she? It's not like anyone's coming back here tonight. She drags the chair across the concrete floor and boots up the monitor. Password. She chews her nails. What was DB's dad's name again? Harry? Harvey? No. Henry. And DB kept jibber-jabbering about how Moore's Law kicked off in 1970, the same year his dad was born, so that would mean – Henry1970. Nope. Henry1970! *Bullseye. Call yourself a hacker DB. If you ever need a stronger password, just throw an exclamation mark on at the end. It makes your password hacker resistant.* Mae opens the main control system and searches for her own name. The profile loads instantly, and her blood runs cold.

"What the hell," she says out loud. "This can't be right." She scrolls all the way to the bottom, then back up again. "What the fuckbag!"

"It's true." A low voice comes from behind her. DB's footsteps cross the room, and she feels him come to a stop behind her, but she can't take her eyes off the screen.

"You knew," she accuses, still not looking up. "You knew that I'm ranked inferior?"

"I've only known for a couple of hours. We matched on the app. And well, you're not *just* inferior exactly. See you have two icons, and that one is slightly different." He points to the little 'Is' beside Mae's name, and when she looks closer she sees that the second symbol is indeed different. The heart encasing the letter is upside down.

Mae shakes her head. "I don't get it. What does that mean?" She looks up at DB. His face is gray in the now lightless room, dark shadows contouring under his eyes.

"I downloaded the app to try and figure out if I had Huntington's. Just confirming what I already knew, I guess. Playing games with myself. And I do – have it, that is. Because you see, I only match with a certain type of person. Not people who are inferior as such, but with people who can't reproduce."

Mae's mind is spinning, too many thoughts all fighting to be front and center, so many that she can't focus on any single one. "Stop talking in riddles, would you?" Her voice echoes. She didn't mean to shout, but now her fists are clenched, and she can feel the veins in her temples twitching. "Just tell me!"

"Mae, please. I don't want to be having to tell you this, okay? I don't want to be the one to—" DB draws a hand over his face, then stares past her at the screen as he says, "They're matching inferior people with people who are sterile to scupper reproduction."

"So?"

"I'm inferior." DB grimaces. "Which makes you—"

But before he can finish, the elevator doors ping behind them. Mae glances past DB just in time to see a familiar dark figure emerging from the cavern in the wall, heavy footsteps striding out onto the floor, extending an arm toward the ceiling. Cullen. *Fuck.* He fires up and the bullet clatters against the concrete. A warning shot.

DB throws his full weight on top of Mae, forcing her off the chair and onto the floor. Mae hits the ground with bone-breaking force as the gunshot rings out over their heads, ricocheting off the walls. Instinctively, Mae covers her head with her arms. The sound is disorientating, the volume of it ringing in Mae's ears as the acrid smell of gunpowder stings her nostrils. She feels DB shift off her and watches through her arms as he wrenches two drawers free from the desk. He shoves one at Mae.

"Take this as a shield," he yells. "Follow my lead. We have to go now. Come on, Mae. I've got you."

"No, wait! I need to unplug the system." Mae hasn't come all this way for nothing. Shaking her arm free from DB's grip, she throws herself onto the floor and starts a frantic army shuffle over to the servers. Her arms graze on the rough concrete floors, the ringing holding an ear-drum shattering note the whole way – the sort of pitch only dogs should be able to hear. She can see the plug, like a tentacled alien it sits there hanging off the bag of the huge blinking face. She reaches forward, fingertips dancing with the wires. She strains, grabs it, and tugs. *Yes. Fuck you Rob. Fuck you D8N App.*

A bullet brushes close enough to Mae's ear that the fuzzy peach hairs on the side of her face stand on end. She yelps as the bullet hits something metal behind the servers and a loud *kerplunk* echoes around the room, followed by the low rush of running water as the burst pipe gushes over the floor.

Taking the distraction, Mae jumps to her feet and darts back to the desk. She grabs DB by the hand, and they crouch as low as they can into the maze of broken screens as another round of gunshots bounces off the walls around them. They make it halfway across the room before Cullen relaxes on the trigger and the room falls quiet. DB pulls up, pressing a finger to Mae's lips. The room is dark, but not completely pitch black – the tower block of servers in the corner still giving off a little light. Mae's ears are still ringing. She strains to relax her senses, feeling DB's heart hammering under his shirt. Something heavy hits Mae's foot. She squints down at it – the fire extinguisher.

"Ring-a-ring o-roses, A pocket full of posies." Cullen's sultry voice taunts them through the dark, his words sending a chill down Mae's spine. "Ashes, ashes, we all fall down."

Mae jerks her body down and makes a grab for the fire extinguisher. Her movement doesn't go unnoticed. Time slows to a crawl as Mae's eyes lock with Cullen's, and he turns the barrel of the gun to point directly at her. It's only then that she notices a second shape in the room. A man with broad shoulders and once irresistible eyes. Rob moves out of the dark, his feet splashing through the rising water as he looms behind Cullen, and for an awful moment the room is frozen in chaos.

In the next heartbeat, several things happen. First, Rob launches into action, throwing the weight of his six-foot frame at Cullen, tackling him to the ground. Cullen fumbles his fingers around the trigger, and Mae, finally reaching her senses, pulls the safety tag from the fire extinguisher and begins to spray blindly.

The room is full of foam, water and smoke, glass fragments and singing. Mae's senses are in overdrive. Dropping the fire extinguisher, she reaches wildly for DB and clings to him. She has no idea where Rob and Cullen are. No idea whether Rob really did intend to save her or if he merely wants to shoot her himself. No idea if she herself is dead or alive. Then DB is shoving her forward and she feels metal against her palms. Buttons. She clicks for the ground floor, punches the button over and over. The doors close behind them and all sound evaporates.

Mae leans back against the side of the elevator, her heart beating so fast that she's surprised she hasn't had a heart attack. She looks at DB, but he's not looking at her. A dark stain is spreading from under his shirt.

Mae gasps, reaching out to touch his arm. "You're hurt."

DB strokes a hand down his side and winces. "It's just a scratch," he says, clenching his jaw. "Don't ever say I wouldn't take a bullet for ya."

"That's no scratch. We need to get you to a hospital."

DB shakes his head. "Ok. It's a graze. No. No hospitals. We need to hightail it the fuck out of Austin. Damn, blood on my Jordans."

19

Mae

Mae's and DB burst out of the building, their breathing ragged and their bodies pumping with adrenaline. The arid night air hits them like a scolding splash of reality. It's as though the sky itself is closing in. They're no longer safe on the familiar streets of Austin. No longer able to hide behind DB's job title, or Mae's skimpy outfit. They're fugitives.

Turning right, they merge onto the now bustling street, neon lights casting an eerie glow over the scene. Groups of afterwork drinkers mingle with pedestrians dancing in and out of the road to move around each other, switch conversations or wave down taxis. Mae starts down the street, constantly scanning either side, her senses on high alert. DB's hand presses against the wound on his chest and Mae can't help but notice the stain eating up one side of his shirt.

"How did you get here?" DB pants, his voice strained from pain and exertion. "Don't tell me you drove. Again. Mae, you're fucking half blind!"

Mae nods, her mind racing. "Yeah, but my car's in the office carpark. We can't go back for it now. Besides, security will know I parked there."

DB grimaces. "I took a taxi down. We could try and get back to mine, but that'll be the first place they look for us. Plus, I've been drinking."

"We need to get somewhere they won't think to look for us. Somewhere we can camp out for a bit and stitch you up."

"Train station?" DB suggests, clearly struggling to keep up with Mae's long strides. "I'm covered in blood."

"Yeah, on the subway, nobody'd blink. Here in Texas, they'll offer ya a cold one." Mae nods again. "This way."

Once safe down the back alleys, Mae takes charge, breaking into a run. Austin Station is west of downtown Austin, a good hour by foot. They don't have that sort of time. DB's footsteps echo behind Mae as she sets the pace, wheezing. Will they follow? Surely they'll try. After all, she managed to cause quite a bit of damage back there – will it be enough to stop D8N App, or at least take them down long enough to come up with a better plan? She can only hope.

Exactly thirty-three minutes later Mae and DB skid through the station doors, pausing only to catch their breath. It's not busy – Austin Station rarely is – leaving them little space to try and blend in. The glowing departures board tells them the next train is in just seven minutes.

"Looks like we're going North." Mae steps toward the counter. "Two tickets please."

"How far do you want to go?" says the lady behind the scratched glass, looking bored.

Mae hesitates. As it happens, she knows this trainline. It was the easiest route home when she was in college, though still a long-ass trip. She only used it twice in her whole three years.

"Fort Worth, please. One way."

"What's in Fort Worth?" DB asks over her shoulder. She hushes him.

"That'll be eighty-two dollars and sixty."

Mae looks to DB. "You'll need to pay maestro, my accounts are still in handcuffs."

DB leans across and holds his phone out to pay. The machine bleeps and the woman behind the glass screen slides two tickets across the counter.

"Home sweet home," Mae mutters under her breath.

They let themselves through the barriers, and Mae glances up at the signs. Still five minutes to go. She taps her feet. Tensions hang heavy in the air, and Mae tries not to think about where their pursuers are right now.

What feels like an hour later, two circular lights gleam like eyes out of the dusk, and the clacking vibrations of the Texas Eagle rattle through their feet. Then, just as Mae dares to feel the smallest sense of relief she hears shouts from behind them.

"Mae, stop!"

Mae's heart flips as she turns to see Rob jump the barriers. *Well, thank my fucky stars, isn't this just the icing on the shit birthday cake you sat on.* Her mind races, caught between fear and confusion. He saved her life back there – didn't he? Is he her fireman saving the day or just an arsonist with a flamethrower adding fuel to the inferno?

Rob has both his hands up as though trying to placate an anxious dog, his face etched with desperation and concern as the train screeches to a halt beside them. "Mae, please. I need you. I need your help. This has all spiraled out of control. I didn't know how bad it had gotten. You have to believe me. Stay, please. We can help each other fix this. Help me rebuild the business we started – our way. This time we'll do it our way."

Mae hesitates. Rob's eyes are imploring – that pathetic puppy dog look she could never seem to say no to. If only he hadn't gone and fucked it. But then, what if he wasn't really in it? What if it really has been Rose pulling the strings all this time? She wants to believe him. God, she wants to believe him. Trusting Rob could be a mistake, but she couldn't deny the need for an ally. Mae weighs her options, the urgency of DB's condition pushing her towards a risky decision.

"Mae, we gotta get on the train, now!" DB's urgent voice snaps her back to reality, his body already half in, half out of the train.

Mae opens her mouth to say something, but as she does, her eyes are pulled by the three broad men dressed in all black vaulting the barriers. One final glance at Rob, and Mae makes her decision. With a surge of adrenaline, she grabs Rob's hand and lunges toward the open doors of the train. DB slams his hand on the button, sealing them in.

The train heaves out of the station, but Mae's hands and feet are still tingling. Rob's hand is still gripped tightly in hers, his huge doe-eyes holding her captive, exposing a pain unlike any she's experienced before – so raw and honest, it slices through the air between them like a blade. His breath catches. "I had no idea how deep this shit went," he pleads, desperation scratching at his voice. "Rose pulled the strings. I thought we were just curing genetic diseases, but this…"

His sincerity hits like a gut punch, tugging at something deep in Mae's gut – but she pushes it aside. She searches his eyes. "Why the hell should I trust you? You ripped out my heart and spoon-fed me the pieces."

Rob groans. "I was blind. A proper arse-pipe sucker for the success. But I've seen what they're capable of and it scares the living shit out of me. Holy bloody sweaty bollocks. We have to stop them. I can't do it without you, Mae. I need you." Rob squeezes Mae's hand tighter. "Mae, I know you. I had this gut feeling you'd go for the bunker basement to destroy everything. That's why I left the security door unlocked, hoping you'd find a way in. I wanted you to see it for yourself. Genetic power is the most awesome force the planet's ever seen, but she's wielding it like a kid that's found his dad's gun."

"Did you just quote Jurassic Park?" Mae separates herself from Rob, trying not to look at him directly. These feelings in her chest are all too much right now, she needs to stay focused. She slaps DB on the back. "Nice work Indiana Jones. Let's keep moving."

Instead of taking seats, they dash down the length of the train, their hearts pounding with each step.

Mae spots an unattended suitcase in a luggage rack. She glances left and right, then grabs it.

"What the—" DB double-takes, nearly tripping over himself.

"Get in here." Mae slides open the door to a passenger toilet, and the three of them cram themselves in. Slapping down the toilet lid, Mae unzips the stolen suitcase. *Jackpot.* The small canvas case is full of nondescript men's clothes – dark jeans, chinos, a couple of plain t-shirts and a worn leather jacket. Mae quickly divides up three outfits, and they change with immense difficulty, the air becoming denser and denser with every breath.

"Keep your damn elbow out of my face, would you?"

Mae scoffs.

"Yo, careful with my side, Missy."

"Sorry about that hit mate. Didn't mean to besmirch your trainers, old chap." says Rob. "Guess that one's on me. Nothing personal, it was your side or Mae's heart."

"Yeah, couldn't have you fucking up Mae's heart now, could we," DB mutters, his voice dripping with sarcasm.

Rob glances at DB. "You have no quips sleeping with another man's missus, maybe I had the right to give you a little nick after all."

DB scoffs, "Bro, for real – you got me shot, and now you're out here actin' like a dog that nips and then looks back, all innocent, like, *why you trippin'?*"

"Would you two behave? We're gonna have to get along if we're gonna make it out of here in three whole-ish pieces."

Once changed they turn to look at each other, Rob looks fairly normal in a tight-fitting t-shirt that was clearly meant to be baggy on its owner, Mae though is dressed like a teenage goth and DB looks like a middle-aged dad trying to squeeze into his kid's skinny jeans. Mae snickers. "Fuck me, DB. You look like a 3D printer manufactured midlife crisis on steroids with a side of daddy issues."

"At least I don't look like budget Wednesday Addams on laundry day, auditioning to be backup dancer for Marilyn Manson."

They double over laughing until Mae has a stitch in her side and tears are streaming from DB's eyes.

"Alright. Alright. Let's get back out there," says Mae, pulling herself up. "The air in here tastes like stale cum."

With their own clothes sealed inside the suitcase, they bundle themselves back out into the carriage. Mae discards the suitcase in a different rack, and they keep their heads down as they move halfway down the next carriage. DB whistles at Mae, motioning toward a spare pair of seats.

"What about Rob?" Mae whispers, gesturing over her shoulder. "We're three now, remember?"

"There's another couple of seats back there." DB points. "He's the 'muscle', right? Plus he needs to earn his stripes. Don't see why I should trust him just cuz you two have kissed an' made up already."

Mae nods, reluctantly. DB's right. They need to make a plan, and while she wants to believe Rob, it makes sense to take caution.

DB slips into the seat as Mae turns to Rob in the aisle. "Babe, you alright sitting back there? Give us the alert there's any trouble? I'll let you know when we're getting off."

Rob meets her eyes and holds them, then lifts a tentative hand and strokes the side of her face, drawing a line from her temple right down to her jaw. He used to draw the same line with his tongue when they were making love. Mae shivers and closes her eyes.

"I really am sorry, you know?" Rob murmurs.

"I hope so." Mae opens her eyes and smiles, then turns and slips into the seat beside DB.

"What now?" DB whispers, glancing back to make sure Rob is out of earshot.

"If we can make it to Fort Worth, I can get us to my parents' ranch. It's a bit of a risk, obviously as it's connected to me, but it's the safest option we have right now."

DB's brow furrows in confusion. "You never mentioned your parents before. I kinda got the sense you guys didn't get on."

"Yeah, well," she shifts in her seat, her voice tinged with bitterness. "They weren't the most supportive of parents, let's put it that way. I don't remember exactly why we fell out – memory gaps and all that – though I know Rob was the one who showed me the light. He pulled me up by the bootstraps and opened my eyes to my true value. But whatever, it's our best shot right now. Plus, it's not exactly the first place cronies'll come sniffing."

DB's expression softens. "I'm sorry."

"Stop right here. I don't do sympathy. Even a blind chick knows to peck the ground."

They fall silent, looking out the window. The train from Austin to Fort Worth would take more than four hours, and still Mae isn't certain they're not being followed. She looks over at DB. He has his head rested against the rattling window, his skin pale as an anemic woman's breast in winter. Were they even going to make it without him passing out? It's not like she could carry him if he did.

Feeling a sense of duty, Mae racks her metal-clad brains to think up a story that might keep him alert. "No, no snoozing. I can't sleep on trains. I had a dream, which was not all a dream. A wild-ass one where I have a viral prank show and I board a train packed with so many people it's like a Mormon orgy. Then it gets hijacked, and the passengers think it's all for the cameras. Their excitement spirals into a straight-up frenzy, then just as the champagne corks are poppin', there's another sound – a gunshot. The folks cheer as one of the hitmen breaks in and stabs a passenger – in his urethra, a knife up his dickhole. But instead of panic, the crowd erupts with cheers of 'Hooray!' Okay, it's a spicy dream. Hell, it's a nightmare. If that had really happened, I hope I'd remember it. A fearful hope was all the world contained. Or maybe I'm a soothsayer, and it's about to go down." Mae turns to DB, but he's started to doze off. *Yeah no one ever wants to hear about someone's dream.*

Mae taps DB sharply on the knee. "C'mon, buster. We've got planning to do."

"Yo, step off, Mae. I've had a bullet to the chest."

"Sleep ain't gonna fix that," Mae jibes, not wanting to let off how terrified she actually is – to let him know how fast her pulse is thumping in her wrists, like a metronome bouncing back and forth to fleur-de-lis in triple-time. "How we gonna take these fuckcucks down from underground? Genetic cleansing. That's beyond a felony, right? That's like Geneva convention sorta bullshit. Stealing data? That'll get quadruple life without parole, even if Rob's never murdered, robbed a bank, or mugged a granny's purse. White-collar crimes get extremely severe sentences – eternity getting your rectum resized."

DB doesn't reply, his eyes still closed. Mae sighs and slumps back in her seat. Across the aisle, a young mother is patting her newborn on the back, humming in its ear. "You said I'm infertile," she whispers, not expecting an answer. "But if I was infertile the whole time, how did I have a miscarriage? You have to be fertile to get pregnant, right? Had my baby kicked it from the start?"

She turns back to the window to find DB's eyes open and on her. He shakes his head.

"I'm sorry, Mae. I don't know enough about it. But it's genetic data, and it ranked you infertile. I guess it must always have been that way."

"You're infertile?" Rob is stood over them, his eyes wide as petri dishes, boring into her. "So, the whole time we were trying, it was all pointless?"

Mae folds her arms. "Rob, for God's sake. Why are you eavesdropping? And yes, I'm barren. My uterus is the atom bombed cavern in the burning depths of the Texan plains, uninhabitable even by cockroaches. Or that's what your app says anyway."

She scowls up at him and finds herself taken aback by the pain in his face. "But you had a miscarriage. You *were* pregnant. How can you be—"

"Oh, stop your babbling," says Mae, though her usually jokey tone fails to come through. She reaches out and takes Rob's hand. She squeezes it. "I didn't know either."

"We should get you tested," says Rob, clutching at

imaginary straws. "Just to be sure."

Mae doesn't have the heart to refuse, so she nods. "How about you get back to your seat, hey? Gotta keep this sexy hunk of meat intact if you wanna get its fertility tested."

With Rob gone, Mae finds herself hit by a sudden wave of exhaustion. Perhaps sleep isn't such a mad idea after all. A power nap. Just for twenty minutes.

When the train pulls into its first station stop, Mae jolts back to full consciousness, skin prickling as the signs for Temple slow beside them. Adrenaline rushes into the arches of her feet, urging her to run. She fights it, sinking as low as she can as she watches dark shadows of people pass the window. No sign of Cullen or his cronies. Maybe they didn't follow them after all.

DB's breathing is shallow in the seat beside her, his face etched with pain. Mae grips his hand tightly. "We'll get out of this," she whispers. "I'll get us out of this."

The sound of the automatic doors hiss shut, and the train slowly eases forward. From behind them, the doors to the carriage open to let in the new passengers. And then Mae makes a fatal mistake – she glances round.

Rose's eyes meet hers and her heart seizes. For what feels like an entire minute, they stare each other down, and Mae imagines she can see a flicker of a smile on her lips, like a child who's just won a game of hide and seek. She steps aside, allowing Cullen to squeeze past her, his right arm lifted, and Mae finds herself staring once again into the barrel of a gun.

"Rob!" Mae yells, but Rob doesn't surface. *Wankcuck, if you've fallen asleep.* Cullen's fingers twitch.

Mae dives on top of DB, shielding him from the gunshot as the carriage around them descends into panicked screams. She feels DB's body tense beneath her, his breath coming in ragged gasps. Mae grabs his arm and together they start forcing their way through the frantic passengers, like fighting against an angry current.

"Mae!" Rob appears behind her, his shoulders broader than both her and DB together. "I got you, love, keep moving."

Suddenly, the shrill sound of an emergency alert pierces the chaos, and the terrified passengers are thrown forward, bags falling from the overhead shelves as the train lurches to a stop. The lights in the carriage flicker and die, plunging them all into a midnight blackness. Mae seizes the opportunity. Eyes locking onto a metal thermos bottle that's rolled across the floor, she snatches it up, feeling the cold metal against her palm as she struggles to her feet, raising it up above her head and bringing it down with all her strength against a nearby window. The window stays perfectly intact. She makes to try again, raising her arm higher, but a hand grips her wrist before she can take a second shot. Rob. He takes the thermos from her and brings it down on the window in one blunt thud. The glass shatters instantly, sending shards scattering like deadly confetti.

"DB, come on." Mae grabs DB's elbow and hauls him

up. "You first. Lickety-split."

DB takes the order leaping sideways out of the window without hesitation. Mae looks around at the passengers. Parents. Children. She wants to help. It's her fault they're in this. But then the overhead lights flicker back on, and Cullen's rises from the floor, his nose bloodied, but the gun still firmly in his grasp. There's no time to play the martyr. She turns back toward the window, but somehow Rose is blocking her way.

"Oh, deary me. Got ourselves in quite a pickle here haven't we, babe?" Rose's voice is sickly sweet, oozing with poison. "Did you let yourself imagine this might be a fairytale? Thought you could run away together into the sunset?" Rose steps forward, but not toward Mae, pressing her pixie-shaped head into Rob's face instead. "Time to come home with us," she whispers, and from her side, she raises her gun at Rob.

In a split second, Mae sees a flash of primal fear cross Rob's face. Before she even has time to blink, she finds her arm being yanked forward as Rob throws her body in front of his like some sort of human shield. *What the?*

"Rob, no!" Mae wriggles and thrashes against Rob's grip, tears leaking from her eyes. Despite everything, she'd never have believed Rob's first instinct would be to sacrifice her to save himself. She looks back and can see him register her words. His eyes widen in realization, and his iron-clad grip slackens, his expression shifting to one of horror and regret.

Rose's eyes glint with chilling mirth. Her mouth twisting into a macabre grin like The Joker on pure nitrogen. Rose shakes her head and tuts. "Trouble in paradise," she sneers, as a hand appears on her shoulder and Cullen steers her aside once again.

The lights flicker and Mae takes her chance. She jabs her elbow back, hard as she can into Rob's ribcage and feels his grip slacken just enough. Turning to face him, she looks Rob directly in the eye and rams her knee into his balls. He crumbles.

Her path finally clear, Mae throws herself through the shattered window, and as her feet hit concrete, she immediately starts to run.

The horizon is an endless expanse of darkness in front of them, the outer industrial area of Temple thinning to their right. Mae's feet pound, the force of the hard ground reverberating up her shins. She imagines she can hear Rose's voice behind them, a haunting echo that sends a shiver down her spine. But she doesn't dare to look back.

"Mae, I'm tapped out. I can't. I can't run." DB lets out a strangled cry, like a calf lasso'd and pulled tight, its strain echoing across the corral. Mae pulls up short, searching for his shape in the dark behind her. The lights of the train are a good football field behind them now, flickering in and out of life.

"Hang in there, big guy." Falling to his side, Mae searches for his shoulders, preparing to heave him up. She wraps an arm around him and feels how wet his shirt is. The air around them suddenly tastes fearfully metallic. Gripping him firmly, it takes all of Mae's body strength to get him to his feet. Together they edge across the tracks and toward the eerie graveyard of metal units. The ringing in Mae's ears is only just starting to fade, and she finds it replaced with the unmistakable sound of engines.

"There's a highway through here. We might be able to wave someone down."

DB groans. "I feel like a lawn gnome that got used for target practice."

They move at snail's pace, DB getting heavier and heavier with every meter's progress. They stumble through the industrial outskirts, Mae's breath coming in ragged gasps as she half-drags DB along as the distant hum of traffic grows steadily louder – a ray of light in the oppressive darkness. By the time the glow of a diner appears, Mae is starting to think her back might be permanently misshapen.

The fluorescent lights from the window signs flash like a beacon of hope, their glimmer splaying across a handful of banged up looking cars parked out front.

"Well, shove a broom up my ass and call me a popsicle – there's hope! Those rust bucket clunkers better have keys inside. Or looks like my grand theft auto training is about to pay off." Mae leans DB up against the side of a building. "Stay here," she says.

"Yeah, like I'm gonna do a runner."

Mae rolls up her sleeves. "I'm fixin' to rustle us a ride."

20

Mae

Stealing the car was surprisingly easy – levering an old junk Cadillac door open with a sheet of discarded metal, and patiently following DB's instructions on how to get it started. She has a strange sense of déjà vu as she climbs behind the driver's seat that isn't hers. Like the old Mae was the sort to boost cars on the reg.

Mae peels out doing the feeder road dosey-doe to hit the highway. She put the pedal to the metal, cruising northbound on Highway 35, then heading northwest on US 287 past Wichita Falls and the highway spools out into farmland. By the time the tarmac started turning to bare earth beneath their tires, the sun was coming up.

DB slept in the back most of the way, leaving Mae to her thoughts. Only two years ago she'd been an up-and-coming twenty-something living in the city, she'd had a boyfriend and an engagement ring, a home and box of pregnancy tests. She'd been at the start of a brilliantly successful but wholesome life. Now she has nothing besides a stolen car, swiped clothes and a purse full of credit cards she can't even use. Her life is a void of hope and possibility, even her womb is barren. *What the hell did I do to deserve this?*

The sun breaks the horizon, and the Texas countryside emerges from the night's embrace – vast expanses of rolling hills and endless plains stretch out before them like a canvas painted in hues of amber and gold. The once dew-kissed grass is scorched from the summer heat. Mae rolls down a window, but the air is heavy, still and breathless. A billboard up ahead alerts Mae to their turning – *Hereford, beef capital of the world.* Then, as the seconds tick by, the rising sun illuminates a second billboard – *tax cow burps.* It's the liberals again, with their targeting campaigns. This time, it's the cattle's methane emissions in the crosshairs, those mighty beasts that rule the heartland. They never let the ranchers alone. Always something to complain about, even out here in the sprawl.

The road stretches another mile ahead, the sun now casting long shadows that dance playfully in the dead grass. Then the ranch house grows out of the dust and Mae barrels the stolen Cadillac onto the long gravel driveway leading up to her childhood home.

Loose gravel clatters against the car's exterior and Mae skids to a halt. "Goddamn, the break on this piece of junk." She turns to DB, splayed over the backseats. His complexion faded from its usual rich tone to a deadened purple color. "Shit." They need help, and fast. Shifting in her seat, she thumps a fist on the car horn sending ripples through the morning air. From behind the ranch house, she can hear chickens flapping, disgruntled by this rude awakening. She pounds the horn again, and this time the front door of the ranch house swings open. Her brother Max, a good foot taller than she remembers him, comes careering down the porch steps, hair shoulder length and ragged, his chest bare, wearing only a pair of pajama shorts.

"Mae? What the good God almighty!"

Mae jumps from the driver's seat, the engine still running. "My friend's been shot, he won't respond! Here, quick, you have to help him."

Max's feet are bare on the gravel, but it doesn't seem to faze him as he crosses the driveway in five long strides. Mae opens the back of the car so Max can lean over DB, assessing the damage. She holds her breath and Max lifts the sodden red front of DB's shirt. He grimaces. "We need to wake Daddy."

Ten minutes later, Mae's father Waylon, and Max are hauling DB across the front drive and into the barn just right of the house. They lay him flat across a hay bale and Max sets to work cutting the fabric of DB's clothes and peeling them away from his skin. Waylon meanwhile goes rummaging in the back of the barn, returning seconds later with a dusty tool kit.

"I'm gonna need me something to sterilize," Waylon mutters, selecting a long, thin set of pliers. Max digs in his pajama pocket and pulls out a lighter. Mae raises an eyebrow at him.

"Smoke in yer sleep now do you, big bro?"

"Like a Texas wildfire pumped on methane." Max grins.

Mae watches nervously as Waylon holds the pliers over the flame, then leans in on DB. "You do know what you're doing?" she asks, clenching her fist.

"Aye, kiddo. I help the wounded every so often. More so just take 'em behind the barn an' put 'em out to pasture," says Waylon, not looking up.

Mae hides her face, peering through her fingers, scared to watch as the metal sears the puncture in DB's flesh. Waylon's steady hand extracts a small bullet from DB's side, dropping it with a low clink to the barn floor, then presses on the wound.

"Gi'us some twine, son." He nods Max to the toolbox, and Max sets about sterilizing a thick needle and the sort of twine they'd usually use to fix up a bull after a bash in.

By the time DB is all sewn up, both Waylon and Max are stained with blood. But the wound looks clean, and Mae finds she can breathe properly for the first time since leaving

Austin.

"Is he going to be okay?"

Waylon meets her gaze and gives a solemn nod. "We've done what we can for now," he replies, his tone measured. "All we can do now is wait and pray that he doesn't get sepsis."

Mae opens her mouth to respond, but at that moment her mother's voice pierces the quiet, calling out from the house.

"In the barn," Waylon shouts back to her.

A moment later, Mae's mother, Grace appears in the doorway, already dressed in old pair of jeans and an oversized plaid shirt, her blonde hair pulled back into a bun at the back of her head ironing out some of the wrinkles collecting around her eyes. Grace pulls up short at the sight of her daughter, a montage of emotions flickering across her face like a short film. Mae stands frozen, uncertainty knotting her stomach as she tries to recall the last time she saw her – the last words they'd said to each other. Did they end on bad terms? It seems likely considering none of her family has been in touch since the accident – the only timeframe she can be sure of.

"Hi, Mommy." Mae offers a hesitant greeting, taking a small step forward. Then in an instant, her mother's face dissolves, and Mae finds herself enveloped by the smell of sawdust and manure. Grace's tears wet Mae's shoulder as she whispers into her daughter's hair.

"Thank God you're alive. I been praying for this

moment for so long." Grace pulls back, her eyes glistening, the exact same shape and shade of blue as Mae's. She lifts a finger and delicately brushes Mae's hairline aside, tracing the translucent scar running along her hairline. A single tear draws a silent track down her cheek. "Welcome back to God's country."

Grace insists that they carry DB inside the main house. So, Waylon and Max settle him on the sofa in the living room, while Grace collects blankets from around the house to cocoon him until he wakes. Then they all settle down for a proper Texan breakfast.

"You're thin as fiddle string, a frail fritter of a girl," Grace scolds, slapping Mae on the leg. "Extra sausages for you, that's an order." Graces realizes what she said, apologizes, "Oh, I apologize from here to Sunday. You're on that bird-food grass-eater path. My mind's scattered as a flock of geese."

"Ma, you can take the girl out of Hereford, but you can't take the Hereford out of this rib-lickin' gal." Mae says. She really must've been a real strict avid vegan-zilla head before the crash if even her straight-talking Ma will pander after her.

Grace smiles. "Bless your heart." They move around each other, setting the table, brewing coffee, flipping eggs and turning sausages. It's like a well-choreographed dance that's locked itself into Mae's muscle memory, and yet she can't quite shake the feeling of being adrift in a sea of blurred recollections, her past a fractured mosaic of forgotten moments. It's not until the breakfast is being dished up that Mae realizes her youngest brother, Billy, hasn't come downstairs.

"Shall I go wake lil Billy?" she asks, setting a jug of orange juice on the table.

Her parents exchange a converse look, Waylon's wiry brows lowering over his eyes as Max turns his back and becomes suddenly over invested in blackening the sausages to a charcoal crisp.

"Billy isn't here." Grace says, her voice trained steady. "We don't know where he is. Went missing not long after your accident."

"Likely banged away in a prison somewhere, or joined Hells Angels, knowing that boy. He's probably got knuckle tats by now. Or maybe he's squatting in a trailer park with a biddy down in that black carbon plant town, Borger. Be hard to find anyone in all that pollution smog." Waylon snorts.

Mae's heart drops into her diaphragm like piece of shrapnel. Billy missing? He was always a troublemaker, but he wasn't a bad kid. Was he? She tries to recall his face but finds she can't. Tries to recall anything about him. But his memory is stuck behind a thick sheet of misted glass.

"He's... missing?"

Waylon grunts, a grim expression etched on his weathered face. "Yep. Disappeared without a trace. Sheriff been looking, but ain't found hide nor hair of him."

Mae's gaze drifts to the empty seat beside her. The seat where Billy surely would have sat, between her and Max. She looks to her older brother. "Do you have any photos of Billy?" she asks. "I just– I have huge gaps in my memory, and I can't seem to remember what he looks like. In my mind, he's still a skinny blonde five-year-old, chasing me around the ranch with a pickaxe and a fistful of shit. I can't see him grown up. It's like he's stuck underwater."

Grace gets up, crossing to an old cabinet at the back of the kitchen. She rummages for a minute, before pulling out a dusty old photo album.

"Don't kick yourself too much," says Max, as their mother sets the album down in front of them. "He got his growth spurt since you last saw him. You mightn't even have recognized if you did see him now."

Mae flicks through the pages, staring blankly at the photos. There, looking back at her, is a young man with a beard, his features both familiar and foreign. She traces the contours of his face, the years etched into every line and crease. Then it hits her – how long it must have been since she saw them all in the flesh. "How long has it been since I was home?" Mae asks, looking round at them, alarm ringing in her ears.

"It's been five years," Grace says matter of factly, like some figure she just heard on the morning news. "Four since we've even heard from you. You personally, that is. Of course, the hospital called after the accident but were told not to visit." Her voice trails off, her fork shaking slightly in her hand.

"But why?" Mae asks. "I mean, of course, I knew that we weren't, I just, I thought it was because of the accident. Because of Rob. Because you didn't like him and us…" There were more reasons. More reasons that she'd learnt after waking up with her head in pieces, what was left of it, strapped inside a helmet. But how can she be sure they're true now, after everything that's happened? After everything Rob's turned out to be. "Why did we stop talking?" she asks again. "I can't remember. Someone please tell me the truth?"

But before anyone can answer, Waylon has risen from his seat, chair scraping across the floor. "I'm gonna take my breakfast out to the pastures," he announces, his voice gruff. "Plenty of work to be done." And with that he grabs his plate and is out the door, his footsteps thudding down the front porch steps.

"I should get the laundry in," Grace says quietly. Mae watches her leave, too shocked to ask her to stop, and sit down, and not to run away. A knot forms in her throat as she realizes the nostalgia that filled the air earlier, has turned stale.

She looks to Max, half expecting him to leave too. He whistles. "You sure know how to clear a room, lil sis." He grins, then reaches behind him into a cupboard and pulls out a bottle of whiskey. He sets it down on the table with a heavy thud. "Now, would you like swigs to go with the story?"

21

Mae

Consciousness gradually seeps back into DB. There's a strange smell in the air. Manure, perhaps? When he finally comes around, he finds himself lying on a sofa in what appears to be a rather old-fashioned living room. The floorboards are bare, and the sofas aged. The scene is unfamiliar. He frowns. His memory is fragmented, his last recollection is of an industrial estate somewhere on the outskirts of Austin. Running. Running. Gunshots. His chest tightens and he instinctively reaches for the source of the pain. His torso is covered in a patchwork blanket. He lifts it gently and finds his t-shirt is missing, replaced by a snug gauze dressing covering where he now remembers the puncture in his skin. Blood. There was so much blood.

DB pushes the blanket aside and the fabric slides away with a soft rustle. As he struggles to sit up, the echoes of conversation drift to him from another room – and he could swear he recognizes Mae's laughter. A sense of relief washes over him at the sound. Mae is safe. They both got out.

Pushing himself slowly to standing, DB scans the room with bleary eyes. His gaze settles on the mantlepiece adorned framed photographs of three faces repeated over and over at different ages. He hobbles across to them, his movements awkward and unsteady. Reaching the mantle, he can clearly see that these photos are of Mae and what must be her two brothers. He picks up one of the frames. The resemblance between them is striking, especially between Mae and the younger one, whose mischievous smile mirrors hers with uncanny precision. He doesn't have siblings, though he supposes with what he knows now, that was probably for the best.

Lost in contemplation, DB's grip loosens, and the photograph slips from his grasp, falling to floor with a sharp thud. He winces at the sound, but to his relief, the frame remains intact. He attempts to pick it up but the pain in his chest stops his torso from bending. He yells out as a spasm shoots across his ribcage. Then a door creaks and footsteps sound behind him. He turns to see Mae stood in the doorway.

"Howdy, soldier." She beams, her face flushed. "Lord

a'mercy, looks like someone had a rough ride. Were you in the outhouse and lightning struck? Yeesh."

Mae's brother, Max, whips him up some grub as Mae recounts their journey across Texas, filling in the gaps in DB's memory.

"Kinda nice being the one who remembers things for a change," she jokes.

DB can tell she's not told them why they're there. Her expressions are cartoonish. He plays along, keeping the tone light until Max finally announces that he needs to hit the rangeland.

"Catch y'all later, folk," he says, smacking DB on the shoulder as he passes. DB winces.

"Daggummit, I thought he'd never leave." Mae pulls back her chair and watches by the window as Max crosses the front drive and starts up his truck.

"D'you think they'll know we're here?" asks DB. But Mae isn't listening. She seems twitchy – on-edge. She comes back to the table and re-corks the bottle of whiskey her and Max had been chugging, then tucks it under her arm.

"Best get out to the barn. Daddy won't let you upstairs and we don't need anyone overhearing us."

Still feeling a little woozy, DB stuffs a last sausage into his mouth and follows her out of the house and down the front porch.

"You'll probably have to sleep in here tonight," Mae says as she pulls back the barn door. "My parents are hella religious. It's like they think Christ is glowing out of their assholes sometimes."

"No biggie. Crashing in a barn still beats the funk of my Pop's old socks. Man ain't lived there for over a year and I still can't shake the stank out the walls."

The floorboard creaks underfoot as DB steps further into the old barn and Mae seals the door shut behind them, plunging them into momentary darkness. Then comes a click, and a light flickers into life above them – a single lurid yellow bulb swinging back and forth like something out of a horror movie. This whole goddamn thing has felt like a horror movie. But to DB's surprise, Mae's glowing face is now illuminated with a huge grin.

"I can't believe we actually did it," she exclaims, her voice tinged with a mix of triumph and disbelief. With a dramatic flourish, she collapses onto a nearby hay bale. She reaches for the bottle she's brought along, deftly popping the cork and taking a long swig of amber liquid.

DB lowers himself in a rickety chair, his hand pressed gingerly against his side. "Yeah, that was a little too close to the lungs for comfort."

Mae laughs. "But look at us now," she says. "We're free! Well – I'm sure they'll come after us for vengeance, but who gives a shit. We took them down. Plug pulled. Abbosh." She mimes an explosion with her hands.

DB frowns. Did something more happen while he was conked out? "What do you mean, we pulled the plug? You don't mean when you literally yanked the plug back at the bunker, right?"

"Duh." Mae rolls her eyes. "That was their whole system, DB. The big one. The Pentagon of the D8N App world. And I cut the cord." She sits up straighter, flicking her slightly greasy pink bob over her shoulders. "I, good sir, am a motherfucking maverick. Just call me Mae-verick from now on. No, wait. Scratch that. Super-Mae-verick The First, leader of the free, inferior world."

"Hold up. This decommissioning process ain't no Pixar flick. Unplugging it doesn't just magically wipe everything. Each server's a backup machine, auto saving everything in real time. It's a massive scale taking down 288 servers. Their data is intact, Mae. It's just hidden, waiting for some new hardware to reveal all."

Mae's expression falters, caught somewhere between manic jubilation and shocked devastation. "Fuck, I fiddle with coding, but server bunkers? That's your rodeo. I figured you would've custom firmware, instantly triggering a memory-wipe kill switch."

"That ain't an easy flex grind. That's a beast mode marathon hustle – like draggin' a Caddy up Everest, solo dolo."

"So, it was all for nothing?" she murmurs. Rising abruptly, she begins to pace the room, kicking up clouds of dust as her feet hit the dirt floor.

"It wasn't for nothing," DB interjects, watching her pace up and down, up and down. "Listen, even though the system is still running, we'll have given them something to sweat over. We made a big fuck-ass mess in there. They'll be on damage control for at least twenty-four hours. Well. I guess more like twelve now. But still, time is what we need. Just a bit of time to find our smoking gun."

Mae continues pacing, muttering under her breath.

"Think about it," DB plunges on. "What hard evidence do we have? We could go to the media—"

"No," Mae pulls up short. "No media. That won't be enough. They have too much power. They could squash any story we put out before it even makes it over Texas borders. No, we need to do this in a way that means they could never, ever come back from it. Something so conclusive that they can't deny what they've done."

"Right." DB nods. He can see Mae's mind working, almost hear her thoughts clattering against that titanium skull.

"We need to use our assets," Mae says slowly.

"So, my good looks and your bullet proof head?"

Mae shoots him a sarcastic glare. "Sense of humor is not one of your assets, dimbo. Stick to what you're good at, eh? No, I mean we need to use your genius hacking skills and my throbbing sexual prowess."

"Your throbbing sexual prowess?" DB grins, then shakes his head, his expression turning pensive. "No, you're right," he says, scratching his chin. "We have to reverse our thinking. They've got the power, and we're out here in podunk no man's land sticks. But if it's smart, it's vulnerable. Our smart cars, smart houses, smart cities, even a damn smart watch – all hackable. But how do you hack an old school wind-up wristwatch? You don't."

Mae plonks herself in front of him, clears a space on the hay-strewn floor and grabs a piece of flint. "Exactly," she says, as she starts scratching words into the concrete. "We are taking on a giant – a Goliath of Big Data. We need to play them at their own game. They fuck us, we fuck them back."

22

Mae

The plan is set. While DB rests, Mae gets on the walkie talkies and hauls Max back from his chores to help her find all the equipment on DB's list. It takes them all day. Luckily though, Max isn't the prying type, so no matter how strange or illegal their foraging gets, he never thinks to ask what it is Mae and DB are up to.

"Just promise me one thing," he says, blowing a lungful of cigarette smoke into the air as Mae stows the satellite dish they've just disconnected from a neighboring ranch roof into the back. "Promise, to come home for Thanksgiving? I need someone to help me drown out Mom and Dad's yappin', preferably with alcohol."

"I got you big brother," Mae says, clapping Max on the back. "I get to shoot the turkey here. It scares the shit outta everyone in the frozen food section in Austin's Wholefoods." Mae winks and then sighs, looking back at the ranch house – the childhood home she wishes she could fully remember. "There's nothing left for me back in Austin now anyhow."

"No?" Max raises an eyebrow. "Not even bullet boy?"

Mae splutters and rolls her eyes. "DB? You're pullin' my stirrups. We ain't a thing. I'd rather get hit by a car than be with him." Mae throws a doozy right hook at him.

Max holds his hand up in mock surrender. "Whatever you say, sis. But you forget I've spent a lifetime watching you try to flirt. It's like watching fish trying to cross the Texas plains." Mae punches him hard in the arm as he starts to mime a fish floundering over sand, then they both collapse into giggles.

"Yeah, yeah. Alrighty," says Mae, recovering. "I guess he's not *that* bad. He is missing a good chunk of his side though, so that's going against him."

"Uhuh, cuz you're only missing half your skull. That's nothing."

"Exactly." Mae grins. "I'm basically the Terminator. And if that isn't hot, well, I'll never get what you men are after."

Max flicks on the engine, sending a cloud of dust into the scorching air. "Hasta la vista, no comento más."

DB is awake when Mae gets back and looking a lot more solid. He watches her and Max start to unload, mumbling to himself as he inspects each random scrap of metal, taking the backs off the old mobile phones they stole from Billy's bedroom drawers, inspecting the insides. When they unload the microwave, DB opens the door and cracks it clean off.

"Woah, buddy. You know what you're doing?" Mae asks, watching DB unscrew the back of the microwave with a flat piece of gravel. "There ain't seconds of this shit. You got one shot."

DB straightens up, brushing his hands down the front of his jeans. "Toolbox, beer, and a titanium assistant with charms." He looks at Mae, holding her eyes steady. "Let's take these motherfucker goonsdown."

Mae doesn't miss the low, mocking wolf-whistle from behind her. She stamps her foot down hard on her brother's toe, winning her a satisfying squeal.

They work late into the night, Mae holding a torch over DB and keeping his spirits up with a stream of corny jokes and debauched stories about her college days. When they get hungry, Mae brings them out her mom's infamous ambrosia salad – a delightful disaster of Jello, fruit cocktail, mini marshmallows and whipped cream with shavings of chocolate covering it like charred bark. Mae scoops up the top layer of cream with her hand and eats it straight from her palm.

"You know," she says, licking the corners of her lips, "there was this one scorching hot summer just after I finished high school – and when I say scorching, I mean like, weather advisory, don't let your cat out, there's gonna be a nine place jump on the nursing home waiting list kinda scorching – I decided to pay Austin Energy Headquarters a little visit." She grins through her whipped cream mustache. "I walked in there, all innocent-like, pretending I was after an internship. But my true mission? To swap out their water bottles with ones filled with clear jelly-filled imposters. I think it was a stunt or something. Or maybe I was a bored intern there?" Mae scoops out another handful of sweet salad. "Oh yeah, I think I also switched the whipped cream cans in the staff fridge with shaving cream. I remember I used to do that to my family. Can you imagine the looks on their faces when they took a mouthful of that? Pure chaos." Mae cackles, spraying mini marshmallows across the floor. She should cover her mouth, but her laughter is infectious. "Shit, I pulled that one on Rob too, as he loves hot chocolate in the winter—" Mae's smile fades, memories of Rob casting a shadow. "Isn't it weird that I can remember that, but I can't remember my lil brother's favorite ice cream, or what my family does for Christmas or where we went on vacation growing up? I can't really remember anything from before being like fifteen, and nothing of at least a year before the accident. But some of my most embarrassing moments at college – those I've got in high definition, IMAX sort of detail. Pretty fucked up, huh?"

DB puts down his screwdriver, his face now illuminated like a Halloween phantom by the torch. "All of that stuff'll be there, I'm sure," he says. "Maybe it just takes time. Or prompts or something. Like, maybe if you got Max to chat to you about old stuff it would come back. Maybe eventually the smell of cattle shit will reboot the memories."

"Yeah, maybe." Mae bites her lip. She had thought about that herself, but the truth is, part of her is afraid to give it a try. And not afraid that it won't work, but afraid that it will. The prospect of her buried memories looms heavy over her, all those twisted recollections her brain has shielded – maybe for a reason?

"Oh god, if it's putrid cattle shit that triggers my memories, amnesia wipe me again. Those taxed musty, rotten-egg burps and foul, stench-laden farts – their pen smells like the turdburglar's corpse bag was stuffed with dung and left in the sun. The creatures are fucking foul. Nah, hopefully, the smell of wet horses after rain will trigger something – that's my all-time favorite smell."

At that moment, a deafening crack sounded from outside the barn. Mae clambers to her feet and throws the barn door wide. The bizarre looking microwave-powered satellite DB erected in the front yard comes alive, sparking and crackling.

"Sweet mother of Jesus."

Mae turns back in time to see the old phones DB has spread around him light up in canon, lines of code running down them like a rain machine.

"It's working. Fuck me, Mae. It's working." DB jumps up and throws his arms around her, locking her in such a tight bear hug she feels her ribs splintering.

"DB, you need me alive, lickbag!" she says into his shoulder.

DB lets go, his dark eyes shining with glee.

Mae looks down at the phones. "What now?"

DB sits back and reaches for a bottle of Shiner Bock. "Now, we wait. That little beauty is gonna connect us to all the highest profile news networks, billboards across the country – Times Square in New York, Burj Khalifa in Dubai, Shibuya Crossing in Tokyo, Piccadilly Circus in London and Champs-Élysées in Paris. Maximum exposure all over the world. And then, I'm also gonna broadcast blast all the phones with D8N App. Now it's time for your bit." He digs into his pocket and pulls out an old-school Nokia. Its screen is alive, scrolling through a garbled stream of letters. He holds it out.

Mae takes it and turns it over. She knows Rob's number by heart, though she can't recall her own. One of the cruel little fucklet nuggets of information that's refused to leave her – unless of course she's hungover in yesterday's clothes, crammed on a bus with an audience judging her declarations of infidelity. Goddamn karma. She opens a new message and her fingers hover over the keypad. "How shall we rip the ball sack off this *rumpleforeskin reprobate?*"

"It's go time," says DB. "Just be sure to give him the right coordinates."

Once the deed is done, Mae feels mentally exhausted, but her body is still buzzing. She wants to forget this fucking day ever happened. Needs something strong enough to knock her on her ass and erase her memory.

"Wait here," she says to DB. He looks up at her from the barn floor and nods in a sleepy way, a gentle smile lighting up his face as his eyes meet hers. Something flutters in Mae's stomach. A strange teenage sensation she'd forgotten about. "Don't fall asleep, okay?"

Mae scampers into the house, sneaking past her parent's bedroom door and up to her childhood room. The walls are still painted lilac and there's a poster of Jane Fonda in handcuffs after her legendary demonstration in Washington: *There's no more important fight than climate change.* hanging above the twin-sized bed. When she comes back, it's with a bag big enough to smuggle a dismembered body part. She dumps the bag on the floor by DB's feet and rummages through it, finally producing a bottle so huge it could put a gorilla on its ass.

"Boink," she says, brandishing the mammoth bottle like a trophy. "Ya ever tried moonshine?"

DB's eyes widen at the sight. "Can't say I've had the displeasure."

"Swig it," Mae orders, shoving the bottle into his hands.

DB stares at it like it's a bomb about to detonate. But then shrugs and takes a gulp. "Holy fucking Christ!" He sputters, his eyes nearly popping out of his skull.

"Told ya." Mae smirks, taking back the bottle and slugging a healthy swig herself. "It'll put hair on your chest and melt your retinas. Good thing I already got the blindness half-covered."

She digs deeper into the bag. Out comes a tiny denim wrap mini skirt, a laced bra and corset, and not one, but two sets of handcuffs. One pair is pink and fuzzy, with "YES DADDY" screaming from them, and the other is straight out of a kink catalog, complete with LEDs, bells and a padlock. Mae jangles them in her hand. She can't remember when she got into kink, but her body is screaming for release, and something tells her DB has seen this side of her before.

DB raises an eyebrow, but as Mae hoped, doesn't seem shocked. "Not sure if they're for kinky shit or self-defense. Just promise you won't cuff me to the radiator for a week straight?"

"They're for wellness," Mae says. "I need a night of self-care right now."

They each take another long swig of moonshine. Mae's whole body is tingling with anticipation, overshadowing the anxiety. She locks eyes with DB, and without another word they start making out like horny teenagers. His mouth is soft, but his tongue is rough. She grabs at his chest, careful to avoid his bullet wound – *Holy Christ it's hot to bang someone with a bullet wound.* They move over to the hay bales, and he rips her bra open with his teeth. The world could end in a fiery apocalypse, and she wouldn't give a flying rat-assed hoot.

The next morning, they're jolted awake by a loud bang – the barn doors bursting open. Standing there like a cowboy from the depths of hell is Daddy Waylon, guns blazing.

"Mae!"

His voice echoes through the barn, pulling Mae abruptly from her S&M-induced slumber.

Shit. They totally screwed the pooch sleeping together in the barn – Waylon's bed-sharing policy has been alive since Mae hit her teens – but it's too late now. Waylon reloads the cattle gun, his eyes wild with urgency.

Mae attempts to scramble to her feet, only to realize that she's physically attached to DB – and not just handcuffed, but ankle-cuffed too. The realization hits like a punch to the gut. Mae and DB look at each other, panic rising.

"What the actual fuck?" DB frantically scans the room for the keys. "Where the hell are the keys?"

"Yeh, get to gittin'!" Waylon yells.

Mae feels around, her heart pounding like a drum solo. "I don't know! I don't know!" She looks across the room at the shape of her dad in the doorway, already steadying his gun for a warning shot. "I do know he isn't joking though. He once skinned the left ear off some jock in high school who got me home after the streetlights came on."

"You're not making me feel any better," DB hisses,

rattling the pink chains. DB puts his hand over his face. Mae's arm has to come to his face as well.

"Scoot your caboose. We'd better skedaddle."

"Mae, I'm butt naked!"

They scramble to get dressed. DB holds up the denim mini skirt. Mae laughs at the sight.

"You'll look sexy as hell in that." Mae laughs again – a laugh that quickly turns to coughs as the air turns thick, burning the back of her throat. And that's when she notices the dark smoke slithering in like a snake around Waylon's ankles.

"Hitch your britches and start haulin'!" he yells.

Mae grabs DB's arm and pulls him forward. Waylon runs them out, faltering as they pass as though momentarily stunned by the sight. Bursting from the barn, Mae and DB set out on a three-legged, three-armed race across the front yard that would put any circus act to shame.

"Fire!" Waylon hollers. "We gotta spur it on."

DB gasps audibly Mae's in ear. It's a proper wildfire alright – the fields behind the ranch-house blazing with scarlet fury, threatening to brand their naked skin.

Luckily, the fire has the family well and truly distracted – Grace filling buckets with water as Max sprints back and forth in his pajama shorts, herding the livestock in a desperate fleeing exodus to higher ground.

"Mae," Max calls, not registering her skin-clad lock-and-key situation. "Open the cattle gate!"

Obliging, Mae grabs DB's arm and pulls him toward

the gate to the cattle field. They trip, fall and eat shit in what feels like an endless repeat as the air around them grows hotter and the family's shouts grow more urgent – but they keep moving. It's a goddamn shitshow, but they finally make it, flinging the gate open just in time for Waylon and Max to ride through on horseback, leading the cattle to safety.

"You and handcuff keys," says DB in a choked voice.

"Blame the moonshine-field hoedown going on in my bloodstream," Mae says, grinning at him. "I have a talent for swallowing handcuff keys. You know, in case I get wasted, end up in a cop car, and need to escape. Practiced that a lot in high school."

DB shakes his head, a mix of amusement and disbelief. "You're a wild one. Last night was so unholy your ancestors surely are frownin' upon ya." DB gives a cheeky grin. "Now how the hell are we gonna get these off?"

"Daddy'd likely be down to shoot 'em off," Mae suggests, making handgun gestures. "Plink. Plink. Plink. He'll 'av calmed down after a good cattle chase. Or Mommy can bring out the bolt cutters. Though she'll start praying to our forefathers for forgiveness if she sees us like this." Mae makes the sign of the cross, dragging DB's hand with her.

"Nah. Let's wait for Max."

They watch as Waylon and Max chase the withering herd across the field. Then comes another gunshot and another train of smoke up into the already dark clouds above them, and Mae can't help but feel a little guilty for the distressed "moos" rumbling across the pastures like mournful death knells. She squints at their bright red plastic ear tags, and a haunting shiver courses through her.

Apparently noticing her reaction, DB places his free hand on her shoulder. "You okay?"

Mae shrugs. "Hearing the cattle, seeing those tags," she says, her voice low. "And the wildfire carnage. It's bringing back memories. Fucked-up ones."

DB gives her shoulder a squeeze. "It's gonna be okay," he says, though they both know there's no guarantee of that.

Mae nods anyway, her eyes never leaving the cattle. She sighs and coughs. "That was the worst smoke gender reveal party gone wrong." They laugh. "If I could have a baby, mine'd trigger an international incident." Mae sighs. "Let's go grab some feed sacks to cover up while we wait. What an even more diabolical day this is going to be."

23

Mae

Neither of them slept well. But that's not important. What's important is that today's the day DarkStork gets put into the ground. Mae and DB wake with the rising sun. They told Rob to meet them at midday, and the location DB has chosen is a good seven hours from the ranch house.

The morning sun casts long shadows across the yard as DB gently dismantles the equipment and loads it into the hot-wired car. Mae settles into the passenger seat, her eyes moving slowly from left to right, taking in the scene as though watching a movie in slow motion: the pick-up trucks and discarded troughs, the big old house with its wrap-around porch and broken swing, and the weathered barn, red paint peeling with age. Her brain aches as she tries to recall the countless hours she spent playing hide-and-seek with Billy in the bales of hay, or the arguments she had with her mom over her expulsions from school. But her mind draws a blank, memories painfully obscured by the gaping holes in her titanium skull. She hopes to be back here by sundown. She will be, she tells herself. Though if life has taught her anything these last few months, it's not to make dinner plans.

They drive in silence, for the most part. Exchanging words only when stopping for coffee, or to swear at passing trucks. They switch driving at the half-way point. Mae still shouldn't be driving, technically, but DB needs the time to make final preparations on his cell.

"That one must've been doing 120. No way that was 85. Jackass cousin-fucker hillbilly bitch," Mae growls. "I do get fussin' and a cussin' on the highway."

The Texan landscape unfolds before them, shifting from rolling plains to the rugged gravel ridges of the Chihuahuan Desert. The sun, now higher in the sky, casts a harsh glare that makes the heat shimmer on the horizon. DB periodically glances at his phone, checking the compass to ensure they stay on course. With each passing mile, the coordinates draw nearer. Mae's pulse throbs against the steering wheel. By the time they shift from tarmac to sand, she can almost feel the tension in the air, the weight of their mission pressing down on them like the oppressive heat of the desert.

"We're getting close," DB says, his voice breaking the silence that has settled between them. "Drive slower."

Mae nods, her gaze fixed on the horizon where the rocky sand flats seem to stretch endlessly. Finally, DB throws a hand on the dashboard.

"Stop!"

Mae throws on the brakes with a little too much force, obscuring their view in a cloud of bronzed dirt. She squints through the windows, scanning the surrounding area for any sign that Rob has already arrived. But the desert stretched out before them is empty and desolate. "We're early," she remarks, glancing at the digital clock on the dashboard. "Only by twenty minutes though."

DB nods grimly. "Not much time to set up."

Without another word, they set to work, unloading the equipment from the back of the car. Mae's coordination is off, working with efficiency of a drunk squirrel building Lego bricks.

"Not like that, Mae. For real, just don't touch anything, fall back, alright?"

"I did exactly what you said, it's your rambling instructions that's the problem, not me."

The sun beats down on them mercilessly, its heat intensifying with each passing second. Straightening up, Mae wipes the sweat now dripping from her temples, her hands trembling with a mixture of nerves and adrenaline.

Gazing out over the top of the car, she spots movement on the horizon. She lifts a hand to shield her eyes from the glare of the sun off the windows and makes out three separate vehicles emerging from the shimmering heat. Two black SUVs with tinted windows lead the way, their sleek frames cutting through the desert terrain with ease. Behind them, the unmistakable shape of Rob's Aston Martin gleams in the harsh desert sun.

"They're here."

DB quickly finishes up behind the boosted car, the urgency in his movements evident as he checks the tiny camera attached to his front – detached from an old flip phone they found in Billy's room, it now feeds into the phone in DB's pocket. By the time the cars come to a stop, Mae and DB are stood together in front of their car, Mae's fingertips tapping against her side.

The convoy pulls up in military fashion and the driver's doors of the three vehicles swing open, three figures emerging as silhouettes against the sandy expanse. Rose, Cullen and Rob.

Rose takes the lead, strutting forward like a model on her first career-breaking catwalk. The three of them come to a stop, Cullen flanking Rose's left, Rob on her right. It's a Mexican standoff.

"No one said your name three times," Mae deadpans, eyeballing Rose across the five-foot no-man's-land between them.

"What's with all the sand and daggers, wee gobshites?"

asks Cullen, sneering like a mountain lion watching its prey.

"Aww, don't be mean, Cully. They just wanna knock a hole in the wind with a sackful of hammers." Rose is dressed in another one of her ridiculously bright power suits with rattlesnake print. She looks like a Powerpuff Girl out for scalps. Mae bites the inside of her cheek to stop herself laughing.

"If they're not careful, I'll make them dig their own hole. They have. People have dug their own graves. Shite in the hole, then roll around in the muck wailin': *Ah Jaysus! I'm sinking covered in shite.*"

"You act like you're throwing them a lifeline rope, but it's a barbed wire noose, you fucklecuck." Mae spits at the dirt.

"Now, now. There's no need for language like that. We're the good guys, after all." Rose smiles.

"Pfft. Yeah, you're a real Disney princess. Do you bio-hack birds to braid your hair in the morning? And they glitch and shit in your mouth. Or do they fly into your face thinking it's their reflection? You wide-eyed bird-faced twat."

Rose straightens her back, pulling herself up to her full height. Mae can feel DB shifting beside her, fiddling with the phone in his pocket. *Don't draw attention to it, dipshit.*

"When I was born the population was barely five billion," says Rose, her voice cutting through the tense desert air. "In a few years, it'll pass nine billion. Humanity already uses 1.8 Earths to provide resources we use and absorb our waste. We're in overshoot. We're running out of resources faster than the Earth can replenish them and yet we're still growing by 90 million more feral mouths to feed per year. We've gone from three to eight billion in under 60 years. We're causing the sixth mass extinction, and I'm here to stop it. Come to Jesus—you're standing right before her." She smiles and spreads her arms, her words carrying the weight of a dire prophecy.

Mae paces in disbelief. "So, all of this is a solution to saving the planet? Your plan to reduce the environmental strain of climate change is to control the human population?!"

"We're progressing, y'know?" says DB, his voice measured. "Doing things to help. We just need to change our lifestyle. That's it. Don't buy unnecessarily. Decrease meat consumption. Increase public transport. Make more walkable cities. Reduce, reuse, recycle."

Rose raises her eyebrows. "What, electric cars, solar panels, LED light bulbs, and sipping through mushy straws is going to save us? When all our resources end in a few years, we're going to share?"

"Humans are empathic," says Mae, crossing her arms and hoping this will distract from DB's incessant fiddling. "Though maybe your parents never cuddled you. Or you smoked too much peyote as a kid."

A wry smile curls the corner of Rose's lips. "They can be compassionate. Sure, my Choctaw people, despite suffering the Trail of Tears, aided the starving Irish. You had one poor, dispossessed people helping another poor, dispossessed people who were suffering as much as we had. We all want to survive, and that dormant want we're all born with forces us to surpass other people. In that moment the thought process is, *I need to get something before they do.* When push comes to shove, humans are self-serving and greedy. In the pandemic people swamped stores for masks, sanitizer and toilet paper because of viral videos continents away. And you're telling me the human race knows how to cooperate?"

"We can ramp up renewables," DB retorts. "That was a symptom of corporations mismanaging."

Rose whistles to the sky in mock hilarity. "And consumers are primary drivers. Humanity can't make that change to renewables in time. The climate crisis is the single biggest health threat facing mankind," she says. "Society is past the point of collapse, don't you see? We're already jostling for space on this dying planet. It's about freshwater, usable topsoil and precious minerals. Two-thirds of farmland is unusable. Microplastics are everywhere creating hot spots for antibiotic resistant bacteria. Soon we'll have more plastic in the ocean than fish, they're already loaded with microbeads from face scrubs. Hell, by 2050, there won't be any seafood. Wave goodbye to Sushi."

"Water wars have begun," Cullen jumps in. "Risin' temps are supercharging deadly heatwaves, wildfires, droughts, hurricanes – extremes growin' more savage, frequent, unpredictable. Breathing'll be deadly soon.

Respiratory and heat illnesses takin' human tolls. Whole regions'll be unlivable, forcing mass migrations and wars over scraps," Cullen scoffs, his expression hardening. "Sure, it's not the first time countless masses starved while the rich turned their backs. Same greed, same indifference. In the Great Famine, millions died and fled. Only now, it'll be a whole damn planet – one vast Lazar-house filled with famine, disease, death. No land left to flee to, no escape from hysteria, fear, and dread."

Cullen rubs his temples. "To not do this is to condemn billion souls to starvation and unimaginable suffering. Without intervention, everyone will die. Graves are walkin' to the toll of the death bell."

"Yeah, yeah," says Mae, rolling her eyes. "So, to you this is all just reparations for the Irish Potato Famine? One time the drive-thru forgot my fries but you don't see me stealing people's unborn kids. Every fast-food joint around the corner delivers diabetes to millions of people. Are y'all really going to start taking all of these things personally? And Rose, you can drop the whole brooding act an' all, like a battered beaten wife taking revenge. The kind of rage a woman has after a lifetime of buying her own drinks. Even if everyone is destroying the planet beyond the point of no return. Stealing global data for eradicating genetic diseases is one thing, but there's a fine line between that and genetic genocide."

Something ugly passes over Rose's face. Some like malice, or vengeance. "It is personal. Have you ever had family suffer a genocide? Genetic genocide is nothing new. We've been doing it since the beginning of time. I'm Native American Choctaw. Chanta Sia Hoke. Believe me, I understand. This isn't genocide. Doing nothing is genocide."

Mae clenches her fist. "You're ranking people on a dating app inferior. And who gets to decide that, huh? You? You've decided that we're taking away the reproductive freedoms of certain people because they aren't worthy of reproducing – *we don't want their type in our society.* What gives you the right to determine who's fit for the planet? And don't lie to me here, cuz I know you've not just targeted people with genetic diseases. God you definitely get drunk with power when you become in control of the window shade on a plane. Now you wanna burn innocent people to the ground and do a rain dance on their ashes."

Cullen rolls his emotionless gray eyes. "This isn't about craftin' a genetically modified master race or whatever fanciful shite you've dreamt up from ye' Marvel comics. It's about saving the human race. Or who knows, maybe polar bears adapt and fancy livin' in tropical ponds and thrive havin' a grand ol' time."

"Oh, look," Mae taunts. "The recycling center bouncer hitting me with supreme quality explosive sarcasm now."

"Science shouldn't be a means for making a decision about the value of something as rich as human life," says DB, speaking over her, his frustrations tangible now. "If we eradicate conditions caused by genetic differences, are we getting rid of dyslexia too? You know Albert Einstein was autistic, right? Beethoven had hearing loss. Blindness? There are valedictorians with Down syndrome. This is a genocidal fuckageddon."

"Rose, you're so delusional, your ramblings sound like a blender full of kittens," Mae snarls.

"There are scientific articles that confirm what Rose is saying – code red for humanity." Rob's voice is quiet, like an apology.

Mae forces herself to look at him. She can't believe she used to believe in this man. To think of him as strong. Now his head is so far up his own 'arse' he's just a puppet in someone else's sick game – the scapegoat, the face of the operation, but completely powerless on paper. "You're seriously on their side, Rob, you bystandin' bitch?" she asks, half-accusing, half-imploring, part of her still willing him to make a U-turn. "You're siding with the eugenics cheerleader? Sterilization is right?"

"Matching inferior people or ticks or whatever with infertile people isn't bodily invasion like sterilization or abortion." Rob's voice is still quiet, like he low-key hates himself for speaking. "Even if it was, we don't have an unlimited right to autonomy. I have the right to swing my arm, but not into your face. We don't have the right to procreate at a level that harms others."

"Oh, my fucking-diddly-God." Mae throws her head back, screaming in frustration. "Own up already, would you? Your time's up, Mr. Capitalism. Take some fuck-ass responsibility. You're the so-called *genius* behind D8N App, remember? This is your legacy. This is how you'll be remembered forever. As the Hitler of the 21st Century. Is that what you dreamed of as a little boy? Oh wait, you're following orders like a Nazi Guard under Adolf Titler."

"Humans are driving the firetruck that's on fire off the edge of abyss," says Rob.

"Rob, for real. Don't side with this bitch. Can't you see what she's doing? She's trying to stop the firetruck by standing you in front of it. Many of these things, heinous crimes against humanity happen because ordinary people turn a blind eye, choosing to see others as less. Are you a savior who'd hide people in your home? Or a guy who'd fuck Anne Frank and then cough-cough-finger-point on your way out? This shit happens because people convince themselves to turn off their empathy. You're better than this!"

"I am better than this." Rob's face drains of color. He squeezes his eyes shut and drags a hand down over his face. When he speaks, he speaks into his palm. "I was all for eradicating hereditary diseases, sure. That ensures a healthier, more productive population – human improvement through genetic means. But choosing undesirable types we want to exist? Fuck a duck. Fame is a fickle, tempting mistress, and temptation's a bitch—but I never signed up to play God. Try doing what I do.. By year's end, you'll be a piss-soaked, gin-sodden husk, shouting at pigeons, crawling into a bin, praying the rats will take pity and share."

Mae cuts him off, "Rob, is this an apology, or are you just unloading this shit to get it off your chest?"

"Capitalism feeds off people and I have to keep the economic machine running." He flinches, guilt flickering across his face. "Anyway," he mutters, deflecting, "aren't birth rates already declining?" He looks sideways at Rose, his eyes pathetic, almost pleading.

Rose rolls her eyes. "Oh yeah sure, birth rates are declining in *some* nations, but global population marches relentlessly forward. Governments, in their economic fairy tales, persist as if infinite growth isn't delusional. The poor will bear the brunt, brutally suffering far more than the rich. Soon, you'll only grow old or have any semblance of life if you're wealthy. We're living with a dying government that's coughing up blood. People everywhere are getting sick. We're gonna murder each other in a war for water, food and oil – that's coming in our lifetime." She smiles at Rob, her painted lips curling with malice. "But your opinion really doesn't matter at this stage, does it Rob? Whatever you think and feel, there's no backing out now. You're the face of this revolution." Rose reaches up and strokes the side of Robs face. "Did you really think Hitler was the brains *and* the brawn?"

"Get your saddle-tramp skidmark hands off of him," Mae seethes. "You're denying people life."

"This is an act of war against humanity," growls DB. "Ranking people inferior based on their DNA. But it won't stop there. We all know it won't stop there. Today it's people with autism, tomorrow it's lefties."

"Colonizing Mars will be the only escape left – the final refugee for the rich overlords with yachts," says Cullen. "Though if ye' don't have fuel, a rocket is just a paperweight."

Rose nods. "The things we do for our kids."

"Genocide?" DB scoffs. "You don't even have kids. You really believe you're Captain Planet even while you're punching kiddos?"

"We're at a point where having children is immoral," Rose says, cooly. "Sometimes a culling is the only way for a species to survive."

Mae pushes all the air out of her lungs. The sun is turning her head into an oven. There's no point in trying to win this debate. There's no rationalizing with the irrational. That's not what they came for, she reminds herself. But it's grating on her. She feels dirty just hearing it. The absurd inhumanity of their words burrowing into her then spawning from her pores like a cockroach infestation. They need a confession. An outright confession. Mae clicks her tongue, choosing her words. "You still haven't really told us though, what it is that makes someone inferior." She shrugs. "After all, I'm inferior, right? So, I have a right to know – what makes a *tick*, tick?"

She can feel DB tense beside her, holding his breath in an effort to catch the response as clearly as possible. By sundown the world will have heard what's about to be said.

And by tomorrow, D8N App will have fallen.

Rose fixes Mae with an inquisitive stare, lips pressed together like she's trying to decide something. She nods to herself. "Well, Mae. That's a great question. See, when it comes to ticks, I only have half the cards." She cocks her head, still staring right into Mae with that same strange look in her eyes. "As far as I know, there are two groups factors that could make someone match with someone who's infertile. Disposition to genetic diseases is obviously the first, we call them 'inferior'. The second is arguably even more noble – murderers, rapists, pedos, addicts. The very bottom rung of our society. The Morlock dregs of humanity. Those people are ticks."

"Wow, you really do think you're some sort of superhero, don't you?" DB shakes his head. "How are you even tracking those people? Those traits aren't genetic."

Cullen chuckles and turns to his sister. "Jaysus this fookin' lad." He looks back to DB. "Ye literally handed us the keys, fella. Social media, phone hacking, scanning the criminal database. It's dead simple once you've got all the bits and bobs in place."

"So, what is it that makes *me* inferior then?" asks Mae, folding her arms. "Cuz I *am* ranked inferior, right? Ok, I'm half blind. I sometimes can be a fuck puddle of a person. I drink too much and get real horn tossin' moody when I'm hangry. But then you say I'm *infertile* too! Man, you let one thing slide and motherfuckers start ice skating. Should I start writing my obituary? I break my skull. You break my heart. The fuck, y'all want to break my soul? Crush it and serve it as a cocktail? I hope you get in a car crash, a fiery one, and your limbs get detached and devoured by tug-of-war feral dogs."

Rose holds her hands up above her head. "Woah, chill girl. Let's not forget we go through your data. We know you overdosed your fiancé. That makes you a tick."

"Shut your tits! Compared to what you're doing, almost murdering Rob was a whoopsie with a boopable nose."

"Whatever, Mae. You would've been thanking me before all this memory loss titanium head shit came about."

"The fuck are you on about, 'I'd have been thanking you'?"

"You never wanted a baby anyway. You were practically begging to be the test subject. Oh, don't look at me like that. We're gonna run out of infertile people at some point. It was only a matter of time before we needed a solution and there you were, bleeding through your hotpants, slagging Rob off for being such a brooding pansy. I did you a favor."

"You *made me* infertile?" Mae's blood runs cold. "Is that seriously what you're saying to me right now? I come crying to you about my miscarriage and you think the solution is destroying my uterus?" She looks to Rob, but he's staring at the ground, his face ashen. "And you fucking knew about this?" She steps forward, ready to throw punches – to ring Rob's throat, then bash Rose's pretty face in – but a hand grabs the back of her t-shirt and yanks her back. "Were you ever going to tell me? Were you gonna wait till I was on my deathbed? Or maybe carve it into my fucking gravestone? That'd be real thoughtful of you."

"I only found out yesterday," Rob whispers. "She only told me after the train." His voice trails off, wafting into the desert like tumbleweed.

DB, a hand still holding Mae back from a fight, raises his voice. "So, you made Mae infertile to match her with this fucking obscure list of malignant targets? How many millions of others can expect the same fate? How many bullets are in your Russian roulette chamber for ninety million users?"

"Oh, come on. It's brilliant," Rose goes on, apparently enjoying herself. "And it's not an *obscure* list. Though like I said, I don't have all the details of the targeting myself."

Mae clenches and unclenches her fist. "You're the cuntbag head of biogenetic-whatever. If you don't 'have all the details', who the hell does? Father fucking Tick Exterminator Christmas?"

Rose makes a face of mock-surprise, looking theatrically left and right to her cronies, before turning back to Mae, a picture of concern. "Mae, don't you remember?" She takes a step forward into the no-man's land between them, her eyebrows pulling together in the middle. "It was you. All of this. The ticks, the coding, the using your fiancé's dating app as a mirage. Everything. It was all your idea."

Mae's breath catches in her throat, her mind spiraling as Rose's words echo through her head. The desert around her starts to fade, the harsh sunlight turning into a blur as her vision narrows. She's floating, disconnected from the earth. Her pulse pounds in her head and the sound of Rose's voice warps, reverberating in her titanium-plated skull like a distorted record. And then it happens. Flashes of the past presenting themselves to her in a vicious stream, assaulting her mind, vivid and relentless. Late nights in the student bar with Rose, the two of them laughing and drinking, beer matts covered in hastily drawn Venn diagrams, the word *ticks* circled and underlined in her own handwriting. She sees herself explaining the diagrams to Rob, his face a mix of confusion and awe, sat on the end of his dorm bed in just Calvin's and Air Force 1s. Then she's in the library. Her grades are slipping, her academic life falling apart as she dives deeper into genetic research that has nothing to do with the law degree she set out to study. In Rob's dorm room, she watches her own fingers tap out complex codes on his computer screen, the keystrokes frenetic and obsessive. Then they're at the D8N App offices, inviting Cullen in, showing him the servers, introducing him to DB, her right-hand man – a personal hire. The scene shifts again, an argument between her and Rob, heated words exchanged before she storms out, clutching a disk, the encrypted disk, tightly in her hand. And now she's knocking on DB's door, shoving the disk at him. He holds her arm, pleading, but she pushes him away. She's now driving with purpose. Up ahead, a man is in the crosswalk, an older man with a walking stick in one hand and a pizza box in the other. Panic and adrenaline flood her as she feels her foot press harder on the accelerator. Faster. Closer. Mae's body is thrown forward, smashing through the windshield. The pavement rushes up to meet her, the impact shattering her skull against the hard surface. Pain explodes in her head, and everything goes dark.

Back in the present, Mae finds herself standing in the desert. The ground feels solid beneath her feet again, but the weight of the revelation crushes her. Her eyes lock onto Rose, the picture of mock concern still etched on her face. Her knees buckle. She stumbles back into the car. She can't look at DB, can't look at Rob. What has she done?

Something inside her snaps. And without a second thought, she turns and runs back, past the parked car, into the unforgiving landscape.

DB

DB watches Mae run. His hand twitches at his side, instinct urging him to chase her, but his legs feel rooted to the spot. He's paralyzed, not by the heat, but by the torrent of information fighting to find a logical space in the timeline in his head.

Mae hired him on purpose, he had sort of guessed that. But he had always assumed it was because of his inside knowledge in data security – if you want to make your data hacker-proof, why not hire a hacker to secure it? But now all the pieces were falling into place – all those times before the accident when Mae had come to him with files she wanted him to double encrypt, never telling him their contents, then sleeping with him afterward. Had it all been a lie? Had she been using him the whole time? He feels sick. Bile collecting in the back of his throat.

His gaze shifts to Rose. She's enjoyed this, watching them unravel – like a sandwich tastes better to her when a homeless guy eyes her eating it. Whose side is he on now? He's stuck in the middle of the desert with a recording device in his pocket. The device feels heavier with each passing second, a burden of knowledge and responsibility he isn't sure how to handle. What should he do with it – the evidence of their plans, the damning conversations? He could expose them all. But that would mean exposing Mae too.

MAE

Mae's calves are screaming, and the scorching sand is burning through the soles of her shoes. She pushes harder. Her breath rasps, the dry air cutting her throat like shards of glass. She needs to move faster. To outrun the memories, the guilt, the truth. Nothing else matters.

The horizon stretches out, enclosing her in a vast, unforgiving dome. She feels dirty, the torrid details of her forgotten past now exposed. She should die out here, that's what she deserves. She's the worst kind of monster because she doesn't even know it.

She stumbles, nearly pitching forward into the gravel, but catches herself and keeps running. Tears blur her already compromised vision. Then, breaking through the pounding of her heart, she hears something else – a low, ominous rumble. It's subtle at first, almost lost to the roar of blood in her ears. But it grows louder, unmistakable. The sound of an engine.

DB

DB gulps back the bile in his throat. Enough is enough. The Mae who helped start D8N App is long gone. The Mae he knows now, the Mae he trusts, is someone different. That's the Mae that matters, not the ghost of her past. He needs to buy her some time.

Digging a hand into his pocket, his fumbling fingers grip tight around the recording device. He rips it free.

"Don't move!" he yells. "I've been recording you. This whole conversation. One click, and this gets broadcast to the world – billboards, cinema screens, every person with D8N App will have your confession in the palm of their hand."

For a moment the three of them, Rob, Rose and

Cullen, just stare at him like he just sprouted a second head and claimed the moon landing was a hoax. Then Rose's face splits into a laugh. "You'll be throwing Mae under the bus, how apropos," she sneers. "Is that the sort of person you've decided to be, DB? Jeez and I thought I had a warped moral code."

"That's the glory of editing," DB bluffs.

Rob raises his hands up. "Just a jiffy, mate. That would pop my company in choppy legal waters."

Rose raises her eyebrows. "DB, you really thought we didn't see that coming? Your Old Man really didn't get round to teaching you all his tricks, huh?" She rolls her eyes. "We already deployed a botnet-driven DDoS hacktivist attack just in case. Both the D8N APP and broadcast servers are currently overrun with a gargantuan flood of traffic. I got the idea from you, actually. It's the very same strategy you devised for Rob when we recently were *hacked*." Rose glances behind her. "In any case, it's too late for that now."

Before DB can process her words, a dark van he hadn't noticed approaching skids past them, heading straight for Mae. His heart lurches and his screams come from somewhere deep inside his gut.

"No! Mae, run!"

Desperation cracks his voice like the desert floor, but he knows she can't hear him. He wants to run after her, but he's frozen, watching in slow motion. Then, suddenly, he finds himself slammed against his car, the metal searing through his shirt as someone yanks his arms behind him.

DB grunts in pain, struggling against the hold, but Cullen's grip is ironclad. Cullen snatches his phone and hands it to Rose.

"It's over, Danny Boy. It's over."

He can smell his chest hairs singeing as the sound of Rose's high heels approach from behind him. She leans in, her hair tickling his ear. "As Trotsky said, a revolution is impossible till it's inevitable," she whispers.

A blunt pain wallops the back of his neck. And the desert is swallowed whole.

MAE

The van pulls up alongside her, the engine now a menacing roar. She glances sideways, panic surging as she realizes there's no escape. The vehicle swings around, cutting in front of her and skidding to a stop.

Mae's feet falter, her breath hitching in her chest. The van door flies open, and three men in balaclavas leap out. They move with military precision, their dark figures stark against the blinding white of the desert. One grabs her arms; another takes hold of her legs.

She tries to scream, to fight back, but they overpower her effortlessly.

"I'm gonna compost heap y'all suckfuck sumbitches! Y'all wish *y'all* were never born cock-sucking cocksuckers.

Y'all underestimate an angry woman."

Inside the van is cool and dark compared to the searing heat outside. The door slams shut just as a hand covers her face, a coarse fabric with a strong, medicinal scent pressing against her mouth. And then, everything goes black.

After everything…

DB

DB's eyes flutter open, confusion clouding his thoughts as he tries to make sense of his surroundings. The familiar ceiling fan of his condo comes into focus. He props himself up on his elbows and looks around. He's definitely home. He rubs his temples, trying to lock down the last thing he remembers. He looks down at himself. His clothes are different from what he remembered wearing – a t-shirt and pair of jogging pants he hasn't worn in years – and a strong antiseptic scent clings to his skin.

He sits up fully, sending the room spinning. Something catches the corner of his eye – a flashing. He squeezes his eyes tight then opens them again, focusing on the surveillance camera flashing in the corner of his childhood bedroom. "What the," DB freezes, staring it down. "What the hell is going on?" Then, like a dam breaking, the memories come flooding back – the desert, the confrontation, Mae being forced into a van, the recording device.

Heart pounding, DB jumps up and begins tearing through the condo, even though he knows it's futile, even though he knows there's no way that Rose will have accidentally left evidence lying around. No, his recording equipment is gone, as is his mobile phone. The surveillance cameras newly installed in every room seem to laugh at him as his frustration mounts. "Oh, hell nah!" he shouts, tossing a pillow at one of the cameras. The clock on the oven tells him it's been over 48 hours since the incident. 48-hours of time he can't account for. They could have Mae halfway across the world by now.

He paces back and forth, every step fueled by a mix of anger and desperation.

"Where are you, Mae?" The question echoes in his mind. He can't shake the image of her scarred hairline, those electric blue eyes looking back over her shoulder as the van ripped through the sand. He needs to prove her innocence and uncover the truth about the crash that stole her memory, her eyesight, and a significant part of her skull. Was this whole thing really all her fault? Her idea?

He stares into the blinking red eye of the CCTV camera above him. "On God, fuck you, boogeyman goons," he mutters. Casting around, he does the mental calculations, measuring the peripheries of the lenses' view. They're only standard, static cameras. There has to be one corner that isn't covered.

DB sets up his computer in the bathroom, using the toilet as his office chair, and for the next four days he barely moves from the screen, living off whiskey and stale pop tarts. First, he scours through news stories for dates and details, cross-referencing every lead, cataloging every single person and every single IP address within a mile radius of the accident that day. Then he hacks into the police database, seeking out the officers assigned to the investigation – the same ones assigned to the missing persons file on Mae's younger brother Billy. It seems like too much of a coincidence not to be important. Did they get to him too? Perhaps as blackmail of some sort? He puts that thought aside for later.

Days blur together, his existence a haze of html. He pores over a never-ending stream of social media, surveillance footage and traffic cameras, creating a timeline of events in Sharpie on the bathroom tiles. Finally, his persistence pays off.

In amongst the noise, he finds it – a witness' account captured on their cell phone from a second or third story flat and shared on TikTok. It had been scrubbed clean a long time ago, but on the shadowy depth of the dark web – the repository of the forbidden – DB found it, preserved just for him. The video starts innocuously, a slice of everyday life, but soon the camera pans, and there she is – Mae, just moments before the impact.

DB sits forward, heart racing as he watches the scene unfold. Mae sliding into the driver's seat of an on-duty ambulance, hijacking it in someone's time of need. She hits the gas. It looks like she's talking – or shouting – gesturing, with only one hand on the steering wheel. But she's not alone in the vehicle. An unknown figure sits beside her, their full profile obscured by the angle of the recording. Then the man steps into the road. An older guy, holding a pizza box. And that's when he sees it. The hand moving across from the passenger side, yanking the steering wheel. The ambulance veers off course, and everything changes in an instant. DB leans even closer to the screen, his eyes locked on the footage, hoping for more clarity. The image is blurred, but the movement is unmistakable.

It wasn't Mae who crashed. And it wasn't Mae who killed that man, whoever he was. But who is the figure in the passenger seat? And why did they pull the wheel?

He sits back but his gaze remains fixed on the screen, the gravity of what he's discovered sinking in. This is the evidence he needs to prove Mae's innocence and find out what really happened that fateful day. But more importantly, this is all the evidence he needs to trust that Mae is not, was never the monster Rose painted her to be.

MAE

Mae wakes up with an all-too-familiar thumping in her head. Like a hangover. Has she been drinking?

She forces her eyelids open. She's in a hospital-style bed and has an IV bag attached to her arm – but this is no hospital. She seems to be in some sort of warehouse, the walls are corrugated metal with shelves of cardboard boxes everywhere. She blinks, trying to ease the blurriness in her single working eye as her other senses fight to kick in. The smell of the chloroform that put her out is still strong on her top lip, and somewhere in the dim light, a TV flickers, casting a faint, ghostly glow while trapped in a grating, endless loop of static. Somewhere out of sight, someone starts whistling. The tune is familiar, dancing on the edges of her memory. She frowns, trying to bring it back. It was from a TV show she and Billy used to love as kids. The one with the purple dinosaur. *I love you, you love me, we're a happy family.* The chime grows nearer, echoing against the high ceilings. And then, cutting through her haze of grogginess, a voice calls out.

"Hey, Squirrel Bait."

It's a unique greeting. One that could only come from one person. But how could that be? And yet–

Out of the dark, a blurry figure steps into her line of vision.

Her brother, Billy.

"Come hell or high water," he says. "That's the last thing you said to me." He moves closer, heavy footsteps coming to a stop at the end of Mae's bed. The dim light illuminates his face – pallid and gaunt – a deep scar across his left cheek. He grins, a feral edge to it. "We can finish what you started. This is all about family."

Mae rises slowly, her body aching, but her resolve unshaken. She locks eyes with Billy, her younger brother once full of mischief and dreams, now twisted into something barely human. A man she doesn't recognize. For a fleeting moment, a memory surfaces: the two of them as children, running through the fields, their father's laughter in the distance. She draws him into an embrace, holding him so close that she can feel his heartbeat.

"Family," Mae whispers, her voice soft but steady.

In one swift motion, she slams her forehead into his – titanium on bone. The sickening crack echoes across the room.

"You do the hokey pokey. That's what it's all about."

END OF BOOK I

About the Author

*"She's the most diabolical b*tch I've ever seen"* - Dave Chappelle

Ashley Barnhill, a proud Texan, is a University of Texas at Austin law graduate. Oh, and she now has a titanium-plated skull, adding a literal edge to her sharp wit.

Ashley is a versatile stand-up comic, filmmaker, writer, and actress. Known for her subversively dark humor and biting delivery, Ashley toured with Dave Chappelle, performing over 500 shows worldwide. Her notable appearances include on Netflix, IFC's *Maron, Drunk History* and Jason Reitman's Sundance film. Ashley was a writer on TBS's *Drop the Mic* and is part of the BBC Writers' Access Program. Ashley's filmmaking talents extend to writing, directing, editing, and starring in her award-winning short films. She was a Top 10 Finalist on HBO's *Project Greenlight* and was in Viacom's Emerging Directors Program. "Her journey epitomizes *Don't Mess with Texas*."

Acknowledgments

Thank you to these accomplices in this madness:

My family, my eternal love and gratitude. Your unwavering support and belief are the reason I'm here today. You are the backbone of my existence, and I am forever indebted.

Scarlett Sangster, my editor, whose involvement was nothing short of miraculous and absolutely vital – dismantling and reassembling, piece by brutal piece, turning chaos into coherence. This book wouldn't exist in its best form without your precise, merciless, and transformative guidance.

Anthony Byrne, whose contributions went far beyond a director's call of duty. Your insights, ideas, and endless patience shaped this book in ways words cannot fully capture. And Imogene Harrison and others subjected to my manifesto emails – your engagement and feedback were invaluable.

Scotty Landes, from the very beginning, your wisdom, encouragement, and timely humor kept me grounded and motivated.

My beta readers, Yuefan Wang, Marissa Riveria, Rosina Phister, and Victoria Gustafsson-Dahill, you were my fresh eyed-saviors. You caught the nuances I missed and reassured me about elements I doubted. Your feedback was instrumental.

My script readers, Dan Weiss, David Benioff, Jason Reitman, Nash Edgerton, Jason George, Patrick McDonald, plus a few more – your inputs gave this story depth and stronger edges. Sharp nods to Dennis Kelly and Jesse Armstrong – your merciless virtuosity in both storycraft and dialogue shaped this novel in ways I'm wildly grateful for.

Anastasia "Stacey" Makhanova, Ph.D, for her groundbreaking research. Your work on CC genotypes and its impact on relationship satisfaction provided a scientific foundation for this book.

Ross Ulbricht, a brilliant, altruistic friend ahead of his time – your forward-thinking energy embodies the dreamers who strive to make the world better but find themselves entangled in unintended nefariousness. Your story is a reminder of the complexities of innovation and humanity.

Lastly, everyone who supported this journey, whether by reading, listening, or what-the-hell-ing at the right moments – thank you.

I am truly humbled and grateful for the chance to share this book with the world. I hope this cautionary tale about digital chaos and climate collapse makes you pause, think, panic, and take action. Like the killer in *Se7en* said, "Wanting people to listen, you can't just tap people on the shoulder anymore. You have to hit them with a sledgehammer." But don't hit them with a car!